The Parent TRAP

NEW YORK TIMES AND *USA TODAY* BESTSELLING AUTHOR

JASINDA WILDER

The Parent TRAP

Chapter
ONE

Delia

I STILL LIVE WITH MY PARENTS. NOW, WHEN I SAY THAT, I don't mean the same bedroom I had at nine or sixteen. A couple years ago, I built, by hand, all by myself, a cabin in the woods on my parents' property. The only things I contracted out were running electricity and plumbing to the spot. I dug the foundation myself, put up the framing, wired, plumbed, roofed, and finished the whole thing. I'm pretty damn proud of my place. It's one bedroom, one bathroom, a living room and kitchen, but it's mine and I built it. It's half a mile from my parent's house, tucked into the woods, with a short gravel driveway peeling off from their mile-long one. I've got natural gas-lit lamps lining the drive, an actual working antique hand-pump well outside—with modern plumbing inside, of course.

I built the cabin with a nice deep porch, and I have a rocking chair I made myself, and I like to sit out on the porch in the evenings, sipping wine and watching the fireflies wink and flash. Sometimes, yeah, I wish I had someone to share the peace with, but…that's not my life.

I'm essentially running a multi-million-dollar construction company. Dad is pulling back, handing more and more of the operations and decisions to me. And despite what I said to him earlier, I have a sick feeling in my gut that he's right about not being around much longer. The thought makes me panic—Daddy is my…my everything. I've spent my entire life wanting to be him, to make him proud. And I have. And without him…? I don't know what I'd do.

We had dinner at my parents' house. Delicious salmon, potato salad, and a couple rounds of 5-hand pinochle with the Bristows from next door—their lifelong best friends.

I'm ruminating, now. Brooding, is more like it.

Of course, the Bristows talk about their son like he's a golden egg-laying goose. They still call him Matty, which I presume drives him nuts. Dell, during a rare visit home a few months ago, said Matthais has been going by Thai, now. Which is weird, and pretentious.

Of course, he's always been weird about his name. Typically, the name is spelled Matthias, as in M-A-T-T-H-*I-A*-S. But according to the Bristows, someone made a spelling mistake on the birth certificate—the argument is whether it was Mr. Bristow or Mrs., an argument which has never and will never be settled—and his name is officially spelled M-A-T-H-T-*A-I*-S, with the A and the I reversed. Same pronunciations—Muh-THIGH-ass.

If you ask me, the emphasis should be on the last syllable. But what do I know?

Going by Thai, pronounced TIE, like the thing that goes around a man's neck, or the people from Thailand, just seems…douchey.

Classic Matthais.

Why am I thinking about him? I've done pretty well putting him behind me, since he left home. I don't think about him at all, honestly, unless my twin brother Dell is around. Those two are still peas in a pod, Dell and Matt. They drive, and I shit you not, matching Lamborghini Aventador hypercars. Matty's is red, Dell's yellow. They vacation in Greece together every summer, sailing on rented or borrowed superyachts and posting douchey pics of themselves with their stupid abs, drinking eye-waveringly expensive scotch straight from the bottle, always surrounded by sleazy, trashy, beautiful women wearing not much if anything at all over their plastic beachball tits.

At least they don't live together, thank god. Dell spends most of his time in LA, while from what I can tell, Matt is all over the place. I don't follow him on IG or anything, because the last thing I want in my life is to know what Matthais Douchebag Bristow is doing day to day.

Getting venereal diseases, if one should be so lucky.

I haven't seen him in person since that day in the

woods—the last day I saw him before he left for college. High school graduation day, a big party in the woods behind our houses. It was a who's who of River Gulch popularity, hosted by the kings of the town, Dell and Matt. I was there…because I'm Dell's twin. I've always hated parties, especially the ones hosted by my idiot brother and his asshole best friend. See, Matt always went out of his way to bully me and torture me and make my life hell. The day of our high school graduation was just the crowning achievement of his douchery. What did he do? The most childish thing he could think of: he threw a garter snake on me. A big, pissed-off snake, right on my shoulder, slipping down my chest, writhing and hissing and twisting and looking for something to bite. Now, it wasn't fear—I'm not afraid of snakes. I'm not one of those girls that dissolves into paroxysms of screams at the sight of a snake. Do I like them, do I want one for a pet to snuggle and carry around everywhere? No. But when a four-foot-long, pissed-off snake is trying to crawl down my boobs, I feel like it's understandable that I react rather explosively. I grabbed the snake behind the head, whirled around to face Matt, who wasn't prepared for instant retaliation. He was wearing joggers, the drawstring untied so they hung low around his hips; being vain, he was shirtless, showing off his stupid, perfect, chiseled abs and stupid, perfect, sculpted pecs. I yanked the waistband of his joggers away from his stupid, sexy, perfect V-cut and tossed that big, pissed-off snake down his pants. And, I walked away. The sound of his angry, frantic yells turning to downright screams of pain as the snake bit him—hopefully on the dick, but I was too committed to my badass slo-mo-walking-away-from-an-explosion swagger to find out for sure—was the sweetest thing I'd ever heard.

And that, while not the revenge I might hope for, was still a pretty nice send-off, being the last time I laid eyes on Matthais Bristow.

Thank the good Lord for small favors, am I right?

I groan out loud. "Stop thinking about that asshole," I scold myself out loud. "He's not worth a single moment of thought."

"Who's not?" a familiar voice says.

Dell.

I huff. "You."

He emerges from the woods, from the direction of the main house. "You wound me, sis."

"You annoy me, *bro*." I flick a finger at him. "Go away. I'm relaxing."

There are two rocking chairs in the set I made, with a matching side table between them. He sits in one, rocking. Pulls a joint from behind his ear and lights it up. "What? I can't come spend a few minutes with my only sister, my *twin*?"

"No." I eye him through the haze of acrid, pungent smoke, waving it away. "I know that look. You want something—what." It's a question, but it comes out more as a statement.

He just holds the smoke in his lungs. "You're crankier than ever. Jesus."

"I'm NOT fucking CRANKY!" I shout.

Dell just lifts an eyebrow. We're not identical twins, but we might as well be. We both have thick jet-black hair, which he styles in that artfully messy thing douchey asshats do, spending hours trying to look like he just woke up like that. His eyes are as blue as mine, like Dad's. Sharp cheekbones. We share DNA, but somehow, he has a jackrabbit metabolism. He eats like he's sixteen, still, and yet has visible abs and perfect skin and he doesn't do *shit* to look like that.

Me?

Strict keto, no cheat days. I run a hard five miles every morning, on top of being on my feet for work sixteen hours a day. And yet, nothing I do makes my hips any less wide. One bite of something not on the infinitesimal list of approved foods, and my ass balloons two sizes. Granted, I'm in way, way better shape than I was at eighteen. I just have to fight for it tooth and nail, while my dick-bag brother can eat pizza and ice cream and tacos and drink beer by the gallon and stay looking like a goddamn model. Not fair.

And he's taller.

Twins, yet I barely clear five-six, while he gets to be an even five-ten. It's stupid.

"Fine. I'm cranky. Dad told his stupid little receptionist that I'm uptight and have no sense of humor."

"Because you are, and you don't." He exhales smoke

through his nose. "Is that the new receptionist? What's her name? Flossie? Barbie? Something dumb."

"Candy."

He nods. "Yeah, Candy." He grins, nodding. "She's hot." A glance at me. "I nailed her."

I gag. "Of *course* you did."

He shrugs. "Perks of the job, right?"

I turn slowly to stare at him. "Perks of the *job*? What job, Dell? You've never worked a day in your useless fuck-boy life."

"Again, you wound me," he says, miming an arrow hitting his chest over his heart. "I'll have you know I got you guys the Oak Glen contract. I was nailing the daughter of the guy who owns the property, and talked McKenna Construction up to her, and she mentioned it to her dad, and he hired you. So, you're welcome. Consider me your marketing department in the wild. A traveling salesman, you might say."

"Nailing. Why nailing? Why do you always say you *nailed* this girl or that girl? It's so…*gross*. Demeaning, and immature, and just…gross."

He frowns at me. "What do you want me to say?" His voice takes on a deep, mocking tone. "I'm *making love* to them? Fuck that. They're hookups. I'm nailing them. It's what it is." He points at me. "Not my fault you're a sexless prude, Dee-Dee. Some of us actually like to live a little, unwind, enjoy life."

His words are an echo of Daddy's from earlier,

except coming from Dell they sound douchey rather than wise.

I swallow the last of my glass of wine before I throw it in his face. Go inside, pause before shutting the door. "You can see yourself home, Dell. And next time you think about dropping by to spend quality time with me? Don't." I slam the door and lock it.

Do I pour myself another glass of wine? Yes I do. Have I had more than my usual allowance of two glasses? Yes I have.

Am I sorry? Only a little.

Sexless prude? SEXLESS PRUDE? Who the *fuck* does he think he is?

A fist pounds on the door. "Dee-Dee."

I ignore it.

Tell my Alexa to play Justin Timberlake very loudly. "DEE-DEE!"

"God help me," I mutter to myself. I pause the music and open the door a crack. "*What*, Dell?"

He's sheepish. "I, uh."

"What could you *possibly* want from me?"

"Do you have any spec homes done enough that I could crash in one for a few days?"

I blink at him. "No. And even if I did, I wouldn't let you. Also, why? You have a three-million-dollar condo in LA."

The trademark Dell grin, sheepish, sarcastic, and gloating all at once. "I sort of told this model I'm…uh, *dating*…that I own my own home up here. I just need it for a weekend. I have a guy who can come in and furnish the place all pimped out, and I'll have it cleaned out and empty again by Monday at noon. Promise."

"A model."

"Yeah. Amber Jane. You may have heard of her."

"Does she have a last name, or just two stupid first names?"

"I dunno. That's her stage name. I don't think it's her legal name." Another of those grins. "We're not quite at the sharing personal information stage."

I cackle. "You're screwing her, but you don't know her actual name?"

He sighs. "I actually like her. I want to impress her."

"Oh, you *actually* like her. Meaning she's *not* just a wet hole with fake tits?" I roll my eyes. "If you want to impress her, maybe you should do something with your life. Like, say…learn to read. Get a job. I've heard the Wendy's in town is hiring. You probably can't fuck that up *too* bad."

He blinks at me. "Jesus, Dee. That was actually really harsh."

"You need a Kleenex to dry your tears?"

A sigh. "What did I ever do to you, Delia?"

I boggle at him. "You want a list? I mean, off the top of my head…*nothing*. You've never done a damn thing for me. Including stopping your shithead friend *Thai* from making my life a living hell for eighteen years. Other than that? Let's see…oh! I know! Mooching off the family business, never being around to help Mom and Dad. Not working, *ever*. Let's see…what else? Oh, I know! The one friend I ever had, you screwed. Remember Vivian Harris? My best and only friend from seventh grade? Whom you fucked in the back of a limo on prom night? Yeah, that comes to mind as something you did to me."

"*She* came on to *me!*" he protests.

"Did it occur to you to, oh, say, *turn her down*? Like, 'no, Viv, you're my sister's best friend, maybe we shouldn't have unprotected sex in the back of a rented limousine.'"

"I wore a condom," he mutters.

"Not what she said. And you wouldn't know the truth if it bit you on the face."

He shakes his head. "I dunno why I bothered. Sorry to have wasted your time, Delia." He turns to walk away.

"I'll make you a deal."

He turns around. "Okay?" A lift of an eyebrow. "I'm not apologizing to Vivian."

"Work for the company for one month. Thirty business days, not including weekends. I don't care what you do. Pick up nails at a jobsite. Drive supplies around—actually, no, I don't trust you with any actual responsibility. You could work with the marketing department—you *do* have an actual college degree, I think. Pick something and do it for thirty days. Or shit, do a different thing every day. I don't care. Just don't fuck anything up."

"If I agree to that, you'll let me have a house for the weekend?"

I cackle. "Dell, if you can work thirty whole days

in a row without fucking anything up, I'll *give* you the house, to own."

"Will I get paid?"

A disbelieving laugh bursts out of me. "*Paid*? You have a twenty-million-dollar trust fund!"

"I just…"

"No, Dell," I snap. "You will pitch in to earn a fraction of a *fraction* of the money you spend in your useless, idle, frivolous little life."

He closes his eyes briefly, and when he opens them, they're wounded. "You really don't think much of me, do you?"

"Not even a little bit, brother."

He extends his hand to shake mine. "It's a deal. Loan me the house for the weekend. I'll work for the company for thirty days, and then you'll sign a spec house over to me."

I ignore his hand. "And if you do fuck up or give up?"

He shrugs, dropping his hand when he realizes I have no intention of shaking it. "You'll get a lifetime of I-told-you-so out of it? Hell, I don't know."

I grab my phone off the table near the door, dial a number.

It rings twice, and then Cal, my lead project foreman, answers. "Hey, boss. What do you need?"

"Hi, Cal. Sorry to bother you this late on a weekend, but I need a quick favor."

"Sure, boss. Shoot."

"Is 2120 in Oak Glen livable?"

Cal hums thoughtfully. "Eh, it's not *sellable*, but yeah you could live in it. It just needs some cabinet pulls, touch-up paint, some switch plates and outlet plates. I think one of the bathrooms still needs the vanity installed."

"And it's not spoken for?"

"Negatory, boss. We had a nibble, but they ended up wanting something already done and we still had a good bit to finish at that point."

"Okay. My brother is borrowing it for the weekend. He says he'll be out by Monday at noon. Can you meet him with the key?"

Cal pauses. He doesn't like Dell any more than I do. "Doesn't he own—"

"Yeah, Cal, he does," I cut in. "It's a long story. Or, actually, it's not long, it's just stupid and I won't bore you with the details."

"Uh, yeah, sure. Twenty minutes?"

"Sounds good, thanks, have a good weekend."

"No problem-o, and you too."

"2120 Oak Glen Circle," I tell Dell, setting the phone aside. "You're welcome."

"I, uh…"

"You don't know where the Oak Glen subdivision is," I say. "God, you're useless. We've been working on that sub for two years, Dell. How do you not know where it is? You literally pass it to get here."

"Oh, that."

"Yes, Dell, *that*. The two hundred spec home

subdivision your family's business is building, the project that has added literally an entire fucking zero onto your net worth."

"Got it. 2120." He offers a wobbly grin at me. "Thanks, Delia."

"Yeah, well, try not to trash the place."

"I'm not throwing a kegger, Jesus."

"You never know, with you."

He just waves over his shoulder as he walks away. I shut the door, lock it, and lean back against it.

I may have been a *teensy* bit harsh on the poor sap, but everything I said is just the raw truth.

I sigh, pick up my glass of wine, and turn on Netflix.

"I'm *not* a sexless prude," I mutter to no one.

And just to prove it, I turn on a super-steamy Polish romance movie, 365 something.

Chapter
TWO

Matthais

"WHAT WE'RE REALLY INTERESTED IN IS DECREASING our clients' overhead costs, decreasing shipping time, maximizing space on shipping loads via breakthrough packaging techniques, and most importantly, drastically cutting each client's total carbon footprint." The young man opposite me, Marcus, is a few years younger than me, midtwenties to my thirty, and he's earnest. A start-up type. Khakis with the front of a polo tucked behind his belt, curly brown hair in an undercut, wearing Warby Parker glasses and Birkenstock sandals.

"Got it." I tap the arm of the chair with a fingertip, thinking through my options. "And my return on the investment?"

He smiled unevenly. "Well, Mr. Bristow, you'd be helping the planet, for one thing. The construction industry uses a colossal amount of nonrenewable resources, especially lumber. There's a lot of movement and drum beating regarding eco-conscious lumber harvesting, but our goal with this company is to eradicate the need for lumber entirely. We have plans for a facility that can 3D print the entire framing sections as a whole piece, which would increase the structural integrity *and* cost less."

"Right, and that's great, but how are you going to make money? And by you, I mean me."

He frowns. "We're a small start-up right now, Mr. Bristow. Can I guarantee you a return like, in the next six months? No. But we have people lined up to try our products. We're starting small, like I said before. 3D printed nails and screws, brackets, switch plates, things like that. All of it renewable, all of it recyclable, all of it engineered to withstand greater forces than traditional products. So whenever the house our product is in gets taken down, that plastic will be recycled rather than just tossed into a landfill where it would otherwise sit unchanging for the next thousand years. You know ninety percent of all plastic ever produced—"

"Still exists," I finish for him. "Yeah, you mentioned that statistic already." I adjust my tie—I hate ties, but I want to look the part. "So, if I invest, you can expand your vision, so to speak."

"We have the vision already. Like I said, we're actively working on designs for large-scale printers that can create entire framing sections, whole roofs as a single piece for cheaper than you can currently get them, stuff like that. We just need cash to build the facilities."

"And you have clients lined up."

"Yes, sir. If we were to take orders right now, I would think we could count on at least half a million in instant sales, just in the little pieces we're currently capable of producing, with the little bit of online marketing and crowdfunding we've done."

I nod. "Okay. I like your ideas. Show me some numbers, some projections." I scratch my stubble, deciding on a number. "I think I'm in for…say, two million?"

Marcus can't quite contain his excitement. "I can have those numbers for you right now, Mr. Bristow. Just… just hold on." He rummages on his desk, flipping through stacks of papers.

"I have another appointment to get to. Just email them to me." I stand up and button my suit coat. "My investment isn't going to disappear in the next twenty minutes, Marcus."

He abandons his search and extends his hand to me over his desk, and we shake. "Thank you for your time, Mr. Bristow."

I give him my best grin. "Hey, we're in business together now. Call me Thai."

"Well, Thai, I can tell you without reservation that all of us here at Tree-Free 3D Construction Supply are very excited to have you on board."

I can't help a laugh. "We might have to work on that name, though. It's a little…clunky."

He laughs sheepishly. "Yeah, we played with a lot of other ones, and believe it or not, that's the best one."

I shake my head. "What about…Green Lumber?"

He chokes on…a laugh? On shock? Not sure. "That's, um, already a company, sir."

"It is?"

"Yeah. Men's, um, supplements." He holds up a fist, and his index finger lifts slowly upward. "For, uh…men's…erectile….issues. Also, green lumber is already a thing, in the construction trade. Just means untreated lumber. Not what we're going for."

I wave a hand. "Whatever. Run a test group or something. A focus group. It's gotta roll off the tongue, and Tree-Free 3D Construction Supply just doesn't."

He nods. "Got it. Focus group." He makes a note on his phone—which is not an iPhone or an Android, but something…else. Nor is it an old-school dumbphone, like a Nokia.

"What kind of phone is that?"

"It's a Light Phone 2."

"A what?"

"Minimalist cell phone. It's e-ink, like on a Kindle. It can only call, text, and set alarms."

I shake my head. "Why?"

He snorts. "Well, because I needed to be free of the distractions and addictions of the smartphone age. I was on my phone literally all the time. Now, when I need to talk to someone, I have to call them, or text them. No more social media. No more doom-scrolling. When I make notes, I send them in a text to my assistant."

I shake my head again. "Weird, man, but you do

you." I pull my phone, the latest and greatest iPhone. "All right, well. Shoot me those numbers, and I'll work on getting the investment rolling. I gotta go, I have an appointment to get to."

I do actually have an appointment. With Destiny.

In this case, Destiny has utterly mind-blowing DDD tits, and considers the art of the no-hands blowjob to be her calling in life.

Sure, the tits are fake and talking to her is like talking to a tree stump, if the tree stump was a vapid bimbo with an IQ in direct inverse proportion to her silicone content. But damn, can she suck.

An hour later, I'm on the balcony of my borrowed San Francisco condo, naked, watching Destiny do her no-hands best. Which is pretty damn fantastic.

My phone rings.

"Dammit," I hiss.

Destiny doesn't pause but does glance up at me through the curtain of bottle platinum hair, batting her eyelashes. My cock plunges through her lips.

My phone goes silent, and I close my eyes again.

Seconds later, it rings again.

"Fuck."

I sit up. "Hold on," I murmur. "Just…hold that thought."

"Uh-huh. Don't be gone long. You're not done yet, mister."

Good lord. That's her idea of sexy talk.

I grab the phone off the island inside. "Yeah?"

"Is that any way to answer the phone, Matthais?" My mother's voice.

Yeesh. What a way to ruin a hard-on. "Sorry, Mom. What's up?"

"Your father tells me you've invested in a company."

"You have to call me for this? Yeah, Mom, I did. It's an eco-friendly construction supply thing. They 3D print stuff for builders."

"You should pitch it to your friend Dell. He's been working for his family, lately."

I snort. "Dell? Work? Not likely. He's lazier than I am."

"It's a deal with his sister, I believe."

Correction—*that's* a hard-on killer, referencing Delia McKenna.

"Great. Look, I have company, so I'm gonna let you go."

"Are you going to visiting home any time soon?"

"I dunno, Mom. I'll let you know. Bye." Click. Phone off.

Where was I? Oh, yes—balls-deep in Destiny's mouth.

She's sitting in my chair, scrolling on her phone. Doesn't see me, at first, even when I stand right in front of her. Then she looks up, startled.

She looks me over, head to toe and back up to the middle. "Well, hello there. What have we here?" She flicks me with her tongue. "Ooh, this is yummy. I think I'll have some of this."

I'm tempted to tell her to shut up and get to it already, but I like to think I've outgrown that kind of rudeness. "Destiny."

She licks, and licks. "Uh-huh?"

"Let's go inside. I think it's your turn, now."

Another hour later, I'm trying to figure out how to get rid of Destiny. She's made herself awful cozy, asleep naked on the bed, on top of the covers. I think she's faking, hoping I'll see her lying there naked and want yet another round, and that one more fuck will lead, somehow, to me letting her stay the night. Which would, of course, lead to having breakfast together. And breakfast together would lead to an afternoon in bed, and suddenly, voila, I'd be in love.

Right.

I shoot a quick text: *Dell, buddy. I need you to call me in five minutes and invite me out. I got a stage-three clinger to brush off.*

Dell answers within seconds. *Got you covered. I want to get a drink for real anyway. Where are you?*

Me: *I'm in SF. Where are you?*

Dell: *River Gulch actually.*

Me: *Mom said you were doing some sort of work for the company?*

Dell, with an eye roll emoji: *Yeah it's a deal I made with Delia. I needed to borrow a house for the weekend and this was the only way that tightfisted slave driver would loan me one.*

Me: *Why would you need a house in RIVER GULCH?*

Dell: *Long story but it involves Amber Jane.*

Me: *The model and cam girl? That Amber Jane?*

Dell: *One and the same. And the short version is yes my friend she's as hot in person as she is in the magazines. Hotter maybe.*

Me: *You still nailing her?*

Dell: *why u gonna claim sloppy seconds?* A crying laughing emoji follows this.

Me: *I mean, would it be worth it?*

Dell: *Youll have to keep wondering. I actually LIKE this chick. We even have actual conversations LOL.*

Me: *ha, right.*

Dell: *It's true. Don't laugh but I might even go exclusive with her. see what happens.*

Me: *By exclusive, you mean cut down to only one other side piece.*

Dell: *I know I know. but fr I like her and I mean exclusive like actually.*

Me: *Well good luck with that, then. I mean it. Call me in five.*

Dell: *Why wait five minutes? Why not tell her your friend texted you and invited you out for a boy's night?*

Me: *Trust me. This is the way.*

Dell: *Whatever u say man. Five minutes, then.*

I putz around noisily, and Destiny pretends to sleep. Once, I even catch her, out of the corner of my eye, peek at me through slitted lids, and adjust her position subtly. Convincing acting, actually. She flops her torso over, so her ass and legs are sideways with her heels tucked up against her butt, but her upper body is facing upward. Doesn't look comfortable, but it does do very interesting things to the lovely balloons on her chest.

My phone rings five minutes later on the dot, and I have a conspicuously loud conversation with Dell, and then hang up.

By then, Destiny has abandoned the sleeping act. "You have to leave?"

Good god, the pout is comical. Pursed lips in a moue, eyebrow lifted.

"Yeah, I haven't seen my buddy Dell in a few weeks, so we're gonna hang." I tug on jeans commando, and she watches me button them with regret and longing; I've been known to have that effect on women. "It's been fun, though."

She rolls her eyes at me. "Wait, hold on. Let me guess...don't call you, you'll call me."

Not far off from where I was going, actually. "You said it, not me."

She sighs. "I kept hoping you'd reveal some, like, hidden depths. Maybe start thinking about getting more than just a quick suck-and-fuck out of me." She opens her door. "I guess I was mistaken."

"I guess so," I say.

"Wow." She shakes her head. "You really are an as-shole, aren't you?"

I nod. "You knew that when we met, though. I've never hidden it."

"And you're just…cool with it? Being an asshole?"

"It's always worked for me. Why stop now?" I wink at her. "See you around, Destiny."

She just huffs and shakes her head and climbs in. Rolls her window down and ducks, peers at me. "Don't call me, Thai—I'll call you."

Her tires squeal as she peels out around the corner and out of the parking garage under the building.

Guess the BJ appointments with Destiny have come to an end.

Dell calls back before I've left the parking garage. "Hey, bro. So, I'll just meet you in San Francisco."

I laugh. "You're three hours away, Dell. How do you propose to do that?"

I can hear his shit-eating grin. "Dad's finally letting me take the helicopter."

"Oh?"

"Legit. It's a little one, and it's only got four seats plus the pilot, but shit, it's faster than driving. He's letting me take it down there."

"That's pretty sick, actually. You gotta take me up when you get here. I've been after Dad to get one for years but so far no luck."

"What a cheap-ass, right?"

"No shit," I say. "Like, come on, dude. You've got hundreds of millions stashed away in literally six different offshore banks. Just spring for a damn chopper." I'm out of the garage, now, tires squealing as I peel out of the garage, because what's the point of having 710 horsepower if you don't drive like it? "So, you're actually working? What are you doing?"

He sighs. "It's such bullshit. I'm working with the marketing department. Errand bitch stuff, making copies, proofreading designs, monitoring mass print jobs, answering phones, shit like that."

"At least it's not manual labor, right?"

He laughs. "As if, bro. My sister is such an overachieving bitch, though, for real. The shit she said to me, you have no idea."

"Just because *she* wants to work for a living doesn't mean *you* have to."

"I can't tell if you're being sarcastic or not, motherfucker."

"Neither can I," I say with a laugh. "What's your dad think about you actually working?"

He huffs dismissively. "I don't think he even knows. The old fart has pretty much tapped out, for the most part. Dee pretty much runs the whole show in all but name."

Old fart? That's his dad. Even for me, that's a bit…I dunno. It just makes me a little uncomfortable. I'm not, like, best friends with my father, but I respect him enough to not refer to him as an old fart.

"So. How's your sister?" I hear myself asking.

Dell cackles. "What, like you suddenly care?"

"Hell no," I say, immediately. "I don't know why I even said that."

"The day you and Delia can spend a single second

in each other's presence without resorting to actual knife fighting is the day I *settle down*." The way he says this makes it sound like a curse, like the worst thing he can think of.

"I could get along with her. She's the one who hates me."

"Because you made it your life mission to make her miserable." A pause. "And buddy, you succeeded."

"The *point is*," I say, loudly, to cover the sting of guilt I feel at this, "that *I* could get along with *her*."

"You *say* that," Dell says with a snort. "But you haven't seen in her years. She's even more insufferable now than she was in high school. She's a legit boss of thousands of people. The authority has gone to her head."

"Thousands?"

"Well, hundreds, at least." He sounds like he's outside, and then I can barely hear him over the roar of a helicopter. "Gotta go, my chopper is waiting."

"I hate you, you lucky fuck."

"You know it! See you soon!"

I hit the shower, rinsing away the smell of Destiny and the stink of the things we got up to.

I still can't figure out why I asked Dell about his sister. The last thing on the planet I want is to ever see that girl again.

Right?

I do my damnedest to put Delia McKenna out of my head.

Chapter
THREE

Delia

"D ADDY?" I FORCE MYSELF TO KEEP MY VOICE EVEN AND firm. "How are you?"

The room is filled with the beeping of machines, the smell of antiseptic. It's not a hospital room—he refused to go to the hospital after his fall, so we brought the hospital to him, transformed what had been his main floor study into a hospice room. Full-time live-in nurse, all the best treatments and medicine money can buy. If it can help you heal, we've got it.

The problem is, he's just…tired. Done in.

He blinks at me, slow and owlish, as if it takes a moment to process my presence and then my words. His skin is papery, translucent. "Hi, honey-bunny. I'm doing."

"Feeling okay?"

He huffs, a weak laugh that still manages his trademark bite of sarcasm. "Fit as a fiddle, my love. Ready to roof." Inside joke—roofing is hellishly demanding work. He pats my hand. "How's business?"

"It's great. We just broke ground on the new section of Oak Glen. I'm working on a contract for a two-and-a-half-million-dollar custom home. Working on upselling them up to an even three."

"Good girl. Upsell, upsell, upsell."

"I know, Daddy."

He nods, closes his eyes and just breathes a moment. "Have you seen Dell lately?"

I choke on my tears. "No, not really. I spoke to him...last week, just briefly. He said he'd come see you this weekend."

Dad's jaw clenches. "I want to see him. I need to talk to him."

"Don't waste your breath, Daddy. Save it for getting better."

Dad's laugh is sarcastic. "I'm not gonna get better, Dee-Dee. This is it."

"Don't talk like that, Daddy. You're gonna be fine."

He pats my hand, and this time it's condescending. "Or just keep thinking that. Not what I recommend, but if it's what you have to do."

"Dad."

"I'm *dying*, sweetheart. I've been hanging on for months, and I'm about ready to let go." A sigh. "I just want to see you and your brother getting along, first. I want...I want Dell to step up."

"If you want me to face up to the fact that you're...

that you're dying, then you have to face up to the fact that Dell isn't going to step up."

"He has to."

"He won't." I blink hard. "He knows you're…" I can't say the words again. "He *knows*, Daddy. And he's visited you, what? Once? Twice in the last six months? He's too busy spending money and collecting sluts."

"I want to talk to him. Get him here. Say whatever you need to, do whatever. Just get him here." A pause, a slow breath. "I have one last plan."

I sigh. "Okay, Daddy. I'll get him here."

His eyes meet mine. "I know you've been expecting me to turn over the reins to you, make you president and CEO."

I have been. I don't know what he's waiting for—I've been de facto CEO for a year and a half, now.

He sighs. "Just…just let me talk to Dell, first."

I kiss his forehead. "I'll go call him."

He nods. "Okay, sweetheart. Thanks."

"You rest. I'll bring him in when he gets here."

I close the door behind me and head out to the back deck. It's evening, and the sun is setting onto the tops of the trees. I call Dell.

It goes to voicemail.

"Fine, cocksucker," I mutter. "I'll just spam you until you answer."

So, I call him again. Voicemail.

I send him a text: *Call me. NOW.*

Copy the text, paste it, send it again, and again, and again.

Call him.

Text him.

Call him. Text him.

Finally, after twenty-two voicemails, each one saying "CALL ME, DELL MCKENNA," and forty-one repetitions of the same text message, my phone finally, finally rings.

"*What* Delia? Jesus fucking Christ."

"Don't speak to me that way, one. Two, you need to get home. And I mean *now*."

"But, I'm—"

"I don't give two shits what you're doing. I don't care if you're having dinner with the fucking Pope—GET… HOME…*NOW*."

"Is Dad…?"

"Still alive…for now. But get here."

"I'm in Miami, so It'll take a while."

"Charter a private jet, then. Use the family account for all I care. Just get here."

"You took away my access to the family account."

"I didn't, Dad did."

"Because you told him to."

"I'm not having this argument with you. Use your own goddamn money. Just get here."

"God, fine."

"I know, Dell, such a hardship, having to come all the way back home to see your dying father."

"Fuck you, Delia. Seriously."

"Right back at you, brother."

I'm woken by the sound of tires on the gravel drive—I'm in the chair on the back deck, still, sprawled out, slumped low, head hanging backward. I start upright at the door closing. I check my Apple Watch—12:41a.m.

I work to my feet, rubbing the sleep from my eyes, and meet my brother in the foyer—he has a Louis Vuitton overnight bag on his shoulder, Versace sunglasses on his head, holding back his thick black hair, and he looks exhausted.

"Took you long enough," I snap.

"Lay off, Dee," he mumbles. "I couldn't find a last-minute charter. The soonest flight I could get was a three-stop going to Atlanta and then Minnesota and then LA, and then I had to get another flight to San Francisco and then rent a car to get up here. I swear, I did my best." He rolls his shoulder. "I had to pay through the fucking nose to upgrade to first class, or I'd have been stuck in the back row of fucking economy."

"Poor you."

He just sighs. "Is he awake?"

I shrug. "He's in and out pretty much all the time, now." I head for the study—Daddy's room, now. "He'll want to see you."

Dell shifts from foot to foot. "I, he—if he's resting, maybe—"

I ignore him and open the door to the study. "Come on."

Dell sets his bag down and follows. Dad is asleep, mouth open. I panic for a split second, but the monitor still beeps steadily, if more slowly than it should. According to the doctors, there's nothing specific wrong with Dad, it's just…age. I perch on the edge of the bed and touch his shoulder.

"Daddy."

He stirs. Blinks awake. His eyes go to me, and he smiles—and then his gaze flicks past me, registering Dell. "You showed up, finally."

Dell's shoulders slump, and he flinches as if struck. "Yeah." He rallies, and goes to the other side of the bed. "I'm here, Dad."

Daddy eyes me. "Can we have some time alone, Dee-Dee?"

"Sure, Dad. I'll be in there. Just let me know if you need anything."

He pats my knee. "Go home. You need sleep, honey-bunny. You have a company to run."

I nod. "Okay. I love you. I'll see you in the morning."

I lift my chin at Dell. "Night."

It's the nicest thing I can think to say to him.

He just nods.

When I close the French doors to the study, Mom is hovering at the end of the hall, a blue silk dressing gown not quite closed all the way, revealing a little more of my mother than I'd like to see, but she's half asleep.

"Is that Cordell?"

Mom is the only person on the planet who still calls him that. He's been Dell since we were two, just like I've been called Delia since the same time, even though technically the name on my birth certificate is Cordelia. No one ever calls me that, and I don't think many people except Mom even know our names aren't actually, legally Dell and Delia.

I tug the robe closed and tie it for her. "Yeah, that's Dell. He's talking to Dad."

"Oh, good. About time that boy got his act together."

I don't correct her. "He'll be here a few days, I think. You can go back to bed."

She frowns. "I want to see Cordell."

I hug her. "I'm going home. I'm not sure how long they'll be talking."

Mom hugs back, her arms thin and brittle and soft. "Good night, Dee-Dee. I love you."

"Love you, Mom."

Despite what I said to Mom, Dell is nowhere to be found the next morning.

Dad won't tell me what they talked about.

Mom spends every waking second at Dad's side, in his bed with him. They watch old movies together and don't talk.

FIVE DAYS LATER

Dawn, or just past. Dad's favorite time of day. Since I was a little girl, too young to tie my own shoes, I've been waking up at dawn to have coffee with Daddy. When I was little, it was chocolate milk in a coffee mug. By thirteen, it was actual coffee.

Past few months, we've had our coffee together in his bed in the study.

Today, there's no coffee.

I bring it to him anyway. He can't sit up to hold it.

He just attempts a smile. "I think…we can skip… the coffee…Dee."

I set it aside. "Okay." I hold his hand instead.

"Where's…Dell?"

I texted him last night, called him. Told him it would be today.

Dad spent most of yesterday holed up in here with Quentin Albright Quince, the family attorney. Dad wouldn't say about what, the only thing he's ever kept from me, that I know of.

"He's…he's not here," I whisper.

Daddy pins me with a look, and even now his blue-blue eyes can pierce, hold authority. "Call him."

I stand up. "Okay."

He grabs my arm, holds on. "Here. Now."

I dial Dell's number. It goes to voicemail. Daddy takes the phone from me, holds the bottom end to his mouth. "Dell, this is your father. I'm about to die, son, and you're not here. This is a moment I swear you'll re-gret for the rest of your life." He pauses for a long time, catching his breath. "I love you, son. I wish I could say I was proud of you, but...I'll be watching over you from heaven. Try...try to make me proud...Cordell. I love you. I'll always love you, no matter what. Goodbye, son."

That's the only time I've ever heard Dad refer to him by his full name.

He presses the red end call button and the phone drops from his hand. "I've done all I can do," he says. "The rest is up to him."

A question lingers in my mind, but I refuse to ask it. Not now. It doesn't matter.

He closes his eyes and the monitor beeps, beeps, beeps.

Mom sniffles.

After a while, he looks at me. "I love you, Delia. I'm so, so proud of you, of all you've accomplished in such a short time."

I blink away tears. "I love you, Daddy. I learned it all from you."

He squeezes my hand, surprisingly strong. "Learn one more thing from me."

"Okay?"

"Have fun. You work too much." He tries a smirk, mostly succeeds, but it's faint. "And get laid!"

"Daddy!" I scold, but my heart's not really in it.

"For real. You've never brought a boy home."

"I go on dates. I've had boyfriends. I've just never met anyone worth bringing home."

"Oh. Well, find one. A good one. Someone…someone who'll make you laugh and…force you to relax."

I snort. "Not likely, Daddy. I was born grumpy, remember?"

He laughs, and in something out of a cliche Hallmark movie, it turns into a dry, rattling cough. "You were. You came out yelling and you never…stopped."

"I don't yell."

"You don't need to. Your attitude does it for you."

"I'm a top boss, Daddy. You taught me."

He pats my hand, squeezes it. "For your next trick, try being…just a girl."

I shake my head, tears falling. "I don't know how."

He sighs. Eyes close. "You'll meet a man who can show you. Let him."

"Okay, Daddy."

He fixes me with that stern, knowing look, rising a little. "Promise."

"I promise."

He nods. Closes his eyes again, sinking back into the pillow. "That's a promise you're making me on my deathbed, Delia. You break it, I'll haunt you." A smirk, his eyes still closed. "In my underwear."

I laugh through tears. "I'll keep it, I promise I will."

He looks past me, to Mom, who's sitting in a chair, watching, dry-eyed but only just barely. "Now let me talk your mom a bit before I go."

Like he's taking a trip.

I kiss his forehead, and leave the room. When I'm halfway down the hall, almost to the kitchen, I collapse backward against the wall, clapping my hand over my mouth to stifle the sobs.

I can't.

God, I can't.

I make it the rest of the way into the kitchen. Above the fridge, there's a bottle of Blanton's Dad has kept there for years. It's his emergency get-your-shit-together-and-deal-with-it whiskey.

I pour a couple fingers into a juice glass and toss it back, hissing as it burns on the way down. I hate whiskey.

It jolts me, as it's supposed to, and I breathe. Gather my nerves.

A few minutes later—ten? Twenty? An hour? I have no idea—I was dazed, or dozing, or just spaced out, I don't know—Mom calls me, her voice soft and weak.

"Delia?"

I run into the study.

Dad is still…awake. Mom is lying on the bed with him, curled up against his side, her head on his shoulder, his hand on her waist, her hand on his chest.

He smiles at me. Reaches for me, and I bend over, hugging him and Mom together. His hand rests on my head. "Kiss me, my dear, I'm off."

I want to laugh—he's so insouciant about it, so flip. But I can't. Don't.

I hug him tighter. "I love you, Daddy, so much."

He tilts his head to the other side. "Over…over there." I lie on the other side of him and he rests his hand on my shoulder. "My girls."

Mom sniffles.

"Dell…" It's a faint whisper.

No one answers.

"Love you, Ginny."

Mom's only answer is to kiss him, trembling. If she whispers something against his lips, it's too quiet for me to hear. Meant just for him.

His hand tightens on my shoulder, ever so gently. "Cordelia." Haven't heard that name out of his lips in living memory. "Dee."

"Daddy, I'm here."

"Be happy."

"I will."

After a while: "Love…girls."

How long later is it when his hand drifts away, off my shoulder?

I don't know.

The front door slams open.

"Dad?" Dell, from the hallway.

The study door opens, slowly. Fearfully—I can hear the fear in the way the door opens.

I don't move.

"Dad?"

I don't answer. Neither does Mom.

Daddy certainly doesn't.

Can't, not ever.

"Daddy?" His voice is choked. Gasping. Thick. Small. "Dad, no."

I get up. At some point, the hospice nurse turned off the machines. She's waiting in the other room. Waiting to do…whatever happens now. For once, I choose to not be in charge of it.

I push past Dell but stop in the doorway, a foot away. Don't look at him. I'll never be able to look him in the eye again.

Words bubble in my throat:

You missed it.

He died and you weren't here.

Where were you?

But nothing comes out. The word died on my tongue.

"Delia?" It's a whisper, thin, from Dell.

I open my mouth, but nothing comes out. I just shake my head and walk away.

Chapter
FOUR

Delia

I STRAIGHTEN MY BLAZER AS I STAND UP. QUENTIN ALBRIGHT Quince has called us into his office for the reading of the will—Mom, me, and Dell.

Mr. Quince needed a few minutes to get everything ready, so we've been in the waiting room outside his office. Mom and I are in side-by-side chairs, and I'm holding Mom's hand. Dell is as far away from us as the room will allow—he's scrolling on his phone, but I can tell he's not really seeing anything. It's just so he doesn't have to look at us.

I put Mom between Dell and me, when we sit opposite the lawyer's desk.

There's shuffling of papers, and Quentin clears his throat. He's old—he was Dad's friend first, from childhood. He looks as emotional as I feel. Being a man, and an old-school traditionalist, he keeps it together.

"Ginny, Dell, Delia." He scrapes a liver-spotted hand

through his thinning hair, which is still as black as it is gray, despite his age. Funny how people age at different rates—Quentin could pass for ten years younger than he is, even though he's six months older than Daddy. "No speeches, no reading the legal nonsense. Doug would've wanted me to cut right to the chase."

Dell fidgets, his hands twisting a thread on his jeans. Mom rests a hand over his, as if we were in church and he was five all over again.

"What I will read is the important parts." He clears his throat. "I, Douglas Bryan McKenna, being of sound mind and failing body, all that stuff." Another hem and haw. "To my beloved, darling wife, Virginia, I leave the home and property, the acreage in Montana, and all of our other nonliquid assets. You'll divvy them up or sell them or leave them to the kids as you see fit, in your own time, in your own way." Quentin pauses, adjusts the gold wire-rimmed octagonal reading glasses on his nose. "To my children, Cordelia and Cordell, I leave the company, split fifty-fifty between them. I purchased back all the shares from Boyd and the others, for more than they're worth. So now, you two own it, totally. Delia—Dee-Dee." Quentin glances at me. "His words, not mine."

"Dee-Dee. Quit your hollering. I know, and I'm sorry. It's not fair, but it's what I feel I must do. Dell— you get fifty percent of the company you haven't spent a single second working for. Why? Because you don't get a cent from the rest of my will if you don't take possession and go to work earning it. Learn from your sister. She's in charge. Listen to her. Work with her. Make me proud." Quentin pauses. Looks from me to Dell and back. "There's, um, a rather enormous sum of liquid assets that he's divided between the two of you, but it's conditional upon you working together for a period of at least six months before it's released." A pause. "Dell, the condition here applies specifically to you. Work with your sister for at least six months, or you forfeit the rest of your inheritance. Meaning, the total sum goes to Delia."

I'm speechless.

McKenna Construction is MINE. It's fucking *mine*. *I've* worked there as a paid employee since I was fourteen and legally able to be employed, and I was Daddy's shadow before that. *I* put in the thousands and thousands of hours. *I* built up the client base. *I* expanded operations as far south as San Diego and as far north as fucking Redding.

I did all that. *Me*.

What has Dell done? Not a damn thing.

Spent money.

Fucked women.

Drank booze.

I strive for calm, and go maybe a little beyond it—my voice is quiet, thin as a razor, and colder than dry ice. "Is that all, Mr. Quince?"

He blinks at me. "The sum to be divided—"

I close my eyes. "I know the sum—I don't *care* about the money." Stand up. Breathe. Don't scream. Don't throw the stapler through the window. Don't assault Dell. "Short answer, please, Quentin: is there any way to go around this? To get me Dell's share, right here, right now?"

"I…no. I'm afraid not. He was very clear. You have to work together."

"There's no…end run?"

A shake of his head. "No, Miss McKenna. He made sure there wasn't."

I nod, eyes closed. "Okay, then." I turn and leave. "I'll be at the office. I have work to do." I leave, and I don't look back. "See that Mother gets home, please." I say this to no one in particular.

I get to the office—my office. Dad's office, the big corner one, which has been mine for months. I have a nameplate and everything: Delia McKenna, President and CEO.

There's a button that tints the windows opaque, both the exterior ones and the windows into the rest of the office. I tint them black. Shut off the lights.

Pull Dad's *other* bottle of emergency get-you r-shit-together-and-deal-with-it whiskey out, and drink it.

I get very, very, very drunk.

Chapter
FIVE

Matthais

"IT'S FUCKING STUPID," DELL SAYS, FOR THE TENTH TIME in as many minutes. "I don't *want* half the fucking company! I never did! You'd think the fact that I have stayed as far away from McKenna Construction as possible over the years would be a pretty significant clue that *I'm not fucking interested*. But no. Ohhhhh no—" He tosses back a shot of scotch; I think he's setting to break some kind of speed-drinking record, especially considering we're drinking very expensive, very old, very rare scotch. "What does the dumb old goat do? Fucking ups and *dies*, and leaves me half the goddamn company. And I *have* to take it or I don't get my fucking inheritance. What kind of an inheritance comes with a condition?"

"The kind for lazy rich boys who haven't done a single hard day's work in his life?" I sip my double on the rocks, smirking at him.

"Much better?" he parrots, then repeats it with emphasis. *"Much better*? Bitch, you're worse."

I'm not wholly faking the glare I give him. "That may have been true once, but it's not. It hasn't been for a long time, Dell. I'm a legit businessman. Do you know my credentials? Econ degree from Yale, internship at Goldman Sachs, business school at Wharton. Thirty million in investments across half a dozen different fields."

Dell just snorts. "Investments," he snorts. "How is that work? It's just spending money, except you don't get a new toy or anything out of it."

I groan a laugh. "Dell. It's an investment. It's not about an immediate return. I invest money in a company in exchange for shares of that company's revenue. I invest money, and if they do well, I make money."

"Cool. Still not work."

"Is fucking too, douchebag. You have to dig into the company. What's their business plan? How do they make money? What's their overhead? What's their plan for the future? Have they actually made any money? Do they have an actual feasible product? You have to do research."

Dell eyes me skeptically. "And you, *you*, Thai Bristow—*you* have been doing this? You, who taught me everything I know about how to successfully pimp it as an idle rich influencer. Your idea of work is putting together a photo shoot for your Insta. Shit, Thai, you know less about work than I do."

I huff. "Dell, for a long, long time, that would have

been true." I shrug, sip scotch. "Like I said, it's just not true anymore."

"It's not?"

I wobble my head side to side. "No, not really."

I finish my double and order another with a lift of an index finger; the bartender, a cute blonde with a sweet rack and a nice little heart-shaped ass, gives me a flirty grin.

"So what changed?" Dell asks.

I sigh. "I...I dunno, man. I just...I was getting bored, honestly. I mean, I'm thirty. Dad was a multi-millionaire on his own by my age, and Mom was neck-deep in medical school still, at one of the most prestigious universities in the world. So, is there, like, a little pressure to live up to his example? Sure. I've resisted it so far, but...like I said, honestly I was just bored out of my fucking skull. Like, with life. I've bought all the cool cars, I've been everywhere on the planet there is to go that's fun, because I'm not into mountain climbing or traversing, like, deserts or jungles. I've banged hot women and famous women and average women and even a few hit up ugly chicks just for the hell of it—and yeah, even a virgin once. And to that, I say never again. Too much pressure, man. Too much fuckin' pressure." I wave a hand in a wild, frustrated gesture. "What am I supposed to *do*? I don't have a talent, like music or painting or photography or...I don't even know. Or some *cause* to be all pissed off about all the time. So what am I supposed to do? You can only spend so much time on Instagram and TikTok and shit, and you can only drink so much before even that gets old. Even fucking you can't do all time, as much as I'd like to. The ol' wang needs a break, know what I mean?"

"Wang?" He chortles. "Did you really just call your dick a wang?"

"It was ironic."

"I don't think that's what ironic means."

I flip him off. "Like *you* know what ironic means? Shit, man, I graduated from Yale. I *should* know. I just wasn't paying attention. I slurped up all that knowledge, spewed it out for the grade, and promptly forgot it all."

"So you wasted…however fucking much money your parents spent sending you there, is what you're saying?"

I shrug. "Sure? Not like they care. They shit money, man. Dad had money before he got rich. My trust fund is largely carried over from him. Mom came from money, too. It's literally stupid. I have actually, literally, factually zero responsibilities. Zero expectations. Nothing to do. I may as well not even fucking *exist*, Dell." I blink as I realize what I just said. "Fuck, man. I didn't…" I frown, wipe my face, and take a slug of fifty-year-old Glenlivet.

Dell is eying me. "Dude, do I have to worry about you?" He's as serious as he's capable of getting. "Because I will, If I have to."

"No. It's just…it's true. My parents would be, like, sad. You'd be sad. But that's…it." My eyes are wide, shock shuttling through my system. "Fuck, man. It's true. I may as well not even exist for all the effect I have on the world."

"Dude, that's bullshit. If you're that worried about leaving, like, a legacy, just do what all rich people do when they decide they want to leave a legacy."

"And that would be what?" I ask with a wry smirk.

"Start one of those charitable foundation things in your name."

"I'm not talking about a fucking legacy, you fucking knob, I'm talking about *purpose*."

"Purpose."

"Correct."

"By which you mean purpose *other* than expensive booze and expensiver women?"

I narrow my eyes at him. "Did you just say... expensiver?"

He tosses back another shot. "Yes, I did. Yes, I know it's grammatically wrong or whatever the hell. I was being ironical."

"Again, not what ironic means, I don't think."

Dell sighs heavily. "Why are we talking about *you*, Thai? *I'm* the one with a crisis, here."

"Crisis? The thing where you have to work with your sister for six months before you inherit millions of dollars on *top* of your trust fund? That crisis?"

"Sounds douchey when you put it that way."

"Because it is douchey."

"You're supposed to be on my side here, Thai." He is genuinely upset, I think.

"I *am* on your side, Dell," I say with a sigh. "But as your best friend, I feel obligated to not blow smoke up your ass."

He's silent a moment, staring into the depths of his scotch, then takes a sip, brow furrowed. "You think I'm the asshole, here?"

I clap him on the shoulder. "Brother, we've always been the assholes. I thought you knew that."

He shrugs. "I mean, sure, in a funny way. Haha, yeah, I'm a dick, what're you gonna do about it? But this is different." He moves the rocks glass in small circles on the bar top, making the amber liquid swirl just beneath the rim. "Thai, I…it's just not fucking *fair*. For Delia, or me. She's the one who wants the company, not me. She worked for it, not me. And now, instead of giving her what she wanted and what she's worked for her whole fucking life, he wastes half of it on me. I don't fucking want it. I don't give a shit about construction. Maybe I do need to find something else to do with my life, but I can guaran-fucking-tee you it's not the family business."

I sip. "So…what are you going to do, Dell?"

He shakes his head. "I don't know. I don't…I don't know." He sips and hisses. More from frustration than because of the burn. "I…Thai, I'm genuinely at a loss. Can I do the work? Yeah. I'm not a dummy, you know? I'm perfectly capable. My issue has always been motivation. The problem here is I just don't…I can't do this. I can't take half off the business from Delia. I don't want it, I don't deserve it, and I just…I won't do it, Thai. I fucking *won't*."

"Then from how you explained it, you don't get your inheritance." I frown at him. For the first time, I realize how serious he is about this. For his sister, and not just himself.

He nods. "I know. I just don't see a way around it."

"You're willing to give up…shit, I don't even know how much it is. Thirty million dollars? Fifty?"

Dell shrugs. "I dunno. Somewhere in there. A fucking lot."

"And you're so dead set against working for McKenna Construction that you're willing to forgo that much cash?"

He nods. "I think I am. I understand what Dad was trying to do, I really do. I've been a useless piece of shit. I get that. But this isn't going to change me in the way he wants. It's not going to repair my relationship with Delia. If anything, it's going to make it worse."

"So…what? You just refuse?" I eye him; I can tell he's feeling the alcohol, but there's no humor in him, no levity. He's more serious than I've ever seen him, and I've known him literally my whole life.

He blinks rapidly, brows furrowing even deeper, and then he straightens, head tilting, jaw clenching.

"I know that look," I say. "That's your lightbulb moment face."

He turns to face me, scotch forgotten. "Buy me out."

I cough around a swallow of scotch. When I'm done hacking, I speak my question through a hoarse and raspy throat. "Excuse me?"

"You heard me, bitch. Buy—me—out. I'll sell it to you for a fucking steal. Nickels on the dime, or whatever the phrase is."

I ask the obvious question: "Why not just sell to your sister?"

"What's the fun in that?" he says, chortling. "At least if I sell you to, I'd get some entertainment out of this whole fucked-up situation." He tosses back another sip, then gestures at me with the tumbler. "Hell, you and Delia might make a great team, if you don't kill each other first. I mean, all that angst and anger could be redirected into running a business instead of at each other."

"I need another shot," I mumble, even though I'm still working on my second double. I glance at him. "You're serious about this?"

"Hell yes," he says. "Listen, I know my dad always thought that the business should go to family, but you *are* family and I think you could do an amazing job of taking the business to the next level. What do you have to lose?" He gestures at me again with his glass. "You've been getting all into this 'I'm a businessman, look at me doing business' thing, right? Investing, shit like that? Well, what better place to invest than a company you know damned well is a certain success. With Delia at the helm, as president and CEO, you have to know that McKenna

Construction is going to not only continue its current success trajectory, but most likely do even better. Dee was born and bred for one thing—to run that business. She couldn't fail at it if she tried."

I arch an eyebrow at him. "One problem with your little plan, bud."

"And that is?"

"There is no one on this planet your sister hates more than me." I laugh at the idea of showing up at the next board meeting—at how apoplectic she'd be. "It may solve *your* problem, if you're willing to give up the millions of dollars you'd get if you just sucked it up for half a year and did the work. And it may be good for me, because yeah, you're right, McKenna is absolutely the safest bet I can think of, as long as I survive your sister when she finds out what you did. And shit, Dell, we do this, *you*'d have to go into Witness Protection because your sister would flat out fucking murder you."

She hates me with damn good reason, something I increasingly find myself regretting and embarrassed about as I get older. I haven't seen her in a good ten years, but I find myself awake at night, sometimes, thinking with a burning pit of guilt in my stomach about all the horrible things I did and said to her over the years. I teased her mercilessly—about her weight, her appearance, the books she read, the things she said. If she misspoke, I mocked her. If she showed even an ounce of pride in something, I went out of my way to cut her down. Looking back, I'm not even sure why I was the way I was to her. I mean, I was a dick to everyone, because my family had more money than god, I was good-looking and popular, which meant I was an arrogant, entitled, egotistical bastard. But Delia McKenna? I went after her harder than anyone.

Shit, I once destroyed, on purpose, her most prized possession, a mint-condition first edition hardcover of *Harry Potter and the Half-Blood Prince*. I took it from her hands and threw it in a mud puddle—it was straight out of *Beauty and the Beast*, honestly. I did it for no other reason than to make her cry. And I succeeded.

Yeah, me owning half the company would give her an aneurism.

"You once claimed *you* could get along with *her*," Dell says, shaking me from my guilt-ridden line of thought.

"I could." Assuming she didn't—rightfully—kick me in the sack, first.

"Prove it."

I sigh. "Dell, buddy. You don't understand. It's not me you have to convince, it's her."

"I thought you're all grown up, Thai." He's got me, and he knows it. His shit-eating grin is abominable. "You mean to tell me you can't do it? You can't be a mature, responsible businessman around my sister?"

I groan. "This is a bad, bad, *bad* idea, Dell."

"Which is why it's a great idea," he says, the shit-eating grin spreading even wider. "One last prank."

"Except this one has lasting, real-world consequences. You're talking millions of dollars—shit, tens
of millions. You're talking ownership of a company with
hundreds, if not thousands, of employees. Their lives.
Their careers, their futures. This isn't something you do
on a lark, Dell. Sure, in a lot of ways, I'm still the same
old me I've always been. But I *have* grown up, Dell. I
genuinely want to start accomplishing things with my
life beyond the playboy bullshit. I'm taking it seriously.
And if I were to buy you out—and that's a seriously big *if*,
here—I'd take it seriously. I wouldn't be a silent investor.
I'd be involved. I'd want to be fifty percent of running
that company. With your sister. Delia McKenna. The
girl whose life I made it my mission to ruin, every single
day for eighteen fucking years. When I say she *hates* me,
that's not an exaggeration." I lean closer to him. "The
day we graduated, that party we threw?"

"When she put a snake down your pants?"

I squirm, remembering. "That snake was inches
from biting my dick, man. Still have nightmares about
it." I shudder. "Anyway. Yeah, that. I followed her into
the woods, and she fucking…she flat out told me she
hoped my plane crashed. And she wasn't kidding." I sigh,
grimacing. "And I can't say I blame her. I was kind of a
monster."

"I was right there with you. Thus the fact that we're
basically estranged."

I wince at the truth that their estrangement is at least
partially my fault. "I just don't know that you and me

doing this to Delia is…a good idea. In fact, it's a terrible idea. It'd be a whole new kind of torture for her."

"I mean, yeah, I know. Best option for her is for me to take some job in the company where I fulfill the terms of the will in such a way that I'm not in her hair, then take my money and run. But…I don't know, Thai. I'm just…I have this…I don't know the words." A long silence, as he considers. "I guess I feel like for the first time in my life, I'm going to take a stand. *I do not want* half the company. And I'm not going to pretend to fulfill Dad's intentions by spending six months making fucking copies in the marketing office. Dad wanted Delia and I to make up, to get along. He wanted me to…" He swallows hard. "To man up. To be a better person, I guess. And maybe…maybe this is my way of doing it. I just…I have to find my own way. I'm going to get the real crux of what Dad was trying to do, I'm just…I have to do it my way."

"And that means selling your half to your sister's worst enemy?"

A shrug. "Better than some random businessman who doesn't know or care about the family?" A wave of his hand. "And yeah, I know, selling out to her is the better way. But since when have I ever done anything the easy way or the right way? And I *know* you'll have fun. And shit, she may be spitting nails at first, but I think this could be good for her." A grin with the tumbler at his lips, words echoing into the glass. "Shit, maybe she'll even thank me, someday."

I know it's a bad idea. A really, truly, spectacularly bad idea. She very well might physically assault me. But then…I haven't actually seen or spoken to her in years. Literally, I haven't laid eyes on her or heard her voice in… ten years at least. Something like that. Maybe things will be different. Better. Less…antagonistic.

It's still a bad idea. And I'm not entirely sure what's motivating me when I hear my own voice: "All right, Dell. I'm in. You sell me your interest in the company, and I become part-owner of McKenna Construction." I point a finger at him. "But if your sister tries to kill us both, it's on you."

He grins. "Deal."

"For the record, I must protest this decision," Quentin Albright Quince says, even as he slides a thick contract across the desk to Dell. "It's a terrible idea. No offense meant to you, Mr. Bristow. And…my understanding of family dynamics leads me to believe Miss McKenna will be…less than thrilled."

Dell signs at all the requisite places. "I'm paying for your services on this out of my own pocket. It's my money, my interest in the family business, so it's my decision." He slides the contract over to me, along with the pen. "I'm doing this with full knowledge of the consequences, that I'm forfeiting my inheritance. That she may never speak to me again. But shit, she already despises me, so what do I have to lose, right?"

"I'm sure she doesn't despise you, Dell," Quentin begins.

Dell snorts. "Don't bullshit me, Quentin."

Quentin takes the contract from me when I finish signing it, looks it over. "All seems to be in order. Mr. Bristow, there's just the matter of payment?"

It had taken me almost a month to shift and liquidate enough assets to afford this. In that time, I'd attended Mr. McKenna's funeral; I'd stayed in the back, well away from Delia and the family, as well as my own family. I doubt they even knew I was there, honestly.

I'd already set up the wire transfer, so it was a matter of completing it via my bank's app. With the wire transfer complete, I return my phone to my suit coat's inner pocket; not sure why, but I felt compelled to wear a suit to this.

"Done," I say.

Dell sighs, fiddling with a corner of the top piece of paper of the contract. "Thank fucking god that's done."

I eye him. "There's still time to undo it."

"Hell no," he says with a laugh. "I'm happier than I've ever been, all things considered." He claps me on the shoulder as he stands up. "If she pitches a fit, tell her the truth: it was my idea and I bullied you into it."

I cackle. "Yeah, you really bullied me. I'm still traumatized."

He shoves a hand in the hip pocket of his jeans.

"Well, Thai…you're a fifty percent owner of McKenna Construction. How do you feel?"

I blow out a breath as I wipe my hand down my face. "Honestly? A little scared your sister might actually physically assault me when I show up for the next meeting." I glance at my watch, in a bizarrely idiotic gesture, considering my next question: "Speaking of which, when are the meetings, Dell?"

He splutters a laugh. "Like I know? I've never been to one."

Quentin sighs; he hands the completed contract to an assistant. "Wednesdays at one thirty," he murmurs. "At the headquarters in town."

I jolt to my feet. "Well shit, man, why didn't you say so sooner? It's one-twenty and it's Wednesday."

Quentin frowns. "You plan on attending the meetings, Mr. Bristow?"

"Of course. I plan on assuming all the roles and duties associated with my ownership stake."

His frown deepens. "I thought, to be perfectly honest, that this was all some…jape, on your parts."

I nod. "I understand your position, Quentin, considering my reputation in this town. I'm not that person anymore. Or, at least, I'm trying not to be."

He leans back and steeples his fingertips in front of himself. "You have your work cut out for you, then, I must admit. You face a very steep uphill battle, where Miss McKenna is concerned."

The assistant returns with a pair of copies of the

contract—one for me, and one for Dell. I hold mine in my hands, while Dell rolls his up into a tight tube and shoves it in the back pocket of his jeans.

I button the middle button of my jacket. "I am well aware of that, I assure you."

Quentin's smile is faint. "Oh, you may think you do. But somehow…I doubt you are capable of fully grasping the position you're placing yourself in. Delia McKenna is the most singularly fierce and determined individual I have ever met, bar none." His eyebrow arches. "You're walking into the lion's den, Mr. Bristow."

Chapter
SIX

Delia

I ALWAYS TRY TO BE EARLY FOR OUR WEDNESDAY MEETINGS. They used to be board meetings, since Boyd and some of the others owned shares of the company, but now that Dell and I split ownership, it's not a board meeting anymore, just a…weekly state of affairs meeting of the top staff of McKenna construction.

I look at the chair at the head of the long table. Dad's place; this is the first full board meeting since he passed.

My first time in his place. Because even though Dell is technically co-CEO or whatever, this is *my* company. I doubt he'll even show, anyway, so no way he gets the head seat. Or the seat at the other end. I make a mental note to put Boyd there, in case Dell does decide to show up.

Sure enough, Boyd, Ned, Sheila, and Constance all file in at the same time; no Dell.

When everyone has coffee and is seated—with Boyd

opposite me—I catch everyone's eyes in turn, and the room quiets.

"Well, everyone, here we are." I try to smile, but can't quite manage it. "Dell is technically supposed to be here, but I doubt any of us will be surprised if he's a no-show." There's a murmur of agreement. "I'm not Dad, but I promise you all, I'll do my best to make him proud, to do this job as well as he did it."

"You'll do great," Boyd says. "We all have complete faith in you."

"Thanks, Boyd." I sigh, viciously shoving down the well of emotions that boils inside me. "Part of me is tempted to ask for a moment of silence for Dad, but I hear him grumbling about wasting time on nonsense, so…with no further ado, let's get down to business."

In my head, I hear the rest of the line from *Mulan*: to defeat…the *HUNS*…

I don't snicker or even smile, because if anyone at this table knew I was singing Disney lyrics in my head, they'd quickly lose all that faith in me.

"So. We're cranking along at Oak Glen. The only hiccup that I know of is an unexpected delay in getting our plumbing subs on-site for the new installs. I still don't have an explanation, but the latest word end of last week is that they'll still get it all done by deadline." I glance down at my own notes of things to cover. "Boyd—where are we with the Karsten account?"

Boyd opens his mouth to answer, but something over my shoulder catches his attention, and his jaw shuts with an abrupt click of his teeth, my eyes widening. My back is to the door, where Boyd's gaze is fixed.

At first, I assume the sudden change in attitude in Boyd means it's Dell.

"Nice of you to show up, Dell," I say, without turning around. I point to a seat at the other side of the table, well away from me, next to Constance. "You can sit there. We were just getting a report from—"

"Actually, there's been a bit of a change in plans, Delia." The voice is *not* Dell's. It's deeper, smoother, darker. It's familiar, and it makes my entire body clench, my teeth grind, my heart squeeze, my mind go blank.

I slowly turn in my chair, working furiously to keep my face neutral. It can't be. Can't be. Can't be.

It is.

Matthais Bristow.

In the flesh.

And…holy hell.

I haven't seen him since high school graduation, and he is…well…all grown up. And then some.

Over six feet tall, by a couple inches at least. Broad, hard, round shoulders. His hair is the perfect dirty blond of a surfer, sun-bleached and sun-kissed. A little too long, a little messy, as if he's been running his hands through it…or someone has. Even wearing a bespoke indigo suit, his body stuns. Trim, hard. His arms stretch the sleeves. His chest pushes against the crisp white shirt. It's perfectly pressed, fits him like he was sewn into it, and he wears it like he was born in one.

Those fucking eyes.

Gray-green. Devilish. Cunning and wicked and intelligent. Full of mirth and humor and mischief. And… if I'm not mistaken, possibly even nerves.

He has one hand in his hip pocket, the other clutching a sheaf of paper. No tie, top button undone, sunglasses tucked into the V.

Adult Matthais Bristow is sex on a stick.

Evil personified, but still, I give credit where credit is due—he's fucking breathtaking.

It only serves to make me even angrier.

Striving for that icy calm which anyone who knows me knows is a thin cover over my volcanic temper, I lean back in my chair, spin a pen around my middle finger. Stare him down without speaking for a long, tense thirty seconds. "What are you doing here, Matthais? This is a private business meeting."

He withdraws his hand from his pocket, goes to the coffee station and pours himself a cup of coffee, leaving it black. The coffee station is on the opposite side of the table as the only open chair, so he has to go back around behind me. On his way past me, he drops in front of me the sheaf of paper he'd been carrying, and then takes the open seat. Leans back casually, sipping his coffee, waiting.

I scan it—it's a contract.

A sale.

Of Dell's stake in McKenna Construction…

To Matthais Bristow.

"No." I toss it back at him. "Whatever game you're

playing, Matty, I'm not interested. Go away. I'm busy with adult stuff."

He doesn't visibly react. "I go by Thai, now, actually. And it's not a game."

I shake my head. "No. I refuse to countenance this… this…*tomfoolery*."

Fuck—I just said tomfoolery. What am I, ninety?

Matthais can't contain his smirk. "No tomfoolery, Delia. Just plain business. Dell sold to me. It's legal, legit, and real. Look at the contract—Quentin Albright Quince wrote the contract and notarized it."

I shake my head. Flip through the contract. I'm no lawyer, but I know my way around contracts. This is legit. The real thing. I'll have to have…well, normally I'd have Quentin do it, but since he wrote the contract, I'll have to have someone else look it over for loopholes.

I toss the contract on the table with a huff. Turn my gaze—glare, really—on Matthais. "What do you want?"

He shrugs. "For now, I'll just listen and learn."

"No…I mean what do you want to go away? How much will it cost me to get you out of this office and back out of my life?"

He sips his coffee, eyes narrowed, and I can see the wheels turning. "Well, see, the thing is, Delia, I just spent a whole hell of a lot of money buying out your brother. So…I think I'll see this one through."

I ignore the stares of the rest of the staff, focus on Matthais. "See this one through. What does that even mean? Why would you buy my brother's shares? You're even more of a useless fuckboy tool than he is. This is a real company, doing real business. I doubt you could pour water out of a boot if the instructions were printed on the heel."

He remains obnoxiously unflustered. "I realize I've earned every ounce of vitriol you have for me, Delia, and then some. But as for my qualifications...check your email. I sent you my CV."

"You have a CV?" I snorted. "Doing lines off of strippers doesn't count, Matthais."

His eyes narrow. "Does an economics degree from Yale count? How about an internship at Goldman Sachs? An MBA from Wharton School of business?"

As he's speaking, I bring up the email on my phone. I force myself to hold a neutral expression as I read, and realize he's not bluffing. His CV is, legitimately and honestly, impressive.

And he's not done.

"Or how about sixteen million in investments across six different industries—does that count? Perhaps the fact that I purchased Dell's entire fifty percent stake in this company with cash? I got into Yale on my own merit. I earned my degrees myself, the hard way. I got the internship myself, by competing for it. And turned down an offer of full-time employment from them, just FYI, because that shit was fucking *boring* as hell." He leans forward, hands flat on the table, gaze fierce, eyes like green fire. "Like it or not, Delia, I'm *qualified*."

"This isn't Goldman Sachs, Matthais. We're a

construction company. We build houses. Do you even know which end of a hammer to hold?"

His lips tighten. "Whatever I don't know, I can learn."

"I know you're not actually stupid, granted…you're just a colossal asshole. But the greater point here, is… why? Why would you do this?" I struggle to stay calm, when what I want is to kick and scream…and cry.

But I swore, over a decade ago, that I'd never waste another tear on Matthais Bristow.

The room is silent. Matthais doesn't answer right away, and I can tell he's legitimately considering the answer.

"Honestly, Delia, that's a very good question. And I'm not entirely certain of the answer. It was Dell's idea. I do mean that, and not as a cop-out for not answering. I know why Dell sold, and that's a conversation you'll have to have with him—I won't speak for him. Why did I agree? Why did I actually go through with it? I don't know. It's complicated, I think. And honestly, I think the longer and more detailed answer to the question you're really asking, Delia, is personal. For you, and for me. Which means a board meeting probably isn't the right time or place to have that discussion."

I'm taken aback by the sincerity in him.

Can he actually be this changed? I don't trust it. I don't trust *him*.

"Matthais—"

"Please—call me Thai."

"Fine. Thai, whatever." I sigh, a long, annoyed, conflicted sound. "I'm not convinced this isn't another one of your cruel jokes. If it is, it's the cruelest one yet, Thai. This is my life. My career. I've worked every single day since I was a little girl for the right and the privilege to sit in this chair. I'd still give it back if it meant getting Daddy back." I pin him with the hardest, iciest, most penetrating glare I can summon. Let my full hatred for him seethe out of me. "I will *not* let the likes of you ruin this for me, Thai. I won't. You spent money on this, and a lot of it. I know how much Dell's half was worth down to the last penny. Even for you, this is a big gamble. Which for anyone else would mean they're serious. But I don't trust you, and I like you even less. But…this is legal, and it's binding." I tap the contract. "I'm going to have it examined to see if there's a way out of it, but I have to assume Quentin did his job as he's always done it—thoroughly. So you're here. I hate it more than I can say. But—all I ask is that you behave with something like adult decorum, if not with respect for the fact that we're running a business. And Thai? Don't get in my way."

Matthais…Thai—he doesn't answer. Just nods. And there's no humor in his gaze. No mischief. That taunting sneer he had so perfected is nowhere to be seen.

Somehow, the name he's chosen, Thai…it fits him. Which is every bit as annoying as his overall godlike hotness.

I stand up, collect my things. "Apologies, everyone, but it seems I have to have a conversation with my brother. Carry on without me, and if anything important comes up, you know how to get ahold me." I glance at Thai. "Except you. Don't call me. Ever."

With that, I leave, and head out in search of my brother.

⚮

I find him at the local airfield, in a private lounge, waiting for a charter to finish being prepared. He's sipping champagne from the bottle, wearing mirrored aviators. Joggers, slide sandals, plain T-shirt, all white. Jet-black hair swept back. Scrolling on his phone.

He looks up as I enter. He flinches, and then covers it with a swig of champagne. "Dee-Dee. What's up?"

I yank the bottle away from him and slam it down on a nearby table, so hard it foams up and spills down the side. I curl my fists in his shirt and yank him halfway up out of his chair—I'm a strong girl. "What—the—*fuck*, Dell? Of all the dirty, filthy, slimy, underhanded bullshit you could possibly pull, you sell out to Matthais fucking Bristow?"

He jerks away, smoothing the wrinkles out of his shirt. Settles his aviators more firmly on his face. "It was a strategic move, believe it or not."

"You wouldn't know a strategic move if your life depended on it."

He reaches past me and grabs the bottle. Dabs the

sides and bottom dry with a handful of cocktail napkins. "Think what you want, sis. I'm not arguing with you."

"No, you're running away."

"Sure am."

"Coward."

He shoves the sunglasses up into his hair. His eyes are…angry. Conflicted. Hurt. But mostly angry. "You know what, Delia? Fuck you. I'm damned if I do and damned if I don't, where you're concerned. Let's say I'd gone along with Dad's bullshit little ploy—stuck around, played at businessman with you and Boyd and the others. If I had tried, you'd have bitten my head off at every turn. Given me the worst jobs. Ignored me. Shit all over me, no matter what I did. Just like always. Nothing I did would have been acceptable, or good enough. Never has been. Never will be." He stabs a finger at me, poking my chest just below my throat. "I stopped fucking around with you years ago, and so did Thai. Yet *still*, you shit on me every chance you get. The shit you say to me is fucking *vicious*, Delia. Why would I want to stick around for more of your verbal punishment? Huh? Ask yourself that. If I'm doomed to fail, why should I bother even trying? It's not like you'd let me do anything that matters, not with your precious *company*. You care more about McKenna Construction than you do me. Or just about anything, for that matter."

I open my mouth to respond, but he's not done.

"I know, I know—Thai and I were assholes, back in the day. I get it. I should have stopped him from doing a lot of the shit he pulled on you. I'm sorry, Delia. I really am. But that was years ago." He shakes his head. "But that's not really the point, here, though. I sold to him because *I—don't—want* that fucking company. I don't *want* to build houses. I don't *want* to play good little soldier to your Generalissima bullshit. I don't want to slave away in the marketing department. I don't want to do any of it. I don't know what I *do* want, but it's not that. And this isn't laziness. I don't care if you agree or believe me or not—I'm doing this because I refuse to be railroaded into a career I don't want." He goes quiet, voice so soft I have to strain to hear him. "I have a lot of regrets in my life, Dee. I'm sorry I let you down. I'm sorry I let—let Dad down." He tugs his glasses back down onto his face, but not before I see the gleam of tears in his eyes; he clears his throat, lets out a gruff sigh. "I'm sorry I wasn't there. I just…I could never measure up. Not to you. Not to Dad's expectations of me. And certainly not to the way Dad looked at *you*, approved of *you*. So why try? That was always my…my thing. Why bother? It won't make a difference. Well…I'm going to do something that *will* make a difference. I don't know what, but I'll figure it out—my way. You get my share of the inheritance, I'm not fighting that. I'm not asking you for anything…and I never will." He checks his watch. "My plane is ready—I have to go. And as for Thai? That was my way of…keeping it in the family."

"Dell—"

"Give him a chance, Dee. He's…he's not the person

he used to be. If you give him a chance, he just might surprise you."

"Dell—"

He grabs his Louis Vuitton satchel off the floor, holding the champagne bottle by the neck, and saunters out of the door without a backward glance at me; he pauses before rounding the corner, but still doesn't look back at me. "Goodbye, Delia. I..." A shake of his head; he almost looks back at me, head twisted so he could maybe see me out of the corner of his eye—instead, he sighs. "Goodbye."

He's gone. I'm still standing in that lounge, stunned, when I hear jet engines spool up, and then roar and vanish as he takes off.

Between Thai appearing out of nowhere, owning half my company, and now this from Dell, my world just got turned upside down.

Problem is, it was already upside down from Daddy dying.

Turn something upside down, and then upside down again, does that make it upside right? In my case, not even close.

My head is spinning along a dozen different axes. So, I do what I've always done in the face of such emotional tumult: ignore it and go to work.

Chapter
SEVEN

Matthais

I HOLD MY SHIT TOGETHER THROUGH THE REST OF THE meeting. Barely, and by the hairs of my chinny-chin-chin. Or some shit. I'm not even sure what that's supposed to mean.

It means I'm fucking dizzy.

It means this was a very massively enormously horribly colossally shit-tastic idea.

Not because I can't do the job—I can.

Why?

Because Delia McKenna pulled one hell of a Longbottom transformation in the decade since I saw her last.

She was far from ugly, growing up. No matter how much I mocked her—and I was absolutely merciless—she was, by the time we graduated …hot. She was curvier than the blond cheerleader size-nothing bimbos I tended to hook up with. She wasn't what anyone would call fat or heavy. She was just…curvy. As a kid, she was what you'd have called kinda chunky, and she was seriously self-conscious about it. And I, being the complete tool I was, drilled into that self-consciousness as hard as I could, at every opportunity.

Then, as she got into middle school and high school and she got taller and went through puberty, that chunkiness translated to thick hips and ass and a more than generous portion of tits. Yeah, I noticed. Still made fun of her and called her shitty names, but I noticed.

Maybe I even made fun of her *because* I noticed. It bothered me, that she was so hot, that I noticed. Maybe that was why I was such a jackass to her, why I was so unbelievably mean. God, the things I called her: Donuts Delia, Dino Delia, shit like that. I mean, they weren't even original or intelligent insults—they were childish as all fuck. Maybe they cut her more deeply because of that. And maybe…maybe I was a classic case of an immature boy mocking someone he actually liked because he didn't know how to express himself.

Ten years later, she's a fully mature woman, and she clearly has worked her ass off to achieve and maintain her body.

Which is, in a word, fucking incredible. Two words, but whatever.

Back in high school, there was just this little bit of… extra, I guess. Some padding around the curves.

Now? All curve, and no extra.

She'd been wearing a peach sheath dress with a jean

jacket, the sleeves pushed up past her elbows, with some seriously killer black heels. Her raven's wing hair was longer than ever, in a thick, complicated braid and twisted up on top of her head. When she'd stormed out of the board room, it had taken every last particle of willpower I possessed to not stare at that magnificent ass.

Her eyes were...pure blue fire. Wild and fierce and electric blue. If I were to only see her in a photograph, I'd assume they were Photoshopped to be that hue.

They sparked, and spat flame, especially when she looked at me.

Honestly, that fire in her eyes was...hot. Ha ha ha. Pun intended, I guess.

But it is, though. She's a challenge.

One I'm not sure what to do with.

She hates me, and with good reason.

She's so fucking gorgeous now that it was legitimately difficult to be in the room with her and not ogle her like a horny teenager with his first lust.

She's dominating—in an in-charge and full of well-earned and -deserved authority. She's wicked smart. Competent and capable.

Which is also hot.

My mind has been wandering during the meeting, so I'm taken by surprise when...what's his name? Boy? Billy? Boyd? Boyd, I'm pretty sure. Anyway, he adjourns the meeting, and everyone begins filing out. Within a moment, I'm the only one at the table.

I have to come up with a plan for catching myself up. I need to know not only how THIS business runs, but how the home-building trade works in general.

I have a lot of work to do.

Question is, do I start with the trade in general first, or this particular company?

I consider the problem for a few minutes—It probably looks like I'm sitting on my ass staring into space, but in reality, my mind is spinning in overdrive.

Finally, I have a workable approach.

There's a corner office, the big one with the best view; the door is closed, lights off. The plaque to the right of the doorframe proclaims it to be Delia's office, naturally. And, just outside the office, an L-shaped desk with two different desktop computers, a phone, a large filing cabinet, an industrial caliber copy machine/printer. Manning this station is what I, in my own head, refer to as a CLT—and cute little thing. Meaning, an attractive young female with whom I enjoy flirting but would never actually go beyond flirting, because my tastes in the bedroom tend to be…um, vigorous. And in my experience, CLTs are just…too delicate. Physically, and mentally. They just can't keep up.

This particular CLT secretary/assistant is the brunette version. She probably wears PINK brand thongs, drinks fruity mixed drinks with names like Sunrise Bahama Blast, and her idea of spicing it up in the bedroom is probably some gentle spanking. She's wearing a denim miniskirt with a frayed hem and a baby doll shirt.

Her hair is loose and artfully wavy, and she probably gets a blowout at least once a week.

How do I know these things? I pay attention. Know thy prey, or something like that. Not that this cute little thing is my prey, mind you. For one thing, I can tell just by the way she watches my approach that I could snap my fingers and grin and have her wrapped around my… finger. And where's the challenge in that? Plus, I learned the hard way to not hunt where I work.

I lean a hip against her desk, one hand in my slacks pocket. Give her the smile, the look. "Hey. I'm Thai. I'm new around here, and I'm hoping you can help me out."

Her eyes blink a mile a minute, and she swallows hard. "Hi, um. I'm Jamie. I'm new here, too. Just started last week, actually." Her puppy dog brown eyes flit from my lips to my jawline to my shoulders. She licks her lips. "What can I do for you?"

"Well, Jamie. I need some information. A lot of information, actually."

Her eyes fix on my shoulders and stay there, only briefly flitting to meet my gaze. "What kind of information?"

"I need to know about our current projects. Estimated overhead, projected profit, who our suppliers are, subcontractors, things like that. Oh, and staffing information—how many employees we have, the pay rate, churn, all that good stuff."

She licks her lips again. "So…everything?" This is accompanied by a little giggle, as if this is a great joke.

"Yeah, basically. Everything you can get me about McKenna."

She frowns. "That's a lot. I'll do the best I can."

"Hey, whatever you can get me will be great." I smile at her again and run my fingers through my hair—that always gets 'em. "Thanks, Jamie."

"No problem…Thai." And, as I leave, there's the sigh.

Sorry babe, but sharks can't survive on minnows, if you know what I mean.

Jamie comes through—by the end of the day, I have a three-inch binder stuffed with reports and printouts and such. It's a ton of dry, dense material, but I've discovered I have a pretty voracious capacity for absorbing this kind of stuff.

I take it home with me—home is a brand-new condo in downtown River Gulch, a short walk from the McKenna headquarters. Not as lux as I tend to go for, but in a nowhere town like River Gulch, this is fine living indeed. Two bedrooms, an office-library, massive master suite with a nice bathroom and closet, plus the building has a decent 24-hour gym and lap pool.

I put something mindless on TV—one of the Fast and Furious movies—pour myself a glass of Glenmorangie and start going through my materials. Hours later, I'm bingeing a not-great sci-fi series, I'm only a quarter of the way through the reports, and my eyes are burning. But it's my first day, so I can't expect to be able to cram everything about the whole company into my skull in one night.

When I finally call it for the day, it's almost two in the morning, and my head is swimming with facts and numbers.

Yet, when I lie down and close my eyes, it's Delia keeping me from falling asleep.

Those eyes.

That body.

That attitude. It was always the attitude that got me. As a punk kid, her fiery spirit intimidated me, and I responded by trying to cut her down. As an adult? Her wild, uncontainable ferocity and stubbornness is complemented by a confidence she didn't have back then.

And that gives me a hell of a hard-on.

"…and on either side of a doorway or a window, you double or triple the uprights," Cal is saying.

Cal is the head project foreman, the top dog out in the actual field, in charge of the day-to-day details of construction across all projects. "There are standard specific dimensions for everything, obviously. Studs are usually sixteen inches apart, stair riser standard is seven inches high by eleven deep." He points up, at the ceiling framing. "Same thing up there. You have standard angles, distances, all that. It's all been calculated and engineered, and it's all covered under building codes. Before you can sell a house you've built, you have to have it certified by a code inspector, right, who checks to make sure everything follows all the rules. Keeps folks safe."

"And you know all this off the top of your head?" I ask.

Cal nods. He's short and broad, powerfully built, and radiates easygoing competence. Graying blond hair, short, neat goatee, with a plug of chewing tobacco between his teeth and lower lip. "Sure. Been doing this for damn near thirty years. My pops was a builder, and I grew up on-site with him, just like Delia with the Old Man, God rest him. I was framing by sixteen, supervising by twenty, and I've been lead project foreman for McKenna for the last twenty years. Do something every day for that long, you just remember that shit. Plus, it's my job to know it."

I nod, and we move on through the partially framed shell that will be a house. Right now, it's a handful of walls kept upright with bracers, and a poured concrete foundation.

I spent the first week in the office, getting to know the HQ staff, learning their filing system, payroll, scheduling, accounting, all that. Now, halfway through my second week, I'm tagging along with Cal and trying to learn the basics of how to build a house. He's been taking me from a site that's just a hole in the dirt through the various stages, until Friday when I finally tour a completed, ready-to-sell spec home.

It's eye-opening. You get this idea that building a

house is complicated, but until you see it firsthand, you really have no clue whatsoever.

There are a million and a half moving parts, and just as many codes and requirements to keep track of, plus the manpower and subcontractors and their codes and their staffing and supply chain...

My head is spinning.

I've been avoiding Delia, truth be told. I want to be able to impress her with my knowledge of the business, next time I see her—

Next time I have to engage in the verbal sparring contest that is having a conversation with that woman.

The days go by quickly, and I'm on my feet more than ever.

My loafers are filthy, and the interior of my McLaren is...hard to think about.

By the end of the day, I'm ready for a beer and my bed.

Cal walks me to my car, and whistles when he sees it. "Man, that is one sweet ride."

I nod. "Sure is." I run my finger through the thick layer of dust on the windshield. "Not sure it's practical for this environment, though."

Cal cackles. "Hell no, it ain't. You're gonna spend any time on-site, you need a truck. Or an SUV, even, if pickups aren't your thing. But that sexy little rocket there? One of these days, we're gonna get a load of fill gravel and you're gonna be paying for dent removal and repainting, if not a new windshield as well." He points at his truck, a two- or three-year-old silver F-150, and it does indeed sport some pretty sizable dents, as well as a spiderwebbing chip in the windshield.

The thought of that happening to my McLaren makes my stomach hurt. "Yeah, I think I'm gonna go pick up a truck."

He digs his wallet out of his back pocket, pokes through it, and removes a business card. "My cousin runs the Ford dealership in town. Tell him Cal sent you, and he'll hook you up." He points at the neon yellow hardhat on my head. "Ask Jamie in the office, and she'll get you your own hardhat with your name on it. Keep it in your truck—wearing one on-site is a nonnegotiable. And it's not just for safety code, either. Someone up in the roof joists drops his hammer on your head and you're not wearing one, you'll be a vegetable."

I hadn't considered that—I'd assumed it was mainly meant to satisfy a safety code, as he said. "Will do." I shake his hand. "Thanks, Cal. See you tomorrow."

As I get into my car, I watch him head back to the site—the guys have knocked off for the day, yet there goes Cal, doing one last walk-through for forgotten tools, checking this, that, and the other thing.

He takes the job seriously, he's good at it, and he genuinely seems to take pride in what he does.

It's a good feeling, knowing I'm a part of it.

Chapter
EIGHT

Delia

ON-SITE AT A NEARLY FINISHED HOME, JUST PAST DAWN. Our guys usually start around eight, and Cal is normally on-site around seven thirty. When I do site checks, I like to do them early, before anyone is there. Especially now that I'm the big boss—I'm young, I'm not ugly, and I'm in charge…and a construction site is all horny and rambunctious men. It's easier, some days, to just not deal with all that. I can, and do, I just don't always *want* to, and seeing as I'm the boss, it's my prerogative.

So imagine my surprise when a big black pickup rolls up right as I shut off the engine of my vintage Bronco—it's a resto-mod, and was the last gift Daddy ever gave me. It's got some kind of ding-resistant paint, a new sound system, and a spray-out interior. The truck next to me isn't brand, brand-new, but it's pimped out.

Tinted windows, lift kit, massive knobby off-road tires, custom exhaust, the works.

My Spidey-sense tingles. New truck, and a blingy one that somehow manages to stop just short of looking like the owner is compensating for something.

The door opens, and out steps Thai.

My breath catches.

His hair is still damp, and he's dressed casually in light wash jeans and a black V-neck T-shirt, with tan Timberland boots. And, fuck me—the jeans are just tight enough to cling to thick, powerful legs without being too tight. The shirt is like a second skin, wrapped around broad, hard shoulders and a wide, tapered torso. He didn't shave today, so his jaw is stubbled with a blond dusting of fine scruff.

It's not right. No one person should be allowed to be THAT good-looking.

Especially someone who's as much of a bastard as he is. He sees me in my truck, gives me a friendly smile and a two-finger salute, and heads toward the worksite.

What's he doing?

I stay in my Bronco and watch.

The equipment trailer is locked of course, but he pulls a keyring out of his pocket, unlocks it, and hauls out a circular saw, a bucket of screws and a screw gun, a tape measure, and a few other odds and ends.

Curious. I really wouldn't have thought he even knew what a circular saw is. There's a pile of scrap lumber just inside the shell of the partially framed house, and he sorts through it for a selection of pieces. Once he has what he wants, he brings it over to his work area.

Consults something on his phone—watching a video, it looks like. Then he nods, shoves the phone in his back pocket, and begins measuring and marking. And he does in fact measure not just twice but three times before making his cuts. I'm not sure what he's attempting to build just yet. He measures, marks, cuts, and after he's made his cuts he measures again, and finally seems satisfied. Then, he begins assembling.

After a few minutes, I understand what he's building: a trunk with a lid. He must have brought his own set of hinges, since that's not something we typically have just laying around worksites. When he's done, he looks up at me for the first time, and gives a lopsided grin. Waves.

I sigh, and finally climb out of my truck, head over to examine his handiwork.

He gestures at the trunk as I approach. "Well? What do you think?"

I examine it. Begrudgingly, I have to admit it's actually pretty well done. "The joins are even, no overlapping or gapping, nice and tight. Sturdy, square…" I move the hinged lid. "I have to admit, I'm impressed."

He grins, and if I was a woman of weaker moral fiber, my panties would probably be melting right now. "High praise, from you."

I shrug. "I mean, it's a box made from scrap

lumber and plywood. But considering the source, I *am* moderately impressed."

He rolls his eyes. "Last time we spoke, you didn't think I'd know which end of a hammer to hold on to. And a couple weeks ago, you wouldn't have been far from the truth."

"Just one question." I gesture at the trunk. "Why?"

He laughs, raking a hand through his hair. And dammit, why does that silly gesture put butterflies in my belly? It's dumb.

"I dunno. I've been watching carpentry videos, and this seemed...attainable." He plays with the lid, opening and closing it. "Next step is to figure out how to make the outside look nice, like with fancy wood."

"Fancy wood. Just...wow." I eye him. "Why are you watching carpentry videos, though? This kind of woodworking"—I gesture at the box—"has very little to do with that kind," and here I gesture at the framing.

A shrug, and a nod. "I know. But it's basic skills, I guess. If I'm going to own half of a construction company, I should at least have an inkling of a clue, right? And as you've pointed out, I don't. So I've got to start somewhere."

I gesture at the tools. "Put that stuff away. Let's talk site checks."

He puts everything back where it goes, locks the trailer, and follows me into the shell. At this point, I don't need a tape measure to know if something is off but I still bring one, just because even if you can reliably eyeball the sixteen-inch space between studs, you still have to *know.*

"So, some basics." I tap a stud. "This is a stud. Basic vertical support post. There should be no less than sixteen inches between studs, and no more than twenty-four."

He rubs the back of his neck. "I've spent the last week and a half shadowing Cal, actually. I can't say I know all the standards off the top of my head like he does, but I do have—" he pulls a small black Moleskine notebook from a back pocket, and hands it to me. "My handy-dandy…notebook!"

I can't help a laugh. "Did you really just reference *Blue's Clues?*"

"Yes, I did." He breaks out in an embarrassed laugh. "Dell and I once got super stoned after school one day, and we spent an entire afternoon watching old school *Blue's Clues.*"

I roll my eyes. "Not surprising in the least. Right about your maturity level, at that point, too."

I flip through the pages: he's filled dozens of pages with notes on construction standards, complete with surprisingly good diagrams. It's like he put himself through a crash course on home building.

"Again, I'm impressed. You did all this in the last week and a half?" I hand the notebook back.

He nods, with another of those laconic *whatever* shrugs. "Yeah."

I continue my check of the shell, measuring and

double-checking, making sure everything is up to my personal standards. "So you really are actually planning on, like, *doing* this?" I walk up the bare plywood stairs to the second floor, eyeballing trusses and ceiling joists from below. "Buying out Dell…it's really not some kind of joke the two of you are playing on me?"

He doesn't answer right away. In fact, when I glance at him to see if he even heard my question, he seems to be wrestling with what to say, how to answer. His jaw is tight, and his brow furrowed.

After a long silence, he just shakes his head. "No, it's not."

I find a truss that's clearly been put in well out of true, at the wrong angle, and with the entirely wrong kind of bracket—I take a photo and send it to Cal. "This, for example, is why we do site checks regularly, and why several people have to do them," I say to Thai. "This kind of thing could be easily overlooked. Now, sure, this wouldn't cause the ceiling to fall in or anything, but it would throw things off. Catch it now, and it's an easy fix. Don't catch it until the roof is going on? Much bigger issue."

He nods. "Makes sense." A pause. "Delia, I know you don't really have much reason to trust me, but—"

"Nope. I don't." I give him an obviously fake, bright smile. "I don't trust easily as a general rule, Thai, and the truth is, you're in large part responsible for that. I don't like you. I don't want you on my jobsite. I don't want you in my life. But like it or not, you legally own half of my company, and there's nothing I can do about that, short of buying it from you, and to be quite frank, I simply don't have that kind of liquid assets. So I'm stuck with you. Which really, *really* chaps my ass. So, whatever you're going to say…don't. I promise you, I won't buy it, and I don't want to hear it."

He stares me down, and I have a split-second twinge of wondering if maybe I wasn't being entirely fair. But then I remember eighteen years of being called Dino Delia and Donuts Delia, and brought cupcakes with Miss Piggy drawn on them, and having my books stolen and ruined, and my glasses broken, and snakes and mud and bugs thrown on me…

Maybe he's not entirely that guy anymore. But that doesn't mean I forgive him.

He holds my gaze for a moment, and then his expression hardens. "Fair enough, I guess." He turns on his heel and heads for the stairs down. "I have a meeting in half an hour with Boyd, so I'm going to go."

I frown. "A meeting with Boyd? Why?"

"I found a discrepancy in your books."

"Like, our accounting books?"

"No, Delia, your Harry Potter books." He pauses on the third stair down. "Not sure yet if it's just an isolated thing, or if it's part of a larger issue. Boyd wanted to go over it with me before we brought it to you."

"You went through our books?"

"I went through everything, Delia."

"What do you mean, everything?"

He snorts. "Your accounting, your projected profit margins, your average materials losses, your churn rate." He hesitates. "I know that your dad had a habit of hiring pretty young receptionists, but that it was never for any reason other than having eye candy around the office. I know the Karsten account is way, *way* over budget and that at the current rate of construction it won't be done for something like two years. I know Doug Mendes in the marketing department is completely useless, faked his credentials and references, and spends most of his day playing Warcraft when he thinks no one is looking."

I blink, open my mouth, but he's not done. Ugh, this again.

"I also know Boyd is on the verge of divorce because his wife has a spending problem and he's been seeing Shannon in payroll for months. I know Constance has wine in her coffee thermos from around ten in the morning onward, but she's totally reliable and, honestly, irreplaceable. I know your lumber supplier is about to jack up their costs by at least double, and you can't afford that, but you're having trouble finding a new supplier—and I may have a partial solution but I doubt you'll go for it." His eyes blatantly rake over me, head to toe; I have a meeting myself in a little bit, to look at a plot of land which could be our next big development project. Meaning, I'm dressed to the nines in a tight black skirt, flattering green blouse, and my best heels. "I also know you're wearing the *hell* out of that skirt."

And then he's gone, trotting down the steps and to his truck. The engine is roaring and he's gone—and I'm still standing with my jaw on the floor.

Did he...

Did he just...*compliment* me?

I actually, literally look up to the sky for flying pigs, or some sign of the impending apocalypse.

The rest of what he said is percolating in my brain, but I'm still currently stuck on the last part.

You're wearing the hell *out of that skirt.*

I mean, I *do* look good in this skirt. I wore it on purpose knowing I look damn good in it, because I happen to know the real estate developer I'm meeting is a bona fide member of the good ol' boys chauvinist club, and responds best to women when they dress like he expects them to. And if wearing a tight skirt and low-cut blouse will get me a twenty-million-dollar contract? Duh.

But hearing it from Thai Bristow?

I'm still faint with shock.

⨳

Surreptitiously, I check in on everything Thai dumped on me.

Sure enough, the Karsten account is bloated and bogged down. I arrange a meeting with the Karstens for tomorrow so I can try and convince them to trim things back so we can get them into their new custom home in something less than twenty-four months and something like within budget. I monitor Doug Mendes most of the day, and sure enough, he does literally zero actual work; most of the time he was, as Thai claimed, playing a video game, and the rest of the time he was either in the break room, on the phone, or outside smoking. Easy fix: I call him into my office and dismiss him with his last paycheck in hand.

I watch Boyd exchange a quiet, intense conversation with Shannon, which does indeed smack of a side romance. Not really my business, though, as long as Boyd does his job and his thing with Shannon doesn't affect his work performance. Same with Constance—I notice she comes out of the bathroom with minty fresh breath rather frequently, which I had noticed before but hadn't really equated with anything in particular other than good oral hygiene; as long as her work doesn't suffer, I don't see that I have any reason or place to interfere on that front, and as Thai said, Constance is one of the few employees who is genuinely vital to our day-to-day operations.

The lumber supply thing is a known for me already, but I'm curious as to his possible solution he thinks I won't go for.

And how the *hell* did he know about Dad's thing with receptionists? It was a running joke by the time he died. They got younger, prettier, and with ever more

ridiculous names. Case in point: our current receptionist is still Candy, who was Dad's last hire. She's younger
than me, pretty as all get out, ditzy, is named Candy…
but she's a damn good receptionist, so I've kept her on.
Dad knew what he was doing, after all.

How did he find all this out in the first two weeks
on the job?

I have misjudged Thai on at least one front, it
seems.

I'm used to being the last one in the office. Dad, who
had a wife and children to go home to, was often here
till seven or eight and sometimes nine. I, single, with
no one at all to go home to, not even a cat, am often
here till at *least* nine. No reason not to, right? I'd just go
home and watch TV with a glass of wine, so I may as
well be productive instead.

I'm going over the Karsten account, trying to find
places we can cut the budget down. When Thai said
it was bloated, he wasn't kidding. I like a nice Carrera
marble as much as the next girl, but does literally every
surface in the whole house have to be marble? And…
thirty grand on a built-in intercom and music system?
Have they not heard of Alexa? Buy a couple of those
and save thirty grand; it's an older couple with no
kids—what possible use will they ever have for an intercom? I appreciate upselling to pad the profit margin,

but it seems Nick, the lead project manager for that account, has gone a little overboard. We want to make our clients happy with the finished project, not milk them for every last dollar and leave them broke in a house they hate because it's overdone.

That's not our company ethos. I make a note to have a talk with Nick later.

I don't feel, see, or hear him, so focused am I on the account file.

"Still here, huh?" His voice is deep, rough, and intimate. Close.

I screech and leap half a foot out of my chair. "Holy *shit*, Thai—do *not* sneak up on me like that."

He perches on the edge of my desk and toys with a tape measure that had been on my desk, flipping the end out and letting it snap back again...and again, and again.

"Working late, I see," he says.

"I'm here till nine most nights, so no, I'm not working late. Midnight would be working late." I take the tape measure from him before I bean him in the head with it. "What do you want, Thai?"

He taps the Karsten file I have spread out on my desk—most of our files are digital, but certain elements I prefer to print out and mark up with highlighters and pens. "What'd I tell you? Over budget, am I right?"

I sigh. "Yes, you were right. About Doug, too." I slap the folder closed and lean back in my chair. "In fact, as much as it chaps my ass to admit it, you were right on all accounts."

He crosses his arms over his chest, and I hate that my eyes are drawn to the thickness of his biceps and the breadth of his chest and shoulders. And how green his eyes are today. "I can help you out with that."

"With what?"

"Me." He smirks, but it's sort of rueful. "Your problem with me is not that I'm incompetent. I think you know that. Really, your problem wasn't even that I was lazy—that never had anything to do with you, except insofar as it influenced Dell."

"Ah, and what *is* my problem with you, then?"

"I'm an asshole."

A disbelieving snort escapes me, unbidden. "You admit it then?"

He arches an eyebrow, shrugs. "I've never denied it."

I think back, doing a quick scan of my memories and realize he's right. "So you just have never bothered with trying to *not* be a dick?"

"Nope, not really." He laughs. "Funny, this conversation is oddly similar to another one I had just recently."

"You mean another conversation where someone told you that you were an asshole?"

"And I maintained that I knew it, that I've always been an asshole, and I've never really tried to deny it."

"It was a woman, I imagine."

He smirks. "Got it in one."

I roll my eyes. "Not a difficult guess. You don't really seem like the boyfriend type."

He narrows his eyes. "And you're the girlfriend type, are you?"

My temper flares at that—I don't care to examine my own hypocrisy too closely. "You know *nothing* about me, Thai—don't act like you do."

"And you know so much about me?" He's maddeningly impossible to get a reaction out of—even as he retorts, he's even-keeled and sports that cocky smirk.

"I just have a hard time picturing you doing the domestic thing. Buying a girl flowers, taking her to dinner and a movie…learning her name, sticking around after sex. Little things like that." My knives are out, but this is Thai—he's earned every last ounce of my enmity and vindictiveness a thousand times over.

He nods, but it seems less like agreement and more like he's saying, *So that's how you want to play it?* "Yeah, you've definitely got the inside track on my sex life, Delia. Must have been spying on me." He stands up. Shoves his hand in his pocket, turns to go but glances back over his shoulder for one last parting shot. "But hey, at least I *have* a sex life. I don't claim to know what goes on in yours, but something tells me when you *do* quit working long enough to engage in sexual intercourse, it's with a clipboard and a checklist. Probably with guys who have three first names, and they probably wear suspenders, and loafers barefoot with jeans and have well-rounded stock portfolios and drive BMWs."

I flush with rage...and embarrassment: the last guy I had sex with was named Robert Michael Duncan. And he wore loafers barefoot with jeans...and drove a BMW.

It was awful.

The sex, I mean. Quick, and awful.

"I don't even *have* a clipboard," I mutter, knowing the response is only playing more fully into his hands.

He laughs—out loud, and with genuine humor, shaking his head as he walks out. "Oh man, Delia. What a comeback." He spins on his heel, shaking head again and grinning at me. "You are too funny."

I just glare. "Asshole."

He just winks at me and shoots me double finger guns. "You know it, babycakes."

He's gone before I could come up with a suitably venomous retort to being called babycakes.

He hasn't changed *that* much, clearly.

Chapter
NINE

Matthais

OHHHHH MAN, I MUST HAVE NAILED THAT ONE RIGHT ON the head.

I don't even have *a clipboard*, she said.

Meaning, the rest must have been fairly accurate. I'd been making it up—I had no idea what her type was. Honestly, I hadn't really thought about her much over the past ten years. Her sex and dating life are a complete mystery to me; I have no memory of her dating anyone in high school. I mean, logically I know she's a normal woman with the usual needs and desires. But I just can't picture what her type would be. What I said to her was just me being a dick, trying to goad her into one of those adorably vicious temper tantrums. Apparently, however, I'd inadvertently hit upon the actual truth—her sexual partners are boring, straitlaced, and probably selfish and shitty in the sack.

I am none of those things.

Based entirely on that interaction, I'd be willing to bet the title to my McLaren that Delia McKenna has never had an orgasm she didn't give herself.

Say what you want about me—entitled, arrogant, narcissistic, whatever. True, not true, whatever. But what I'm certifiably *not*? Bad in bed, quick, or unaware of what my partner wants and needs.

Delia strikes me as someone who doesn't know how to loosen up. How to unwind. How to stop controlling everything and just let someone make her feel good.

She probably has sex with her bra on, and the lights off.

I shake myself like a wet dog—why the *fuck* am I thinking about how Delia McKenna has sex? That is the absolute last thing on the planet I should spend mental energy thinking about.

Even if I wanted to, Delia would never get anywhere near me. Not like that. She's more likely to stab me with a pen than let me go down on her.

I'm not even aware of having driven, yet somehow I find myself parking and heading up to my condo. It's dark, and quiet, and lonely, and empty.

I genuinely hate this part of being perpetually single: the empty apartment. It's not like I'm not used to it, and it's not like I want a live-in girlfriend getting on my shit about coming home at a certain time and *keep it in your pants, Thai* and put the toilet seat up and all that shit.

But I *do* get lonely, sometimes.

Yeah, fuck this.

I have no interest in being here alone.

I grab a bottle of scotch, a bag of chips, and a Bluetooth speaker, and get back in my truck. I don't really have anywhere in mind, I just don't want to be there. If I'm going to be alone, I'd rather be outside.

I just drive, at first.

After a few minutes, it becomes obvious where I'm going: The Spot.

As kids, Dell and I created a "clubhouse" in the woods behind our properties—a real, honest-to-god hundred-acre wood. We hauled all sorts of stuff into a clearing and created a place just for us to hang out and dick around. Milk crates, storage tubs, an old bookshelf, a broken Lay-Z-Boy, a Stop sign we stole, a dirty white Igloo cooler we'd keep filled with lukewarm beer. Then, when we hit high school, we upgraded it from a kiddie clubhouse into a teen hangout. We dragged a couch out there, strung some white Christmas lights from the tree branches and connected them to and a gas generator. We even stole a stoplight and leaned it against a tree trunk. We tried out a bunch of cool names for it, but in the end, the kids we invited to parties there named it for us: The Spot. It was *the* place to be, back in the day. You hoped and prayed Dell and I would invite you to one of our parties, which I imagine are still legendary. The Spot is where the snake incident happened.

I haven't been back since returning to River Gulch. I've been meaning to, but my deep dive into the world of working at McKenna Construction has taken up all my time. This is the first day since coming back that I've put work aside before I physically passed out.

It'd shock Delia, probably, but when I do find something I like doing, I tend to be a workaholic about it.

I have no intention of seeing my parents at the moment, so I go the back way—there's a path to The Spot from the other side of the woods from the houses, and when Dell and I were setting up a party, we'd use the back way so we didn't risk alerting our parents that we were up to anything. It's just a barely visible two-track through the trees, which you have to know about to even know how to find. It's been almost a decade and it's overgrown from disuse, so it takes a while to find it. I flick on my brights and aim them at the tree line—no way my truck is getting in there. Not without totally ruining the paint, at least, and I just got this thing. So I shut it off, grab my stuff, pocket my keys, and head out on foot.

It's farther than I remember. A full ten minutes of walking down a dark, overgrown trail, which my cell phone flashlight only dimly illuminates, and then I finally emerge into the clearing. The couch is still there, but it's garbage now, rodent-eaten and -infested, likely. Avoid that. The stoplight is still there, rusted and much worse for wear. The firepit still has old ashes in it, rotting stumps where we used to sit.

Man, this place seemed a *lot* bigger back in the day. Now, it's just a tiny little clearing in the forest. I could toss a pebble underhanded across the entire space. It used to feel so big, so cool. We were gods, back, then. Kings of the world.

There's a stacked pile of firewood—I check it, and a lot of it is rotted, but the stuff in the middle seems like it'd burn okay. We used to keep a Zippo in a little hollow in the old dead tree near this stack of wood…still there, and it still works. It's been an age since I made a fire, but old skills come back easily. Make a little nest with dried leaves and bark, gradually feed larger and larger sticks to it…within a few minutes I've got a nice little fire going.

Put some Miles Davis on the speaker, kick back in my old spot under the tree.

Not as fun alone, but better here than that empty condo. I don't say *home*, because it's not, not really.

I sip scotch and let my mind wander, thinking back to the good old days with Dell, when were the kings of River Gulch. All the guys wanted to be our friend, and all the girls wanted to get with us. Or…most did, at least.

A stick cracks, followed by a flashlight beam, bright and white, a spear in the darkness. Behind the beam comes Delia, double-barreled shotgun under one arm.

"Oh." She lowers the flashlight. "It's you."

I eye the shotgun. "Who'd you expect? Sasquatch?"

She shrugs, gestures around with the now-off flashlight. "There's actually been quite an increase in black bear activity in these woods, last couple years. I'm not about to go traipsing around in here unarmed." She gestures at the fire. "Saw the fire from Mom and Dad's back deck, and I came to see who was making a fire in our woods."

"Just little ol' me." I frown. "You can see this from the house?"

"If you're looking." She smirks. "You and Dell weren't as sneaky about those parties as you thought. Our parents just didn't care."

I grin. "As a punk kid, I thought it was the best. As an adult looking back? I kinda wonder if maybe someone should have shut *some* of those parties down. We got *blasted* in here, back in the day, man."

She laughs at that and edges closer, her gaze flicking to the bottle in my hands—it's nothing special, just some 10-year Lagavulin. "Yeah, someone should have, for sure. I guess they all just figured kids would be kids."

I extend the bottle toward her. "Peace offering?"

She sits on the log with me but leaves a full arm's length between us. Takes the bottle and swigs from it, two good pulls, swallowing with a hiss that tells me she's no stranger to whisky. "Thanks."

"It's kind of a wonder to me that we never really got into any trouble, you know? Like, there never any real fights, just some drunk scuffles. No one ever got pregnant that I know of. No one wrecked or hit anyone."

She hands the bottle back. "Leslie Donovan got pregnant."

I laugh. "That explains where she went senior year. But are we honestly surprised, though? Leslie was…"

Delia snorts. "No, I can't say I'm surprised. She was

the first girl I knew of who claimed to have had sex…in eighth grade." She looks at me sidelong. "You and her ever…?"

I stare back. "You really want to know, or are you just looking for an opening for a dig?"

"I'm genuinely curious. I know Dell says he did, once, at a party. That was…junior year, though, according to his claims, and she got pregnant start of senior year. So, you know, it wasn't his."

"Do you know whose it was?"

She shakes her head. "Nah. She just up and vanished. It was as much of a surprise to me as anyone else—we weren't really friends. I hear she went to live with her aunt and uncle down in San Diego, but that's all I know. No guy I know of ever claimed it, and she never came back to say. And even the fact that she got pregnant is, honestly, more hearsay than hard fact. I never heard it from her, is what I mean." A glance at me. "So. Did you or did you not ever sleep with Leslie Donovan?"

I sigh. Nod, once. "I did." A tip of my head sideways, and then I sip scotch. "Sort of."

"How do you *sort of* sleep with someone?"

I hand the bottle to her. "I, um…" I groan. "It's not something I talk about a lot." I grin at her. "Not for the reasons I think you'd assume, though. I actually asked her out on a legitimate date, and we actually went on one."

"You and Leslie Donovan went on a *date*? When?" She's incredulous.

"Junior year, toward the end. This was after Dell and

her hooked up—and I can confirm his claim, FYI. I was there." I laugh. "Not, like, you know, when they were doing it. But at the party. So unless they went into the bathroom together and came out twenty minutes later and didn't actually *do* anything…"

She shudders. "Ick."

"Hey, Leslie Donovan was hot."

She shakes her head. "Sure, but that's my brother."

I shrug. "True. But you brought it up. Anyway. We went on a date. Charlie's for dinner, the theater for a movie. Afterward, we went for a drive. Found a little spot north a ways—"

She drops her head and nods, laughing. "I know the spot. Every teenager who grew up here knows it."

"And so do the cops, apparently," I say with a rueful laugh. "Because we were literally seconds away from going at it when along comes who but Officer Alsworth knocking on the window. Sort of ruined the mood."

She snorts. "And you never tried again, anywhere else, later?"

"I was going to, but then I found out she went out with Tom Crawford the very next night and slept with him. So I was like…maybe not."

"Why? You can screw a different girl every night but she can't do the same thing?"

I swig, hand it to her. "You know, I never thought of it that way. But yeah, I guess that kind of was my mindset, back then." I take the bottle back after she's done. "And honestly, it wasn't a different girl every night."

"No?" She's supremely skeptical.

"Nope." I've had enough, so I cap the bottle and set it down—Delia doesn't object. "It was a different girl every weekend. I was doing homework on the weeknights."

She wipes at her lips with a thumb, and it has to be the whisky in my system, but for the first time I notice her lips—plump, pink, with a perfect Cupid's bow. They have sparkles on them, as if the lipstick or lip gloss or whatever she put on them had sparkles in it.

"You know, I always assumed you paid one of the tutor nerds to do your homework for you." She shrugs. "Just the truth."

I laugh. "Nope. I earned that salutatorian on my own, thank you very much."

She blinks. "You were, weren't you?"

I nod. "Yup, I was. Didn't have a chance at valedictorian, though. The girl who earned that was a serious overachiever. I think she had, like, a five-point-oh GPA or something ridiculous."

She shakes her head. "I don't think that's even possible." A sigh. "It was four-point-two-seven."

"I heard four-point-five."

"There were a lot of rumors. It was four-two-seven. And I didn't blow the principal to get it, either, despite what the rumors claimed."

I cackle. "I heard that one. I knew it wasn't true, though."

"Why, because you started it?"

I tilt my head. "No, that wasn't one of mine. Could have been, but wasn't."

"So how did you know it wasn't true?"

"Because you just weren't that type. You never did anything but homework, study, and work for your dad." I smirk. "Also, I always kind of assumed you just didn't… do…*that*. To anyone, let alone an adult for extra GPA points."

She frowns. "I don't know whether to be insulted by that or not, actually."

I laugh. "I'm not sure how I meant it, myself."

"I mean, on the one hand, I worked my ass off. Anyone who actually knew me knew that was true." She stares into the fire, which is going low at this point. "But you assuming I wouldn't blow anyone? Like, you assume I'm just this…sexless robot? I'm glad you knew I wouldn't suck off an adult—Mr. Greely especially, because *gross*."

"Whoever started that rumor about you and Mr. Greely must have started it about a few girls, because I heard it about you, Tanya Moynihan, and Kelly Tanner."

She snickers. "In Kelly's case, it could be true."

"She barely graduated—what are you talking about?"

A snort. "Yeah, and I think it's possible she did something with Mr. Greely to let her graduate, because that girl did *nothing*. Literally, nothing, ever. She failed *gym* class because she refused to change. She failed lit class sophomore year because she kept turning in book reports on *Marie Claire* articles instead of the books." She glances at me, and I can tell she's feeling the scotch. "I'm not a sexless robot, Thai Bristow. I've had sex. I *like* sex. I've even given a blowjob before."

I genuinely don't know how to answer. My previous observation of her plump, pink, sparkly lips suddenly seems less innocent, with that statement out in the air.

Delia…blowjob.

It doesn't compute. She's not a sexless robot, I know that intellectually. She's got more curves than a mountain road, and in the past few weeks I've seen her dress to accentuate it, if not flaunt it. Logically, it's only sensible that she's not a virgin. But—

My brain, that strange, deviant place, feeds me an image.

Of Delia.

On her knees.

That thick, lustrous black hair loose and wavy around her shoulders, maybe a few flyaway wisps in her eyes and sticking to her lips. Which are parted…to close around my cock. Blue, blue, crazy blue eyes staring up at me as her lips stretch around me.

Sink down.

I blink, and the image vanishes, and suddenly it's just Delia and I again, several feet between us, on a log in clearing in the woods.

Clothed.

And enemies.

What the fuck was that?

That will *never* happen.

I don't even want it to. That's Dell's sister, his twin. And she fucking *hates* me.

Yet we've had this whole conversation, and it's been remarkably…civilized. Only a few digs have been exchanged.

"Nothing to say to that, huh, Thai?" She rolls her eyes.

"No, I just…" I huff. "I believe you."

"Oh, well," she laughs, "thanks for that. I'm so glad you believe me when I say I'm not a nun."

"I mean, no shit. No nun I've ever met wears skirts like *that*."

Knee-length, green and white plaid, tight around her hips yet stretchy enough to move with her. White button-down, unbuttoned to show enough cleavage to hint at a *lot* more left unseen. Incongruously, she's wearing mud-stained pink camouflage Crocs with the outfit. I can't help but snort at the sight of them.

"Don't laugh at my Crocs. I only wear them to do yard work."

I frown and laugh. "You? Yard work?"

She nods. "Me, yard work. I have an actual house of my own, Thai. With flowers. I also have a fireplace and I chop my own wood. I do adult things like that."

I laugh. "Hey, I do adult things."

"Have you ever mowed a lawn? Chopped wood? Weeded a flower bed? Bought your own groceries?"

"Believe it or not, I can actually cook rather well."

She cackles. "Bullshit. You can not."

"I can!" I point at her. "There's a lot more to me than you give me credit for. What did you think I was doing the last ten years? I can *cook*. I was sick of living on takeout, you know?"

She shakes her head. "I would never have pegged you a cook. Takeout, maybe grill a steak at most."

I snort. "Seems like you wouldn't peg me for much of anything good."

A nod. "That's fairly true, actually."

I laugh. "As long as we're clear, I guess."

"Any other surprises?"

I smirk. "Oh, plenty. But I'm gonna keep those secret, for now." I grab the bottle and stand up, kick dirt over the dying fire; the light in the clearing fades until I can barely see her in the dim orange glow of the coals. "I just like that look on your face. Like, you're so shocked I can do…literally anything at all other than breathe with my mouth closed."

"Nah, I know that. You're not Dell."

"That's not entirely fair." I find my speaker, which is still playing jazz, and turn it off. "Dell's just…a little lost, still."

She doesn't respond for a long time. "I don't want to talk about Dell."

"Fair enough." I kick more dirt onto the coals until the coals are covered—now it's totally dark in the clearing.

A memory occurs to me, and I laugh, thinking about it. "Remember when we played spin the bottle out here?"

"Yes." Her voice is tight, angry. Pained.

That kills some of the humor I'm feeling. "I thought it was funny. We were out here, in The Spot. You, me, Dell, god who else was here that night?"

"Dane Couzens, Olivia Heffernan, Callie Bellows, Rob Prescott, and Leslie." Her voice is quiet and cold.

I feel like maybe I've stepped onto thin ice, here.

"We played spin the bottle. It was harmless fun."

She whirls on me, and I can feel her anger, even though she's little more than a shadow in the darkness. "Harmless fun? Thai, that was one of the most embarrassing moments of my life, thanks to you."

"Thanks to me? What'd I do?"

"You don't even remember?" She laughs, but it's bitter and disbelieving. "Allow me to enlighten you. It was my turn, so I spun the bottle. It landed on Dane Couzens."

Ohhhh shit. I'm starting to remember. "You had a crush on him, didn't you?"

"Yes, I did. A major one. I thought I'd kept it to myself pretty well, because he was your friend and I knew if you found out, you'd do something mean, and also I knew Dane was part of your Big Swinging Dick club of assholes and idiots. He was just cute, you know? I was attracted to him physically. He had a nice smile, and when he laughed, it lit up the whole room."

"His laugh was infectious," I agree. "You couldn't help but laugh when he did."

"I still have no idea how you found out. But you

did. And when I spun the bottle and it landed on Dane, I was, like…all mixed up. Giddy, because I'd get to kiss Dane without having to tell him I had a crush on him. But also scared that he'd find out. But the moment that bottle landed on him, you got this look on your face. It was the look you got when you were about to do something horrible to me."

I close my eyes, remembering this, now. All I'd remembered, originally, was being here, in the dark clearing of The Spot, playing spin the bottle. I'd gotten to kiss Olivia *and* Callie that night. I'd remembered laughing. Having fun. I'd forgotten *why* we were laughing, apparently.

"Shit," I whisper.

"Now you remember?" She's quiet another moment. "You whispered something to Dane, and he started laughing. And he looked at me, right at me, and was like, 'Matt tells me you have a crush on me. That's cute and all, McKenna, but I'm not into bestiality.'" I can hear the hurt in her voice. "Not into bestiality. That's what he said to me. And you all laughed. Like, you all laughed like it was the funniest thing ever. Ha ha ha, Delia McKenna is a hippo. Delia McKenna is so ugly, so fat he wouldn't even kiss me playing spin the bottle."

"Delia, I—" I stop, because what the hell can I say? That's who I was.

She wasn't ugly, or fat. I was just a bastard.

"Want me to walk you back?" It's all I can think of.

She picks up her shotgun—I see her movements as

shadows moving in the darkness, and then she switches on her flashlight. "I'm good."

"Sure? We had a bit of scotch, and as you said, these woods—"

"I'm fine. I can handle myself."

I hold up one hand palm out. "Suit yourself." I fumble my phone out of my back pocket, juggling the bottle and the speaker, manage to turn on my own flashlight. "See ya."

I make it a few steps. "Thai?"

I stop, turn; she's in the same spot, still, watching me walk away. "Yeah?"

"Don't drive yet."

I nod, even though I know she can't see the gesture. "Yeah, no, I won't. Thanks."

The spear of her flashlight beam bobs away, into the forest, and I'm alone. I walk back to my truck, trying to figure out how I feel about that whole situation.

Delia clearly thinks the worst of me, and I can't say I blame her.

When I get to my truck, I start it and put it in gear... and then back into park. Shut it off. Lean my seat back all the way and close my eyes.

Instead of sleep, I see Delia.

That green plaid skirt wrapped tight around thick, generous, juicy hips. The white button-down tailored to her trim waist, bulging around her breasts, gapped at the buttons showing teasing hints of white lace and silk of her bra.

I see again the unhelpfully graphic and detailed image I had earlier, when I thought about her lips—Delia on her knees, her thick long wavy hair loose around her shoulders. Sparkling lips parted, ready to take my cock.

I groan, open my eyes and push the image away, savagely.

Will *NEVER* happen.

She sees me as…some kind of subhuman monster, some kind of soulless, black-hearted deviant.

A civil conversation mostly devoid of brutal digs at my intelligence and character is likely as good as it's going to get.

And the worst part of it is, I earned it. She doesn't know who I am *now*, just who I was then.

I push that line of thought away. But my mind stubbornly goes back to her.

I don't even *want* anything with Delia anyway. Physical, mental, let alone emotional.

I don't want to see her naked.

Well…okay fine, maybe I do. I mean, shit—she's suddenly a gorgeous woman with an incredible body. So yeah, sure, I can admit my lustful curiosity.

But I'm also entirely cognizant that Delia McKenna would bathe in acid before she allowed that. I doubt she's even aware of me as a male.

Chapter
TEN

Delia

I CAN'T SLEEP.

It's not the scotch—I'm nice and floaty and buzzed, but far from anything like drunk. I'm sleepy, but can't fall over the edge into unconsciousness. I get close, and then…

I see Thai fucking Bristow.

I see his stupid, perfect hair. Blond and thick and messy and too long and perfect.

I see his stupid, perfect eyes. Green with hints and streaks of gray. Expressive and deep and full of humor and intelligence. Eyes that *see* me. See through me. Eyes that make me feel…exposed. Naked.

He hasn't said or done anything I can pinpoint as being lecherous or inappropriate. Hasn't given me the leering once-over. I haven't caught him staring at my cleavage or my ass. Nothing I can call him out for. But yet, somehow…around him, I may as well be dressed in nothing but a lace teddy.

I wonder what he would think if he knew I own a red lace teddy—an expensive, sinfully revealing one.

Sure, I've never worn it around a male before, but I do own one and have worn it. Alone, in my own house. Under a bathrobe.

I didn't look at myself in the mirror while wearing it.

But it counts, right?

He's made comments that make me feel like he sees me as a woman. As a physical creature, as an object of male desire. A sexual being.

No nun I've ever met wears skirts like that.

Begs the question, how many nuns has he met?

More to the point is the phrase, skirts like that. The emphasis, skirts like *that*.

Hopefully, the dim light of the fire hid my blush when he said that.

The moment I got home, I stood in front of my full-length mirror and looked at myself. At the skirt.

What did he see? My giant ass?

"Hey, Donuts Delia—did your dad bring you to school with a crane?"

"Yo, Delia. Watch out for that chair. It was a bit wobbly the last time I sat in it. I wouldn't want it to break when you sit down."

"Hey, Delia. I got you something." A Weight Watchers meal.

I hear his voice in my head, even still, every single day when I look in the mirror. The things he said.

I groan and toss and turn in bed, trying to quiet my spinning brain.

Stop thinking about Thai Bristow.

Stop thinking about how thick his arms looked. How tight and round his ass was in his slacks as he walked away from me last night. He'd been still dressed for work—khaki slacks, Timberland boots, collared, short-sleeve polo shirt, brown leather belt. Not quite dressy, not quite casual.

Stop thinking about him, dammit.

Although, thinking about how hot he's gotten is better than thinking about how mean he used to be.

I wonder if he has a six-pack. He and Dell both pranced around shirtless from April to November, and they both always had hard, visible abs despite rarely doing anything remotely resembling exercise beyond running away from me after pulling some lame, cruel prank on me.

He probably still has a six-pack—arms like that and shoulders like that don't come from nowhere.

The guys I tend to go out with and sleep with aren't the hardbody types, let's just say. Thai's accusation as to my type was scarily accurate.

I kick the blankets off and sit up with a frustrated huff. "Stop thinking about Thai Bristow," I scold myself out loud.

Think about somebody else.

Anyone else.

I reach out and grab my phone. I have to distract myself.

Bring up a website I would never admit under torture to even knowing the name of, let alone that I frequently peruse in search of visual fodder for distraction and release.

I find a video.

The guy in it is all hard lines and sculpted muscles... and thick, throbbing member. He's rough, demanding. The woman in the video is tiny and frail-looking with bolt-on boobs, but she takes him like a champ, acting like she loves every second of it. I ignore her. Think about him.

Pretend it's me in the video, doing things that are a million and a half miles outside of who I am and what I like and what I do—I pretend I'm openly sexual. Hungry for him, eager. All the things I simply don't have the courage to actually be.

I wouldn't know how. I wouldn't know where to start. I'd laugh, or more likely, I'd just never let myself even get close to a situation like that.

My sexual experiences are carefully choreographed. We go on no less than four dates before I let him kiss me. It's more like six dates before I let him get any farther. When we do, it's at an upscale hotel in town. Lights off. I undress—there's no messy trail of ripped-off clothing. That frantic, Hollywood passion and frenetic, absurd need is fake. I've never felt anything even close to it, nor has any male ever shown a hint of it for me.

Thus, not real.

I take my clothes off, there's a careful fumbling as he puts on a condom, and then we lie down and he enters me and does the thing, and then it's over.

That's sex, in the world of Delia McKenna.

Is it any wonder I've never been super desperate for it?

In my fantasy world, however…

There's a man who has the body of a god rather than a marshmallow, and he *wants* me. Can't get enough of me. Touches me like he owns me. Demands I give him my body, my desire. He drags screams out of me. I've never screamed during sex. Barely manage a whimper, most of the time.

But like now, when I'm pretending? Watching this stupid fake scripted video and wishing it was me, I slip my hand under the waistband of my underwear and touch myself and a moan escapes me and I close my eyes and picture the sculpted, hardbody god levered over me with one thick, rippling arm like a pillar beside my face he's staring down at me with blazing gray-green eyes and his hair is messy and wild and sun-kissed and his skin golden and he's looking at me like he's never seen me before. And he's touching me. It's his fingers at the apex of my thighs, swirling around my sex in light deft touches. His lips would touch my skin, scour and explore. I'd grip him and caress him and he would be unable to hold back, needing me and wanting more of me. Maybe he'd even pull away and kneel over me and bury his hands in my hair and bring himself to my lips. I'd act like I don't want to, but secretly I would—secretly I *do*. And I'd make him grunt and groan with wild need, he'd be crazy with how I'm making him feel.

He'd rip himself away before he finished in my mouth; he'd need *me*.

He'd need to be inside me, unable to wait any longer.

And when we joined, it would be…

Wild.

Delirious.

A frenzy of screams and primal roars.

I'd come again and again and again, and he'd hold back and keep making me come, and finally, in unison with me, he'd explode, helplessly.

The fantasy brings it out of me. I'm seized with tremors, moans escaping my clenched teeth, hips flexing.

It's only when I'm limp and gasping and finally toppling toward a fitful sleep that I realize:

It was Thai in my fantasy.

∞

I can't look at myself in the mirror as I get ready for my run, the next morning. It's just past dawn, the sky beyond the trees pink-gray-orange. I wear what I usually wear to run: tight black yoga shorts and a super compressive sports bra, hair in a braid, earbuds in, running shoes laced tight.

In the debauched hinterlands of my brain, my fantasy from the night before plays on repeat.

I do my best to repress it, ignore it.

Pretend I'm not hyperaware that I did in fact maybe make myself orgasm while fantasizing about Thai Bristow, my archenemy.

I put on my hip-hop running playlist and step out my front door. Do a few jumping jacks and high knees to get my blood pumping, and then head out at my usual slow but steady jog. I have a five-mile circuit that I could do in my sleep, with my eyes closed: down the driveway and to the dirt road, turn left, two miles along the dirt road until I come to the stile that marks the border between our property line and the thousands of acres of state forest that's on the other side. Around the stile, jogging along the two-track used by the forest rangers, along the western edge of McKenna land. A mile of that, and the trees give out, with the county line road as the northern boundary of our property—it's this county road that Thai would have taken to get to the far side of the woods. I'm in the groove, now. Feeling the beat and my heart is pounding and I'm sweating and my breathing is nice and rhythmic and deep. Just me and the music and the pound of my feet, just the rising sun and the occasional squirrel darting across my path, or a crow wheeling on a wingtip overhead.

I almost don't register it, at first, as I near it—a truck,

parked along the tree line. Who would be here, at this time of day? It's either state forest land or private property for miles in every direction, so it's highly unlikely to be a hunter or hiker—it's not hunting season anyway. But then as I get closer, I realize I recognize the truck—it's Thai's.

Draw closer and slow to a walk as I approach it.

He's asleep, seat tilted back, head to one side, mouth open.

I tap on the glass with a fingernail. He stirs. Tap again, a little louder. This time he jerks and bolts upright, blinking.

I back up as he shoves the door open, rubbing at his eyes. "You okay?" I ask.

He wipes at his face with his palms. "Huh?"

I laugh. "I asked if you're okay."

"Oh." He draws in a deep breath, stretching, arms going up and behind his head. The hem of his shirt rides up, and I catch a glimpse of golden-brown skin and a hint of hair in a thin trail under his navel. Finally, the stretch ends and he blinks a few times at me, then looks around. "It's morning?"

"You are *not* a morning person, are you?" I say, with a laugh.

I'm still breathing hard and sweating from my run. I feel a drop of sweat trickle down my throat, and down into my cleavage.

Thai's eyes follow it. Linger.

Drop lower. To my belly, my hips. My legs.

Back up, to my breasts.

Then, finally, to my eyes, after that long, perusing, appreciative, lingering scan of my body.

I resist the urge to cross my arms over my chest, over my stomach. I have a flat belly, and I've worked my ass off to get that. No visible abs, but I know I'm toned.

He shakes his head, as if just then realizing he was staring. His eyes drop, turn away. "No, I'm...not a morning person."

"What are you doing here?" I ask.

He scrapes his hand through his hair a few times, but it's tangled and snarled. "I, uh...I was going to drive home after we talked last night, but figured I probably shouldn't. So I lay down to rest and maybe sober up a bit, and then next thing I knew, you were tapping on the window." He glances at me—at my eyes. "Out for a run, huh?"

"Stunning powers of observation you have," I say, the snark automatic.

He snorts. "Well, we did just establish that I'm not a morning person." He rolls his shoulder, twists his torso to work out the kinks in his back. "You run a lot?"

"Five miles every morning."

"At dawn?"

"I've woken up at six without an alarm for years now. Just habit, I guess."

"Sounds horrible." He laughs.

I can't help but laugh. "Yeah. Funny thing is, every morning I grumble and complain as I'm getting ready. I try to talk myself out of actually running. Like, I'm just too tired, my legs are still sore, I didn't really eat anything bad yesterday, I don't feel like it, that kind of thing. But I force myself out the door. I force myself to just start running. The first half a mile, mile…it just sucks. My legs hurt and my lungs burn, and I hate it. And I want to quit, turn around and go home. But I don't let myself. Force myself to keep going. And then, it's kinda like magic. Somewhere around mile two, two and a half, something shifts. I can breathe better, and my legs feel good and I'm in the groove and I'm not even really aware of when it happened." I laugh. "And then by the time I get home, I feel proud that I did it. I never *want* to run but I'm always glad to *have* run."

He nods. "Sounds like me and going to the gym. The first few sets suck and are hard and I hate every second of every rep. Then somehow, by the third or fourth set, I'm just…bam, I'm in it. Y'know?"

My eyes go to his arms again, his shoulders. He was lean and sharp and hard as a teenager—as a man he's… he's not brawny, not some muscle-bound macho maniac. But he's just…*dense*. And still hard.

An image flashes into my dumb brain: his thick arm pillared beside my face, his hair messy and around his face and drifting above me as he moves, golden skin bare and taut around sculpted muscles.

I flush, and I'm sure my face is beet red; to hide it, I turn away as if to keep my muscles warm, even though that ship has sailed—my run is over.

I feel his eyes on me.

Ignore.

"I need coffee in the worst way," he says.

I sigh. "Alright. Let's go."

I turn, and he's eyeing me with an arched eyebrow. "You say, with resignation."

I can't help but laugh. "I always make a pot before I run so I can have coffee as soon as I get back."

He just stares at me, as if not comprehending my meaning. "Okay?"

"I have to spell it out? I'm two and a half miles from home and cooled off, so you may as well just drive me home, and in return, I'll provide you with a cup of coffee."

His arched eyebrow of disbelief rises higher in further disbelief. But he has the good sense to just nod. "You've got a deal. Hop in."

I round the hood and clamber up into the passenger seat—unlike the interiors of most construction guys I've ever met, Thai's is neat and clean and smells good. No garbage, no piles of Mt. Dew bottles and empty dip cans and McDonald's wrappers.

Thai makes the larger circuit around the county road and back to the road we live on, pulling into our driveway with a familiarity of long practice. His face seems pensive, thoughtful. At the last minute, I realize he doesn't know about the house I built and is heading by old habit toward the main house, where Mom lives.

I point at the pull off. "Actually, I'm here."

He jams the brakes and skids in the dirt and gravel, slewing sideways a bit, and then we're entering the tunnel of trees that leads to my little clearing.

He pulls to a stop in front of my house. Stares. "This is you, huh?"

I nod. "Home sweet home."

"When'd you have this built?"

I know it shouldn't bug me that he would assume I *had* it built—it's a normal, natural thing for anyone to assume. But yet, it does. Knee-jerk irritation, just because this is Thai we're talking about, I suppose.

"Um, well? I built it myself about three years ago."

His head swivels, and his eyes meet mine. Clearly, this is unexpected. *"You* built it? Like…"

I laugh, because his confusion and disbelief are comical. "I run a construction company, Thai. I'm not just a secretary, you know. Before I was Vice President or CEO or whatever, I was on-site every day. I, personally, me, Delia McKenna, am a licensed and insured builder in my own right." I point at the house. "I borrowed the heavy machinery and cleared the trees, leveled, dug and poured the concrete foundation, framed it, hung the drywall, blew the insulation, roofed it, installed the flooring. The only things I outsourced was running the plumbing and electrical from the road, and installing the actual electrical service. But I did the lighting and the outlets and toilets and sinks myself."

He grunts in surprise. "Damn."

I can't help a grin of pride. "I'm not just a figurehead."

He shakes his head. "No, I know that. But…I dunno. I guess knowing what to do and how to do it is different than being able to actually, you know…*do* it."

I nod and shrug. "Actually, I do know what you mean. And that was part of why I took on the challenge—I wanted to see if I could take what I knew from supervision and management and apply it to actually being able to do it and have it meet code as well as my own standards."

"I'd say it looks like you succeeded."

You'd think, considering it was a little cabin in the woods, that I'd have built a traditional log cabin, but I'm actually not a fan of log cabins as a rule, so instead I'd built a little Cape Cod style with cedar shakes and a pair of dormers and a nice deep front porch. I like to think it looks like a Thomas Kincaid painting in the evening, when it's in shadow and the front windows are lit up.

I hop down from his truck, which considering the lift kit and 35" tires is a considerable drop. He follows, and I focus all my willpower on not being self-conscious about my shorts. They literally cannot get any shorter or tighter without being considered an undergarment, but I only wear them to run, and only early in the morning, and most of my run is off the roads and away from any possible traffic. Meaning, the only reason I feel okay wearing them in the first place is because it's highly unlikely anyone will ever see me.

And now Thai Bristow is behind me, watching me walk.

And I'm deeply, intensely aware that the spandex is so tight it's a second skin and they're so short the bottom curve of my ass cheeks is visible. Especially now—they hiked up while I was sitting and I don't dare pick the wedge out while he's watching. But then, which is worse: having a wedgie while he's behind me, or picking it out while he's watching?

I can't let him know how miserably self-conscious I am. He can't know.

I've worked hard on this body, and I am genuinely proud of it. Of myself. Of how I look.

But this is Matthais Bristow.

His very name, in my mind, is a harbinger of torture and torment and misery.

Don't let on. I hold my head high and walk as if I don't have a care in the world. Even put a little swagger in my step, faking a confident pride I don't really feel.

I feel him behind me, and ignore him. As if his presence in my home isn't throwing me for a loop. Thai Bristow is in my *house*.

Suddenly, it seems like a small space. Filled with him.

He looks around while I pull mugs from my open-face cabinets, and I try to see my kitchen from his eyes: white subway tiles, poured concrete counter-tops, natural oak shelves with industrial pipes for braces. Exposed oak beams overhead—actual antiques sourced from a local two-hundred-year-old barn. Dark, polished walnut floors. There's a little island in the kitchen, just big enough for three stools. Porcelain farmhouse sink. Mustard yellow Smeg appliances for a pop of color.

The living room is open to the kitchen, flooring and beams carrying through. Thick white shag rug, over-stuffed leather couch, flat-screen TV over a German smear brick fireplace with a floating mantle made from the same antique oak beams as the ceiling.

"This is…" He spins, taking it all in. "Truly incredible, Delia."

My cheeks burn. "Thanks. I'm pretty proud of it."

"You should be."

I hand him a mug of coffee. I know he drinks it black—he was at our house most mornings, and Dad would offer him coffee, and he always took it straight black. Still does.

He takes the mug from me, but stares into it suspiciously. Sniffs it.

I cackle. "It's not poisoned, Thai."

That eyebrow goes up. "How can I be sure?"

I reach out, take it from him, sip, hand it back. "There."

He nods, apparently satisfied. Takes a sip. "Mm. Good coffee."

"Life is too short for crappy coffee," I say.

Awkward silence.

It's weird, being in a room with him and not wanting to verbally eviscerate him. I wonder if this truce will last—if this is actually the real Thai, or if this is some long con he's pulling on me.

"Why'd you come back, Thai?"

He drinks his coffee, considers the question for quite a long time, actually. "The truth is, I'm still not...I'm not entirely sure. Part of it is that I was just...bored. But...this isn't a dig, truly, but it's just something I don't think you can understand. You've always had a purpose, a...a *raison d'être*." He shrugs. "I haven't. I honestly went to college only because it was something to *do*. I got into things and found out I actually enjoyed business—or some aspects of it, I guess. I discovered I had more of a capacity for..." A sigh, which seems more of a self-effacing laugh than anything. "For doing stuff, I guess, then I'd ever really considered. Growing up, Mom and Dad didn't expect anything of me. I didn't really try, in school. I was just...I dunno. Salutatorian by virtue of just...not being into sports and it was just easy."

"Why didn't you play football?" I ask, something I'd always wondered about.

He laughs. "It was too much fuckin' work. All that running, all that gear to put on and lug around. I was more interested in partying and girls."

I cackle. "Well, that's an honest answer for you."

He looks around at my living room again, and his eyes go to my built-in bookshelf stuffed full with books. Stands up, wanders over to the shelf and scans the titles—mostly romances, some thrillers, some murder mysteries. A collection of books from my youth, near the top—battered, dog-eared copies of *Twilight* and *Harry Potter*. His gaze goes to the top row, the books that harken back to our shared youth. I have the complete Harry Potter series, there, the original hardcovers I'd bought as they came out. There's one missing, though.

"You're missing one," he says.

"Yeah, I know." I can't help the way it comes out. "Gee, I wonder how that happened."

He happened. Took it and threw it into the mud, and then stepped on it. Just because.

His expression, as he turns around, is closed off. But I can't help wondering if I'm imagining the regret I see, just before his face shutters.

"When Dell first came to me bitching about what your dad did with the will and the business...I sort of realized that I've never had a purpose in life. It was kind of a shitty thing to realize, honestly. That I don't matter. That I've never done anything even remotely valuable. And here Dell had this ready-made thing in his lap. All he had to do was *try* a little. Give a little bit of a shit. It was something to *do*, you know?"

He shakes his head and shrugs. "Once I realized how much I hated living in Manhattan and how much I hated the corporate bro atmosphere of big finance and just quit the whole scene, I had nothing. I wasn't about to come home and live with Mom and Dad again. But I saw no reason to buy a house anywhere because I had nowhere I belonged. I mean, don't get me wrong, I can fly into any one of a dozen cities around the world and I'll know people. I can crash parties on every populated continent on the globe, and shit, I even know someone at a research station in Antarctica. But…down deep? Nowhere was home. I literally was just renting or borrowing condos and going to parties and…" He stares into his coffee. Seems embarrassed. "Honestly, a lot of it was just chasing hookups, if you want the honest truth."

"And that led you to buying half of my company… how?"

He laughed. "It didn't. I'm sure you're well aware that I have a, um, let's just say generous trust fund. Comically so. Plus living expenses provided by my parents that they've just never bothered to pull back. So I honestly don't ever have to work. I could live in ridiculous luxury forever and never lift a finger. But I was bored. And I had all this money and nothing to do with it. I mean, I've done all the things. Skydiving. Scuba diving. Sailing. Private jets to private beaches in Tahiti with, like, squadrons of models hanging around in a whole lot of not much. Fast cars. Old cars. New cars. I even bought a fuckin' yacht once, but then I realized you need a whole crew and a captain and the whole nine yards and that just seemed like way more work than I'd expected, so I sold it."

"Poor you," I quipped, deadpan.

"Right? Poor me. Talk about first-world problems. This was a one percent of one percent kind of problem. But I was just fucking bored out of my mind. So one day about a year and a half out of Wharton, I was hanging out with some guys from school, the business-y sort of guys with stock portfolios—your kinda guys, actually." He smirks, and I glare, but it feels kind of cursory, at this point. "And they were talking about this company they'd bought stock in. Sounded cool. I think they make, like, I dunno—some part for Wi-Fi routers, I think. It was a new company that had just done their IPO. So on a whim, I looked into it. Like, I Googled them. Called their receptionist and asked a few questions. Asked my friends for some information. Their IPO had done really well, so I was like, fuck it, let's do this adult business thing, and I bought stock. A *lot* of stock. Not quite a controlling interest, but close."

"What was the company?"

"Albion Networking Systems."

I've heard of them—they've been making the rounds trying to sell us some kind of whole smart home system. "You invested in Albion?"

"Yeah." He shrugs.

"How involved are you?"

"Not very. They have their own thing going. I know they've been looking at getting into the whole smart home arena, but I guess they haven't had much success yet. And this was a few years ago. I've done a lot of other deals since. VC and angel investing, mostly."

"Albion sends us marketing materials every once in a while, and one of their reps comes by every quarter. But most contractors aren't really interested in new technology unless it cuts their overhead down or drives their profit margins up. Smart home systems is more overhead and you're not guaranteed a return on it."

"That's what they're up against. But I guess the people who know this sort of thing are all saying at some point in the not-so-distant future, all homes are going to be connected, what we call smart, and the builders who get in on it now are the ones who are going to set the standard when it starts to really pick up."

I'm a little floored, right now. Because he's right. It's something I've thought about myself. I just could never get it front of Dad in a way that stood a chance—he just wanted to build houses. He was a traditionalist. But… now I'm in charge. Mostly.

The other person with controlling decision power is…Thai.

And he's talking about something that's been a secret desire of mine for a long time.

He notices I've gone quiet. "Did I just step in something smelly?"

I shake my head. "No, not…not really."

"Then what?"

I sigh, clutching my mug with both hands; I'm on the other side of the island from him, yet it feels like he's filling the kitchen, too close to me, too much, too in my space. "It's just something I've thought about."

"What is?"

"What Albion has been trying to sell us on. Dad always just shut it down cold, but I've been thinking for a while that it might be smart to start incorporating that as an option in new builds. Smart switches, bulbs, thermostats, stuff like that."

He leans over the island. "Now, I haven't looked at their package, but I can tell you it's way more comprehensive than that. It's built-in Wi-Fi, a central hub controlling the entire house, like...Tony Stark kinda shit. Voice-controlled house. Like, you just say 'turn on the kitchen lights,' or turn on the oven to four-fifty, or turn the air conditioning to sixty-eight.' It's not just a house with lights and a thermostat on some goofy app on your phone. It's a truly connected, next-generation house. Built-in, from scratch. They've even got AI that will learn your preferences and adjust things automatically."

I can't help but be intrigued. "Really? I'm...that's...wow."

"It's seriously next-level shit, Delia. And what I learned when I was buying them was that when you buy in, it gets cheaper. If you're building, like, sixty new homes, the parts and labor is cheaper because it's in bulk and it's going in as a new build rather than trying to retrofit one existing structure. The more you buy in, the cheaper it is, so it's really geared for builders with big numbers. Again, this was a few years ago, so my information is probably a little out of date. I'm sure they've upped their game since I invested."

I finish my coffee and pour more—offer him some. "Well that's cool, but don't think I haven't noticed that you never answered my original question."

"Why did I come back? Why did I buy Dell's shares of McKenna?"

I nod. "Yeah. It's hard to even try to trust you and your motives when I have no clue what your motives even are."

He rolls his shoulders, sighs. "Buying Albion put me on a path, of sorts. I saw a pretty immediate positive valuation, so I figured okay, why not? Let's do it again. So I started sniffing around and found another company. This one was just a baby one, though. No IPO, no stock offerings, just a private company with a good idea, and they needed an investor. So I invested. They were a tech company on the verge of going public with their product...some sort of chip or something that makes Wi-Fi go farther with better signal strength or something. I dunno exactly. Again, not a controlling interest investment, but sizable. My investment put them into manufacturing and they were a hit immediately. Including with Albion, who saw their product as a no-brainer. So that's nice and symbiotic." He shrugged, sipped coffee. "So then I bought into a medical supply company, just to diversify. I've invested in something like dozens of companies over half a dozen different industries, and I'm seeing great returns. But none of them really *interested* me. Like, I'm not on the board, I'm not part of running them. It's all just making me more money, which is nice, but... I don't need it. I needed something to do, and I honestly enjoy the work, the process. But investing my money in something is not at all the same thing as investing my emotions. My *self*. My time."

"I'm starting to see. But what I don't get is why *McKenna*?"

His eyes went to mine. "Dell didn't just walk away out of laziness. I'm sure you talked to him. I'm not trying to defend him or make this about him—I know you don't want to talk about him. My only point is, he had valid reasons. But I was just like, you have something, here, Dell. Something real, something valuable. And I told him, when I agreed to his plan, that if I was going to be all in on McKenna, I was going to finally be *part* of it. In it." He huffs, rolls his shoulders. "So, why McKenna? I don't know, Delia. I really don't. It was familiar? I don't know."

I frown. "So, it wasn't…" I don't want to say what I'm thinking, not in so many words. But I do. "It wasn't just to fuck with me?"

He shakes his head. "No, Delia. Not at all."

There's a distance in his eyes, though. "What? What aren't you saying?"

"Just that…I think when Dell first suggested it, I think he assumed I would be looking at it as a prank on you. Like, haha, guess who owns half of your company? This motherfucker, the asshole who made your life a living hell for eighteen years." He shakes his head again, not looking at me. "I don't know that I can delineate or…or quantify all my actual reasons for going through with it. I think part of it was that just from a financial standpoint, it was smart business. I know McKenna is successful. I know it's a good investment, even if I had nothing to do with it. I know you would make it even more successful than it's ever been. Plus, it does potentially dovetail with the investment I made before this one."

"Which is?"

"They're an indie startup. They 3D print construction supplies from recycled, sustainable, and recyclable materials. Their initial products are just things like switch plates and screws and braces and brackets and all that kind of piddly shit. But the product that their whole vision was based around was framing sections, printed whole, in bulk."

I blink. "3D printed framing sections? Made of plastic?"

He nods. "Yeah. But, like, superplastic, or something. Special polymers engineered to withstand something like triple the amount of stresses that traditional framing can support, at least in part because the sections are all one piece, no joins, none of that."

I gape. "And you're just now telling me that you own this company that makes this product?"

"Well, I don't own it. I'm just an investor." He arches that eyebrow. "And I wasn't sure I was quite at a place with you where I could make those kinds of suggestions. I was going to wait until you weren't ready to knife me in the throat every time you saw me."

"I'm not going to knife you in the throat," I say, with an eye roll.

"You once told me you hoped my plane crashed."

"That was then. You had just thrown a snake on me, also."

He snorts. "Yeah, I suppose that's relevant." Another shrug. "But if you're interested in the framing thing, I can set up a meeting. I know they'd love to have a big account with a reputable builder."

"Do it. I think it could be good. Now that I'm in charge, I can make those kinds of decisions." I can't help but let out a groaning sigh. "I wish I could be happier about it. But Dad would never have gone for it. And it just makes me miss him all the more, even though I know modernizing the business is necessary and important."

"I'll get ahold of...god, what's his name?" He frowns. "Marcus? I think his name is Marcus. Anyway, whatever the hell his hipster name is, I'll call him and have him make us an official pitch."

"Sounds good." I glance at the clock on the oven. "Shoot, it's getting late. I have to shower and change before I head into the office."

He swallows hard and sets his mug down. "Yeah, me too. Can't wear the same clothes in to work two days in a row." He smirks. "My boss is a real ballbuster."

I laugh, and it makes my stomach feel oddly warm, and kind of...flippy. "I'm not your boss, for one thing. We're co-owners. And two, I don't give a shit what you wear."

He quirks that eyebrow yet again. "So if I came in wearing board shorts and a tank top, you'd be cool?"

I shrug. "I mean, it would be unprofessional, not to

mention impractical on-site, but...I'm not your boss." I make a face. "And I'm not a ballbuster. Am I?"

He laughs. "How should I know? I barely know you, in some ways. And in others, I know you too well to be an objective source." A thoughtful expression crosses his face, then he shakes his head. "But if you're asking me, I'd say no, you're not a ballbuster. You have expectations and standards, and you personally work your ass off, but I've never gotten the impression that you expect perfection and go around busting people down if they don't measure up."

I'm oddly relieved, in a way I don't dare think too closely about. Because this is Thai, and I don't quite believe that this thoughtful, intelligent, hard-working person in the same Matthais Bristow I so hated, once upon a time.

He heads for the door, pauses. "Look at us, having civil conversations and shit, right?"

I laugh. "I guess it *is* an improvement."

"See you at work," he says, and then he's gone.

And it's weird, when he leaves, how empty my house feels.

Even weirder is how hard I have to work to *not* think about Thai in the shower. Or being in the shower with him.

Gah, what's *wrong* with me? I *cannot* think about Thai Bristow that way. It's not safe, and not healthy.

I don't like him that way.

I really need to find a date—get my mind

off Thai and my stupid fantasy. My stupid, fake, never-going-to-happen, absolutely cannot ever happen again fantasy. About Thai. And how sexy he is. And the things he could do to me, if I didn't hate, loathe, despise him.

Maybe I could call Tyler—I don't do booty calls or friends with benefits, but Tyler is someone I've gone out with a few times, and I know the sex is decent.

So maybe it is a booty call. I just dress it up with dinner and a movie and call it dating.

But when I bring Tyler up in my text thread, I can't bring myself to actually suggest we meet tonight.

I just…can't.

And I refuse to examine myself closely enough to figure out why.

Mainly because if I did, I'd have to admit I don't *actually* hate, loathe, despite Thai at all, anymore.

Ugh.

This is getting…complicated.

Chapter
ELEVEN

Matthais

DAMMIT.

I really wish I hadn't seen her like that.

In those fucking shorts.

In that fucking bra.

I mean, it was a sports bra, meant to contain and compress. For utility, not the male gaze. But...damn. She wore the *fuck* out of it.

And those shorts? God*damn*.

I knew the woman had a killer ass, but until this morning, I didn't understand just how killer.

Fucking...magnificent. In those shorts she may as well have been naked, and the lecherous male in me did not mind at all. The way it moved? Hypnotizing. A little jiggle, but still taut. Round enough to make my dick sit up and take notice.

If it was anyone else, I'd be thinking about how I

want to bend her over my bed and slap that ass till it was pink and she was begging for me.

But this is Delia.

My best friend's sister. I know there's some kind of taboo about that, but I've never gotten it. Maybe because I never thought about Delia that way. Until I came back into town and into her life, that is.

And realized what a freaking smoke show she is.

Did I notice, back in the day, that Delia was a fine-looking piece of woman? Yes, I did. Did I ever allow myself to think about her sexually? Not on your life. If my mind so much as tweaked in that direction, I'd do something to hurt her, just to stop myself. Why? God, I don't fucking know. I'm not sure I want to know. Is that cowardly, of me?

I strip out of my slept-in clothes and twist the water on. While it's heating, I brush my teeth and say fuck it to shaving.

Find myself leaning onto the sink, staring into the mirror—but I'm not seeing myself.

I'm seeing her.

Bent over this very sink.

Her eyes on mine in the mirror.

Body shaking as I drive into her—

I twist away with a groan, scrubbing my face as if to scrub away the images.

I don't want her.

I don't.

But when I get into the shower, my cock is decidedly

singing a very different tune. My cock is thinking about Delia. About what it would be like to peel those shorts off, unzip that bra…feel her skin on mine, taste those luscious tits.

I have myself in my fist, in a tight, punishing grip. Telling myself not to do it.

But I can't fucking help it.

I picture her naked, reaching for me, saying my name not with vitriol but ecstasy…shaking all over as I make her come a thousand times.

What makes me come, though? An image that should scare the absolute hell out of me.

I come while imagining myself on *my* knees in front of her. Making *her* come. With my mouth. Making her scream my name until she begs me to stop.

I explode with a teeth-gritted bellow, and then I watch the shower water rinse it down the drain…

And feel like a tool.

There are a million reasons why it'll never happen, why even thinking about her like that is wrong.

I'm torturing myself with fantasies that will never happen…

And shit, it's not like I actually *want* them to happen…

Right?

The resounding lack of affirmation in my own head at that question definitely worries me.

I clean off, dress, and head to work. It takes real effort to put her out of my mind.

All that effort goes to waste when I finally make it to the office, later that afternoon; I'd spent the morning working with Cal, going over the finishing touches on a house that's just about ready to go up for sale.

Why does it go to waste?

Because Delia clearly dressed just to mess with my head.

Denim miniskirt with knee-high leather boots. Low-cut yellow top that pulls my gaze where it doesn't belong.

I spend the rest of the afternoon around the office, doing my damnedest to not stare at her various assets and actually get work done.

Such as, arrange for Marcus to come in and make a pitch.

Such as get Albion's top rep to come make a pitch, rather than whatever undergrad newbie they've clearly been sending.

Also yet another reason why I have to put a stop to thinking about Delia sexually—this is work. She's my coworker. My *partner*. It's not like that and can't be like that and will never be like that, and letting my lust for her curves play games with my head is only going to endanger the work I've put in toward getting her to trust me.

Or, at least, not hate me.

If I let on that I'm thinking about her sexually, all that will go out the window. I can almost hear her recriminations.

That's how you think of me, Matthais Bristow?

Not if you were the last person on earth, and there aren't any goats…are there goats?

Eat shit and die.

Granted, the last one is more old Delia and less so the newer Delia who can actually have a full conversation without sniping at me.

But if I let on that I was thinking about her naked, that I'd jacked off thinking about her? She'd blow a gasket.

I *have* to put her out of my mind.

❧

A week later, and the struggle is real. I've managed to avoid using Delia as jerk-off imagery, but only barely. It's required a lot of visual stimulation by way of the internet.

I know what I need, I've just been too busy to do it: a hookup.

I don't know that I can bring myself to troll for a hookup locally—anyone my age is almost guaranteed to be someone I know and very likely have already hooked up with. Anyone younger will be the younger sister or cousin of someone I know. Anyone older, the divorced mother of someone I know.

No, I need to go farther afield to find someone to distract me.

So, finally, I take a weekend off and head to San

Fransisco. Rent a penthouse for the weekend and hit a nearby bar.

I know some guys in town, so we meet up and play some pool, shoot some shit. Keep an eye for someone to take my mind off of...

My current problem. Leave it at that.

Finally, late in the evening on Saturday, in walks Distraction.

She's five-seven, bottle-blond hair, with expensive breasts on full display. Little red dress, fuck-me heels. Smoky eye makeup. Little white clutch purse that costs as much as my truck, most likely.

Not that I drove my truck—oh no. When you're trolling for a hookup, you go McLaren. Even girls who say they're not impressed by expensive cars can't help but be impressed with the McLaren.

This chick, Distraction, clocked my car out front, and pegged me as the owner within seconds of walking in.

Beeline for me.

And that's the night.

That easy.

Ricardo, one of the guys I'm playing pool with, sees all this and just laughs. "Man, you don't even have to snap your fingers. The girls literally come to you, man. Not even fuckin' right, bro."

"You know, I tried snapping my fingers, once," I say with a laugh.

"And? Did it work?"

"Hell no. She slapped me silly."

"Good to know." Ricardo is being coy, though. The man has more game than I do. Tall, dark, and handsome, plus he's got the Latin thing going for him.

"Hey." Her voice is low, husky. Fake, but it works. "I'm Violet."

"Hi there, Violet." I give her a grin, the one that works every time. "I'm Thai."

"I like your name." She eyes my scotch. "Buy me a drink?"

"What'll you have?"

A shrug. "Something sweet."

This is where men with less game would bust out a line like, *something sweet like you, huh?* I don't fall for it. I just push off the pool table and weave through the crowded bar, wait for the bartender to see me, and order her a Riesling.

Once she's sipping and watching me line up my shot, I try to figure how long before I make the move of asking her if she wants to get out of here. Not long, judging by the way she's watching me.

"Is that your car out front, Thai?" She leans a little too close, and she's wearing a little too much perfume, but she's intentionally offering me a nice look down her top.

"Sure is." I grin at her. "You want a ride?"

Her grin is hungry. "Hell yeah I want a ride." A lick of her lips. "I'd also like to ride in your car."

Can't get any more obvious than that.

Except Ricardo elbows me. "Yo, someone is staring at you over there, man."

I play it cool. Don't look. "Oh yeah? You know her?"

"Naw, man. But she's giving you a *look*, bro."

I sink my shot, circle the table as if to line up the next one, and scan the bar.

"You have *got* to be kidding me," I mutter.

Delia.

Here.

In a little black dress and tall heels, with her hair in an elaborate updo. Sapphires drip from her ears, gleam at her throat.

And she is indeed giving me a look, but one I can't quite parse.

Not a glare.

Just…a look.

And she's on the arm of a man.

Even if I was the type to be threatened, even if she and I had a thing for me to be threatened, I wouldn't be. The guy is everything I said her type was. On the short side of medium height. Slim and sleek. Slicked-back brown hair. Wearing pleated khakis and a plaid button-down…on a date. Yeesh. Right down to the loafers.

Nice-looking.

My dude wouldn't have a clue what to do with the sexiness that is Delia. He'd waste it—she'd be wasted on him.

Bet he couldn't find her G-spot if she drew him a map.

I stare back, and I sense tension—from her, from myself...from Violet.

"Is that someone you know?" she asks.

I turn away from Delia, with effort. Sink my shot. "Yeah, something like that."

"Do you need to go say hi?" Her tone tells me my shot with her rides on my answer.

Do I? What's protocol, here? Do I bring Violet over? Do I give her the chin lift? Ignore her? Leave Violet here and say hello to Delia...and her date?

I glance at Violet, and somehow I know that there's no chance in hell I'm going anywhere with her tonight. I can't. I just can't. I want to—or at least, part of me does—but...seeing Delia with a date has just...thrown me off.

I sink my last shot, winning the round with Ricardo. Toss back my drink. Meet Violet's eyes. "So, something came up, actually." I gesture at Ricardo. "But I'm going to leave you in Ricardo's very capable hands. I promise, he won't let you down. Will you, buddy?"

Ricardo gives her his most winning grin. "You know it."

I shoot her an apologetic smile. "I'm sorry, really. Just, you know. One of those things."

"What, is she an ex?" Violet asks, frowning.

I laugh. "It's complicated."

And then I walk away, heading for the front door. I tell myself not to do anything stupid.

But yet, as I near the little table where Delia is sitting with her date—right near the front door—I know I'm about to do something monumentally stupid.

I spy a sleek, low-slung red BMW parked out front, near my McLaren. And I know I'm about to really piss her off.

I try to tell myself not to.

Just say hi.

That's it.

Instead, I lean down close to her, as if embracing her with familiarity. Whisper in her ear: "Is that his BMW out front?"

She pulls away. "Matthais." Cold, distant, formal.

"Oh, it's Matthais, now, is it?" I laugh as I stand upright. "Well, Cordelia. It was nice to see you." I extend my hand to her date. "I don't believe we've met. I'm Thai Bristow. Delia and I are…business partners."

He shakes my hand, and I can tell he's puzzled by the whole interaction. "Tyler James Thomas."

I only just barely stifle a snicker. "Nice to meet you, Tyler James Thomas."

She's fuming. I can feel it boiling—I always could feel her fuming, bubbling with anger. Back in the day, I made a game out of making her pop, little digs and needles and snipes until she'd just…BOOM.

Not anymore. I'm a grown-up.

And I don't want her to hate me anymore.

I wonder if I'm going to regret that decision.

Probably.

✦

Next morning, my dumb rabbit brain wakes me up at stupid o'clock in the morning. Oh-dark-thirty. The last time I was awake at this time, it was because I was *still* awake.

Why am I up at five thirty?

Shut up, brain, go back to sleep.

Nope.

I grunt in annoyance as I kick the blankets off and wriggle to a semi sitting position. Rub my eyes. Stare through my open bedroom door at the coffee maker which I can see from here, wondering if I'm really, actually awake and going to stagger my bleary ass over there and make coffee.

Fuck.

I am.

Counting scoops of coffee beans is hard. Filling the reservoir is hard.

God, I am *not* a morning person.

I nearly fall asleep standing up waiting for the machine to brew enough in the pot that I can pour myself a cup, and when I have a mug curling steam up into my face, I take it and collapse onto the couch.

Now, I can drink coffee and try to wake up and figure out why the blistering dawn hell I'm awake at five thirty in the fucking morning.

It comes to me, halfway through the mug.

Delia.

She runs at six.

If she's running, chances are she'll be wearing something I'll enjoy seeing her in.

Which means…

My idiot caveman hinter brain woke me up at five thirty in the thrice-damned morning just so I can go run with Delia…for the sole and express purpose of seeing her in booty shorts and a sports bra.

I must be cracked.

It's been nearly a month since I last got laid which is…three weeks longer than I've ever gone since freaking eleventh grade. So yeah, I'm wicked horny.

But getting laid isn't even in the offing, here. She won't even be topless or anything. I could see more skin if I went to the beach.

Shit, if I'd stuck around at the bar last night, I'd have enjoyed a couple rounds of little miss Violet and her various sexy bits, naked and all to myself.

But I didn't.

Delia walked in, and I promptly forgot all about Violet.

Why?

Because my dick and my brain are in disagreement. My dick wants a piece of Delia McKenna, and my brain knows I have a better chance of winning the lottery… twice in a row.

Apparently, the compromise I'm coming up with is waking up at the perforated colon of dawn to go running—which I loathe, by the way, even after I've been for the run—with Delia, just because at least that way I get to pretend I'm not spending the whole run ogling the jiggly-sway of her fine-ass…ass.

I am pathetic.

I finish my mug of coffee, change into running shorts, a T-shirt, and a ball cap, dig my running shoes out of my closet. Pour a to-go coffee and ignore the little voice in the back of my head which says I'm in no shape to be running five miles.

The macho man part of myself is all like *of COURSE I can keep up with Delia, how fast can she run, anyway?*

Which I immediately tag as horseshit, because I'm a slow runner at best and if she runs five miles every day, she's clearly going to be way faster than me. Or if not faster, I'm going to sweating like a pig and huffing and puffing, whereas when she woke me up in my truck last week, she'd been breathing hard and shiny with sweat, but clearly was not actually winded.

This is a bad idea.

Yet, within a couple minutes, I'm stopped outside her driveway—meaning, at the entrance where the main driveway splits off and leads to her house.

I'm idling, trying to decide if I have the guts to get out and knock on her door and ask if I can go running with her.

I'm a coward, clearly.

Afraid of Delia McKenna shooting me down.

Cursing myself in a dozen different ways, I pull into

the entrance of her driveway but don't pull all the way to her house. Instead, I shut off my engine and stand leaning against the hood, listening to the engine tick and pop, waiting.

I hear her footsteps in the gravel before I see her. She doesn't see me—she's scrolling on her phone, looking for music to listen to most likely. I wait, but she doesn't look up. Even when she's going directly past me, she doesn't see me. Not me, not my giant truck. Lost in zombie land, I guess.

I happen to glance at her phone as she passes me—she's answering email.

"Delia."

No answer.

So I follow after her to the end of the main driveway where she finally wedges her phone into a special pocket built into the waistband of her shorts at the small of her back. Today's selection of running gear is a pair of bright neon 90s purple shorts with a white sports bra, the straps of which at her back are a complicated web.

Her hair is in twin braids.

She jumps up and down a few times, then does some high knees.

That's when I sidle up beside her, nonchalant.

She screams and jumps a literal foot into the air. "What the actual fuck, Thai?" she demands, breathing hard with her hand clapped over her chest. "What are you doing here?"

"Sorry, didn't mean to scare you." I point back at

the opening of her driveway. "You did walk directly past me and my truck."

She blinks. "I did not."

I laugh. "You did. Where do you think I came from? I didn't walk here from my condo."

"Condo?"

"Uh yeah. You don't think I'm living with my parents, do you?"

"I guess I didn't think about it, honestly. I suppose I assumed you were, but now that I think about it, I know there's no way you would."

"Not a chance in hell. I've seen them exactly twice since I've been back, once when I first got into town, and I met them for brunch last week. They spend most of their time at their place in Majorca."

"Where?"

"Majorca. Spanish-owned island in the Mediterranean. They own a place there. I have a feeling at some point they're going to sell that place—" I gesture in the direction of the fifteen thousand square foot monstrosity I grew up in, "—and live in Majorca full time."

She eyes me. "You're not a morning person, self-admittedly."

"Nope!" I agree with fake cheerfulness. "And I'm also not a big fan of running."

She laughs. "So...why are you here, at six a.m., dressed to run?"

"I have *no* idea!" I say, still faking the bright and chipper voice.

She laughs harder. "Glutton for punishment, maybe?"

"That, or I just really, really love your ass in those shorts." And…that just came out of my mouth.

Her head swivels slowly to pin me with a glare. "Funny."

I shrug. "Who's joking?"

Her cheeks color, but she gives no other indication of what she's thinking or feeling. Finally, she huffs. "Keep up, if you can."

She accompanies this by bursting forward into a fast run—even when I was running several times a week with the guys at Wharton, I was never able to keep the pace she's setting.

Can I bench double my body weight? Yeah. Pull-ups with fifty pounds chained to my waist? Four reps. Three plate back squat? Five by five.

But put me outside for a run? I'm doing great if I break a nine-minute mile, and according to my watch, as I push myself to catch up, says she's rocking an 8:22 mile and is probably only going to speed up as she hits her groove.

So the whole plan where I fake running slower than her just to have a legit excuse for staring at her ass? Turns out I don't have to pretend.

The view is glorious, though. Worth the early hour, and maybe even worth having to fucking run.

"You're staring at my ass." This comes a mile in.

I'm sweating already, and my lungs are asking me what the hell I'm thinking.

"Yes," I gasp. "Why do you think I'm even doing this?"

"Well then…if you want to stare at the ass, you have to keep up with the ass," she says, and puts on speed.

"Challenge…accepted."

It's the hardest, most punishing, most brutal forty-plus minutes of my life. By the time we're a quarter mile from her driveway, my breathing is ragged, my legs are jelly, and sweat burns in my eyes. And even she's breathing hard, but as we near the driveway she only speeds up. And speeds up. And speeds up. Until a good hundred yards from the mailbox, she's at a full sprint.

I swing my arms as hard as I can and do my best to match her sprint, and it feels like my legs are pumping on their own, without my input, and they feel like lead tubes.

I slap the mailbox as I stumble to a stop, and hunch over, hands braced on my knees.

"Up," Delia pants, pacing in front of me, hands laced on top of her head. "More oxygen in your lungs. Hunching over makes your lungs compress."

I mimic her stance, upright, pacing, hands on my head. "You do this every day?"

She nods. "Yup."

"You were showing off a little, today, though, right? Just to show me up?"

She smirks at me. "A little." She checks her watch.

"Today was just under a minute faster, which in running terms is actually quite a big improvement. So I guess I should thank you for motivating me to my best time yet."

"You're welcome."

She's coated in a sheen of sweat, her skin glistening. Sweat darkens the center of her sports bra, between her breasts. Beads of sweat trickle down her cheeks and throat…and down between her breasts. Her stomach, flat and taut, goes concave as she sucks in slow, measured breaths. Her thick, strong thighs tighten with each step.

Her eyes narrow. "You're staring."

"You're sexy. Hard not to stare."

She blinks. "Who the fuck even *are* you, right now, what have you done with Matthais Bristow?"

I struggle to slow my breathing. "Still me, I just have a better relationship with the truth than I used to."

She shakes her head. "The truth. The truth that all of a sudden you think I'm sexy?" She faces me, hands braced on her hips, now. "What you're saying is that I'm sexy, *now*—now that I don't have belly rolls and an extra fifty pounds on my ass? That truth?"

Any answer I give to that feels wrong, so fuck it. As long I'm blurting out uncomfortable truths…

"Yes, Delia, that truth. I'm comfortable enough my own fault to admit that I think you're sexier now than you ever have been." I pace closer, until mere inches separate us. "You want more truth? How 'bout this one: a good part of the reason I was such an unmitigated fucking bastard to you was that I *liked* you—I was attracted to you, and I hated myself for it."

And goddammit but that *is* the truth, which I've been desperately trying to avoid.

She nods. "Ah yes, the old truism parents like to feed little girls—if a boy is mean to you, he must like you. I reject that—if a boy is mean to you, maybe…he's just a mean little shit."

"In my case, it's true both ways. Doesn't excuse it, but it's true. I was mean to you because I liked you, and because I was just mean. Not just to you. Ask Tim Harrington how he feels about me. I was even worse to him—he was a boy, so I could physically pick on him. And I did. Brutally." I shake my head, turn away, sick to my stomach. "I can't flinch from the past, Delia. I'm not going to stand here and act like I wasn't a piece of shit human being. I was. And nothing I can do or say will ever change or make up for that."

"Why did you hate yourself for liking me?" she asks.

I shrug, hands out, palms up. "Fuck if I can even say, now. Status? I was the king of the school and you were…"

"I was Dorky Delia. Donuts Delia," she fills in.

"Yeah. It wouldn't have been *cool* for me to be with you."

"So it wasn't because I was fat."

"You weren't ever fat."

"I was." She shakes her head, eyes distant with old pain. "You made sure I knew it."

"I was wrong."

"Doesn't change that I was fat." She meets my eyes, then. "Why do you think I started running? Because of you. Because I didn't want to be Donuts Delia or Dino Delia anymore. I was already dieting all the time. I tried everything, every fad, every trend, every diet. I read every article in every magazine if it promised six ways to beat belly fat or whatever. Nothing ever worked."

"Clearly, something did," I say, gesturing at her. "Look at you now."

"Yeah, look at me now." She smacks her left ass cheek. "Still pear-shaped."

"Delia, you're not—"

"You know what worked? Not eating and running. No carbs. No treats. I only eat between noon and seven. There are no skip days, no cheat days. I run five miles, hard, every day but Sunday. And I've done it for six years." She holds her arms out. "This is the result."

"Pretty spectacular result, if you ask me."

"I didn't." Her cerulean eyes are hard, icy. "Just like with the run time today, I have you to thank for the motivation to finally and truly lose the weight and keep it off. Every run, every mile, every day—hating you was my fuel. Your voice in my head, mocking me, calling me names. Asking Dell and your other asshole buddies if you were the only one seeing hippos every time I walked past. You, bringing cupcakes to class for no reason other than to mess with my head. I don't even *like* cupcakes, Thai. Did you know that? I never have. I always preferred cookies and ice cream. Not that I've had either in years.

One bite of a cookie and my ass balloons immediately. If I so much as look at ice cream, even the so-called healthy keto ice cream, I gain five pounds. But the point is…" She trails off, head shaking. "I don't even know. I just know I ran to escape you. I fasted to get away from your voice in my head. It never worked. And just when I was starting to make progress, starting to feel okay in my own skin, finally able to get through a day without hearing your cruel, mocking voice in my head, finally able to look at myself in the mirror and go, hey, I look alright—that's when you blow back into my life like a fucking tornado. You've set me back years of progress, Thai. *Years*. Because now I have to figure out how to be okay and be confident and like myself *with you in my life* on a daily basis."

A long, tight, sharp silence.

But she's not done. "And then—and *then*, Thai Bristow, you have the big brass balls to crash my run, and tell me you like my ass, and that you think I'm sexy. What the *fuck* am I supposed to do with that? Huh? Answer me that, if you can."

I have nothing. "Delia, I…"

She nods. "Right. Exactly. Nothing." She pushes past me. "Why don't we keep this to work only, okay? Don't show up. Don't run with me. Don't give me the cute little chitchat in the office when it's just us late at night. Just…leave me alone."

She doesn't wait for an answer, just walks away and doesn't look back.

Chapter
TWELVE

Delia

A PPARENTLY, I'D BEEN LYING ALL THOSE YEARS I'D SPENT telling myself that Thai Bristow had no more power over me. That I was stronger because of his torment. That if I could survive him, I could survive anything.

Right now, I feel weak.

I kept my back stiff and my head up as I walked away from him. But as soon as I'd closed my front door, I collapsed to the ground, back to the door, and sobbed.

You know what did feel good, though? Thai couldn't keep up with me. I ran his ass into the *ground*. Eat my dirt, Bristow.

Small comfort, but I'll take what I can get.

I let myself cry for a few minutes, and then I force myself out of it. Like usual, I have to talk myself out of it out loud.

"Suck it up, Delia," I growl. "Stand up and dry your eyes."

I do it, working to my feet, scrubbing my eyes with the heels of my palms.

"Now take off your clothes and get in the shower. And *do not* think about Thai Bristow."

I begin the struggle of peeling off my tight, sweaty clothes, and when I'm finally naked, I twist the shower on and start taking my hair out of the braids and dragging a brush through them.

The bathroom is wreathed in steam. I grab a bottle of water from my fridge and suck half of it down at once, and I'm about to get into the shower when something unexpected and unwelcome happens:

Someone knocks on my door.

"I swear, if that's you, Dell, I'm going to hit you," I murmur to myself. Leaving the water running, I wrap a towel around myself and head for the door, grumbling obscenities under my breath.

I yank open the door, fully expecting it to be Dell, slinking back for a handout. "Dell, goddammit—"

It's not Dell, and my words die in my throat.

It's Thai.

He's taken his shirt off, and he's more incredible than even my fantasy could have imagined. He's ripped. Powerfully built, with razor-sharp abs and massive, anvil-hard pecs. Not an ounce of fat on him. He's still glistening with sweat.

A bead trickles down over his pec. I'm seized with an absurd but powerful urge to lick the sweat off him.

"What—" I have to swallow hard and try again.

"What do you want." It doesn't come out as a question, but rather flat, robotic, without infection.

He just blinks. His eyes rake over me, head to toe. I didn't bother actually tying the towel around me—I'm just pinning it mostly in place with my armpits, since I had assumed it was Dell.

His throat bobs.

He can't bring his eyes up to mine.

"Thai," I snap. "I thought I made myself clear—leave me alone."

"You did," he says, his voice low, and unsteady. "I didn't listen."

"Obviously. Following instructions seems to be hard for you." I start to close the door. "Goodbye, Thai."

His foot blocks the door from closing. My mouth opens to protest, but then somehow he's in my space. Looming over me, massive and hard and radiating heat and smelling of sweat, but not unpleasantly. I don't know what's happening, and I suddenly can't figure out what to do about it. How to stop him. My voice is lodged in my throat. My blood hammers in my ears.

His hands close around my face, fingers behind my jawline and under my ears, thumbs brushing over my lips and then across my cheekbones.

And then he's kissing me.

It's not one of those sudden assaults on my mouth that you read about. It's slow and intentional. He gave me plenty of opportunity to pull away, or smack him, or knee him in the sack. Slow and intentional…and deep, and powerful, and skillful.

This man knows how to kiss.

He's mastered the art.

His tongue is a symphony against mine, and his lips are an aria on my lips. His kiss works me to a fever, steals my breath and leaves me dizzy.

His body is huge and hard against mine. I feel him, all of him. Chest like a cliff face, abs like an iron washboard, thighs like tree trunks…and the thick ridge between us, at my belly. Lined up flush with my own sex, as if we'd been made to fit. He would barely have to dip at the knees to enter me.

He doesn't stop. Doesn't need to breathe. Slow, and thorough.

I can't help but respond—his desire is obvious even without the evidence pressed against me. It's obvious in the way he kisses me. In the way his hands roughly cradle my face. In the way he towers over me, hunched to reach down to my mouth with his. It's in the growl I feel in his throat and chest as he kisses me and kisses me.

My arms reach up, curl around his neck. My hands slide into his hair, and I'm heedless, in the moment, of the fact that my towel drops away. All that matters in this wild instant is his mouth on mine and his body against my body.

My hands scrape against his shoulders, and then my fingers dig into the meat of his chest. Need is a fury within me. To touch, to be touched. His hands are huge, strong, and rough. They're like sandpaper on my skin as he rakes his palms over my shoulder blades and down my spine, and he's got them wrapped around the small of my back, pulling me closer.

I whimper into his mouth.

What sorcery is this? His kiss is a drug—a phrase I've heard but never understood. Yet now it's real—he kisses me and I am high with it, soaring on the wings of chemical, hormonal, physical bliss. I have never never *never* been kissed like this, didn't know it was possible.

He pivots, and I hear my door crash closed with a loud slam and then I feel the wood against my back and his hands clutch my hips, fingers digging into my flesh, gripping hard.

I feel need soaking me.

I'm naked, and I don't even care.

Glad of it, if anything.

His mouth tears away from mine, and I gasp at the abrupt loss of his mouth on mine, whimper to express somehow that I want his kiss back.

I get it—I get his kiss back.

Not on my mouth.

He kisses my throat. The hollow at the base of my throat.

The no-man's-land between my throat and the apex of my cleavage. My hands tangle in his hair and my eyes are closed and my head tilted up and all I can feel is his mouth on my skin, kissing me and licking and nipping.

His mouth on my skin tells me in a way no amount

of words ever could that he finds me beautiful. More than beautiful.

That he needs me.

It's not want, not desire—it's *need*.

His mouth travels lower. One hand cups my breast and lifts it reverently, kneads it and thumbs the nipple until I'm gasping with the sensation. And then his mouth covers my breast and he's suckling and licking and I'm delirious.

The other breast receives the same attention, and I'm gasping, moaning. Who am I? Who is he? What's happening? I know none of the answers in this moment and don't even care.

This feels *incredible*, and it's all I care about.

I don't dare even breathe as he drops to his knees. Stopping him never even enters my mind.

I am a creature of pure physical need, right now, and all I care about is what he's doing to me. I don't care who he is. I don't care what comes next. All I care about is *more*.

I never knew it was possible to feel this way from pure desire, from raw need, from nothing more than his mouth on my flesh.

My nipples are hard, my skin tight. My breathing is hoarse and ragged. My knees dip, but he's holding me up. One hand cups my ass, squeezes, caresses, holds. The other is on my tits, exploring one and the other and both. And his mouth is on my belly. Kissing my hipbone.

Who am I, allowing this to happen?

I don't care. I'll be whoever I need to be, if only he won't stop.

I want to feel good. More. More.

I hear myself saying it. "More." It's a raw, ragged whisper. *"More."*

His cheeks, unshaven for days, are rough on the tender silk of my inner thighs. When his lips touch my sex, I cry out loud, a wordless sound of incredulous, wondrous need.

He growls.

And then his tongue parts my folds and flicks against the aching flower of my clit, and I'm lost, lost, lost. He's doing this. To me.

My knees threaten to give out, but somehow I know he won't let me fall. I sag against the door and thrust myself against his mouth with a wanton, growling whimper of savage desire. Hold on to his head, fingers knotted in his hair. Rock against his tongue.

And holy hell, if I'd thought he was skilled at kissing my mouth, it's nothing compared to his artistry at kissing my sex. He has the mouth of a god. Teasing, driving, maddening. He brings me to the cusp within seconds but then slows and draws me away, and then higher and closer to the edge once more, only to pull me back yet again.

One hand is still reaching up to fondle my breasts, and the other now traces my folds as he pulls his mouth away for a moment, and then I feel his finger entering me. Just one, but it's thick and he knows my insides, knows where to touch me, and I cry out. With one finger inside me, he brings me to the edge a third time.

Pulls that finger out. Immediately, I feel myself clench around the loss of his touch—but he's there again with two fingers sliding through my wetness, and I whimper, rock against the fingers as they penetrate me and then his mouth fuses over my sex where I'm aching for him and throbbing for more. His tongue swirls and flicks and his fingers drive in and out with a hooking motion, and each time his fingers find my depths, I'm wrenched closer and closer to the edge of release, and now I am fraught with need—not just need now, not a nebulous but potent feeling of mere desire. No, this is more. This is a need on an atomic level for release.

"Please," I rasp, whispering hoarsely. "*Please.*"

His answer is a growl against my sex.

His answer is to push me over the edge and push me past it into wild delirium with mouth and with tongue and with fingers, tweaking my nipples and cradling my breast and tonguing my clit with furious circles and driving his fingers inside me with nearly violent speed, but it's what I need, what I want.

"Oh…oh…oh *fuck*," I cry. "Yes…god, yes. *Yes!*"

My scream is frantic and wild.

I shake, and I explode, and everything inside me clenches, detonates, implodes, all at once. Heat and pressure and release and insanity, it's all a whirlwind inside me, and I'm trembling and crying with broken sobs of release, because I have never even conceived of such a climax. My orgasm wrenches through me viciously, beautifully, wringing me into trembling paroxysms.

I cling to him, gasping.

He stands up, and I'm disoriented, shaky.

For the first time since his lips met mine, I look him in the eyes. And I see…

Pure, potent, undeniable masculine need. His eyes rake over my naked form and in his expression I read appreciation for my body—it's written on his face in bold, all caps.

"Fuck…" he snarls. "Delia, you are *so* goddamn… *beautiful.*" Like he can't believe it. Like he can't believe he's saying it. Like he can't believe what just happened any more than I can.

His voice, his words ruin the spell.

Thai Bristow just barged into my house and kissed me.

Thai Bristow just *went down on me.*

And it was beyond incredible.

I *LET* him.

I *begged* him for more.

My eyes fill with confused tears.

Panic sears through me like a bolt of lightning.

What did I just do? What did I just allow Thai to do to me?

"Thai…" I whisper, my voice barely audible. "You have to go."

His eyebrows lower in in confusion. "Delia, I—"

"Go. You have to go. I can't—that wasn't…" I shake

my head, yanking away from him, snatching my towel and covering myself with it. "Please. Just go."

His expression clears, as if he came to some realization. "Ah. Got it."

"That…that shouldn't have happened. I shouldn't have allowed it."

Savagely, angrily, he yanks open my door. He doesn't look back. He's gone, door slamming closed behind him.

What have I done?

Chapter
THIRTEEN

Matthais

I DON'T EVEN KNOW WHO I AM, ANYMORE.

I drive home, but my mind is not on the road. Fortunately, I know this town and all its roads like the back of my hand, even now.

Everything hurts.

My legs ache. My lungs feel singed, scorched.

My head throbs, my mouth is dry, my throat parched.

My cock is a raging monster, so hard you could drive nails with it.

Worst of all, my pride—my heart.

I had hoped she would look at me differently.

I was hoping she'd see—she'd *feel*—the genuine truth and desire in my kiss.

Instead, she looked horrified at what she'd done, and asked me to leave.

So, I left.

She let me in. She let me kiss her. I fucking...I know for a fact I left zero room for doubt as to what I intended before I planted it on her, before I ever touched her. And...once we were kissing, I *know* she liked it. She was legit whimpering, moaning. Hands in my hair, eyes closed. She was the one who let her towel drop—I didn't snatch it off.

She was into it.

She wanted what I was giving her, and damn right she got the best O of her life. I have no doubts on that score.

I'm not upset about anything so dumb and pedestrian as not getting off myself. Yeah, it sucks. Yeah, my balls ache and my hard-on refuses to quit.

It's about the way she acted afterward. Like she'd just been caught slumming it with some trash bag.

Sure, I've earned her enmity, but that shit still stings.

It occurs to me, as I pull into my condo parking lot and jam the shifter into park, that she had been out on a date with Tyler James Thomas, he of the pleated slacks and three names and loafers.

Did she fuck him last night?

God, I don't want to know.

Except, shit, I kind of do. Because I just had my mouth on her.

Even that can't put a damper on my erection. I have a messenger bag on my passenger seat; it's after 8 a.m. and I'm likely to encounter someone either in the hall or elevator, and I can't exactly hide the monster in my shorts, not in its current state.

Sure enough, as I exit the elevator on my floor, there's a young woman with two small kids waiting to get on. I sling my bag in front and paw through it as if looking for something as I pass them, hoping I'd gotten the bag around in front in time.

Another thought occurs to me, a few steps from the elevator—I probably smell like...Delia, let's say.

And that poor girl I passed probably got a whiff.

Not my problem.

Get home.

Lock the door behind me.

Throw the bag and my phone onto the couch, kick off my shoes, strip naked on the way to the shower. I ache, throb.

The water gets hot fast, and I step in. Put my back to the spray and brace one hand on the opposite wall. This time, I feel no compunction about bringing up a mental image of Delia as I grip myself. Fuck, though—she has no right being that damned sexy.

Her tits are even better than I imagined they'd be. Perfect teardrops—plump and round at the bottom, big pink nipples dead center. Squishy but firm. Natural. God...those tits.

All of her was...just perfect. Everything I never knew I wanted in a woman's body. Ass for days, to explore and play with. Her sex was trimmed but not shaved, tight, wet, responsive. She clenched around my fingers like a vise.

The way she moaned.

Please.

She'd rocked against my mouth, begging for more. Her scream as she came had been the sweetest music my ears have ever heard.

I kept an image of her in my mind as I stroked myself, not fast this time, not roughly jerking myself and just getting it over because I was embarrassed to be thinking about *her*. No, I think now I've earned this. And there's no embarrassment, because Delia McKenna is fucking *gorgeous*.

I wish it was her hands around me, right now.

Her mouth.

Her sweet slick wet folds sliding against me.

Taking me.

I empty myself with a gritted-teeth snarl.

But yet, mere minutes later as I wash off, I'm still thinking about her. And within seconds of thinking about her, I'm harder than ever.

It's going to be a long, *long* day.

I manage strained cordiality with her, throughout the day. When I get a call from the Karsten build that they need me on-site to approve some changes, I'm relieved. Just to be away from her.

She won't look at me in the eyes. And honestly, I get it.

After the things she'd admitted to me after the run, I get it. I earned her hatred, a thousand times over. But...the more time goes by and the more time I spend around her, the more I realize I'm really not that guy anymore. Working every day puts a new spin on things. Accomplishments feel good. Making decisions, getting shit done, making a difference...it all feels good, in a different way than making a monetary investment and seeing it pay off.

The following week, Marcus comes into the office for a presentation of...wait, they changed their name. Tree-Free Construction Supply, with an updated logo, a pine tree in a circle with a line through it, Ghostbusters' style.

I clap Marcus on the back as he enters the conference room. "Tree-Free." I shake his hand. "Simple, easy. I like it."

He grins. "Only took four focus groups, three surveys, and a week of solid debate to settle on it and the new logo, but we're happy with the final product."

"Worth it. It works." I take my seat at the far end of the table. "So, I'm not gonna try to jump your pitch here, but are you scaled up for full framing yet?"

He sets about organizing his notes and pulling up his PowerPoint. "Yeah, we are. That's the short version. The longer answer is my presentation." He glances at me. "Do I have you to thank for this opportunity? McKenna was always one of our big fish, the account we dreamed of one day landing. This is…way sooner than we could have imagined."

"Yeah, you guys just came up in conversation one day, and it turns out my partner and I share some ideas."

Delia breezes in, and I keep my expression neutral. Inside, I'm dying.

She's wearing a skin-tight black leather skirt, strappy calf-height wedge-heel black sandals, an emerald blouse that seems to accentuate her cleavage without showing any actual skin at all. Her hair is loose, brushed to a glossy shine, wavy, dangling to mid-back.

Teasing me, dressed like that. That's what she's doing.

Not really—it's no different than how she always dresses, and it's perfectly standard business attire for a successful CEO.

The problem is I'm just horny for her, and now everything she wears drives me crazy.

And I can't show a whit of it.

Marcus is frozen, staring at her. "Who the hell is that?" he hisses to me.

I grin, amused. "That, my friend, is Delia McKenna. CEO of McKenna Construction, and my partner."

"You're a full partner? Not just an investor?"

"Fifty percent owner, and co-executive with Delia. Although, she's the real expert. I'm still new to the business, while she's been running this show since she was a kid, and I mean that literally."

Her intensely blue eyes fix on me for a second, and

I knew she heard me. Then to Marcus. "Good morning, Marcus. I'm Delia."

He rounds the table and shakes her hand, a little too eagerly. "Yeah, hi, I'm Marcus, with Tree-Free Construction Supply. I just want to express how grateful I am for the opportunity to even be here. Of course, I hope you like our product, but just being able to make this pitch is a huge win, in my book."

Everyone else is floating in, and Delia looks distinctly uncomfortable—he's still shaking her hand, and she's clearly trying to politely pull her hand back, but he's oblivious. Nerves and excitement have clearly gotten the better of him.

To the rescue.

I leave my chair and grab him around the shoulders with chummy familiarity, giving him a rough, playful shake. "Down boy," I say with a laugh. "It's all good. Now, I think we're all here, so you can get started whenever you're ready."

Delia gives me a wide-eyed look of amused amazement, and then a wincing grimace. I just wink at her, and then while I'm up pour myself a cup of coffee…and one for Delia. Black, with a touch of creamer, how I've noticed she likes it.

Back in my seat, I ignore the way Delia is staring into her coffee as if trying to understand how it got there. As if me doing something nice for her is some kind of apocalyptic miracle.

Marcus has his laptop connected, has his presentation

cued up, papers and notes shuffled and straightened. "All right. Here we go."

Once he's started and talking about his product and vision, he's smooth and professional. He starts small, goes over their line of minor products, detailing their specs and how many different places have orders for them and sharing rave reviews, and then he pauses to dig a clear plastic divided organizer from his bag, in which is a sampling of the smaller pieces, so everyone at the table can get a feel for the actual product.

"And now, for the product I'm sure you're all eager to hear about—our framing sections." He changes the slide, and it's a video. "Rather than tell you about them, we put together this short video to *show* you what we can do."

It's a slickly produced piece of marketing, showing the production of the framing sections from start to finish, and then there's a time-lapse of a house being built, using Tree-Free products exclusively.

When the video ends, he holds out his hands in a *ta-da* gesture. "As you can see, you can use our framing sections in conjunction with traditional lumber and all that. But obviously, our goal is to provide a whole line of products, from framing and roofing trusses and shingles to subflooring, flooring, wiring, plumbing, lighting… everything. If you use it to put up a building, we have plans for it. Including basic two-by lumber, which will cut more easily and with less mess than wood, for a fraction of the price and a fraction of a fraction of the total impact on our planet."

I look around, and I can tell everyone is at least intrigued, and some are visibly impressed.

Delia is harder to read. "These are built to match the standard pre-built framing sections you can buy from anywhere else?"

Marcus nods. "Absolutely. Exactly the same dimensions in every way. They're interchangeable."

"And you claim that they're stronger?"

"I'm not just claiming—it's proven fact. Wait—here, I brought documentation…" He rummages in his folder and comes up with a stapled stack of papers, which he sends around the table to Delia, who flips through it. "Stress tests show our product is demonstrably superior, and not just a little bit, but a lot. You can see the numbers for yourself, there."

She nods. "I see. And cost?"

Marcus goes into an in-depth discussion of cost breakdown, but I can see on Delia's face that she's sold before he gets halfway through. It's a duh, though. Superior product for less. Easy win.

"And what about your capacity for order fulfillment? Can you provide uninterrupted, reliable delivery, on time, every time? This is a brand-new thing you're doing, and even putting in a test-size order is a risk for us."

"Great question, absolutely." Marcus whips out a calculator and does some fast math. "The honest, no-BS answer is that we are not quite ready to be your comprehensive, sole supplier just yet. We simply don't have the infrastructure in place—*yet*. We're still a young company, still building it all out. But here's what I'm offering. Order, say, a thousand units. I can fulfill that in a matter of two weeks, and that's a guarantee. I'll give you a thousand units for ten percent off what we would normally charge per section. Try them out. See what you think. I'm confident you'll order more. And once we have cash flow, we'll start going gangbusters building out our process. I know the numbers you guys are doing, in terms of framing section orders…if you take this chance on us, give us six months, and we can be your sole supplier."

Delia looks at me, a long, steady, thoughtful glance. Questioning. Is she asking what I think before making her own decision?

I shift in my chair. "Okay, full disclosure here—I own a stake in Tree-Free. But I bought in because I believe in what these guys are doing. And I think it's on the cutting edge of what will eventually be the standard." I tap the table. "Responsible tree harvesting is a joke, and you all know it. Sustainable, green, all that? Lip service, and I bet you all know it even more than I do. Trees take years to grow and require acres and acres…yet we can't seem to stop clear-cutting forests left and right even to save our own air." I point at Marcus. "This? It's the answer. What he hasn't emphasized is that the materials they use to create their products is all recycled. That's part of the infrastructure he's talking about—they collect plastics from all over the place, stuff that doesn't normally get recycled, and they break it down and do some sort of science-y shit to it, to make this polymer. So not only are they *not* using trees, but they're taking plastic *out* of the system and actually recycling it. Now, I'm not, like, some tree-hugging save the whales freakazoid, right? But I do like being alive, and I think at this point, it's kind of obvious to anyone with half a brain that the shit we're doing to this planet is killing it, and thus…ourselves. And I feel like this is one small thing our company can do that will make an actual difference."

Delia eyes me speculatively. Looks around the table, sees the nods. "Okay, I'll bite. One thousand units." She spins her pen around her middle finger. "But Marcus, I have to be clear, here—I have no patience for supply breakdowns. Fail to fill our orders, or cause us delays, and I'll cut the contract so fast you won't know what hit you."

"Understood." He nods, the eager beaver that he is. "Absolutely understandable. That's why I want to start small, just a thousand units. I can do more, a lot more, but I want to start small and earn your trust."

Delia slaps the table. "Smart man. Okay, well, if you're all in agreement, I'll leave you with Boyd to work out the details. I have another meeting to get to, so I'll bid everyone goodbye for now." She pauses at the door. Glances back at me. "Thai…you coming?"

I wasn't aware of any meeting, but I'll play along. "Sure thing. See ya, Marcus." I clap him on the shoulder. "Nice pitch. Now just follow through, buddy."

He grins at me. "I'm on it—I'm all over it."

I grab my things and refill my coffee on the way out, put a lid on it, and find Delia waiting at the elevator. "Did I miss a meeting memo?"

She has a folder open, hands it to me. "No, but you are, as you told Marcus, co-executive and my partner. So I have to start including you in big decisions. Like this one."

It's a proposal for a development deal. Sixty prime acres just off a major highway, not far from a booming little town. Sixty acres divided into two-acre lots, with an HOA banquet center, a park, gated...and the front elevation proposals are not your average mid-threes spec home. These are upscale, all brick, four thousand square foot minimums.

"This is a major proposal," I say, flipping through it. "This is big time."

"And there's room to play," she says. "They already love that proposal. If we can save costs with Tree-Free products? Even better. More off the top for us, and it looks better for the developer, and keeps prices down for the owners. Win all around."

I close the folder as the elevator opens. Step on, but I'm thinking. "And you know, I just talked to my guys at Albion. They've got their VP himself coming out to pitch us next week." I eye her. "We could work that in. High-value lux places like this? I think it could be the perfect place to try and incorporate a whole-home connectivity system, as an experiment."

She muses as the elevator descends. "I'm not sure. I

agree in theory, but this has the potential to be the most lucrative deal McKenna has ever done. One gamble is scary enough—and 3D printed framing is a big gamble. *Two* new, experimental elements? I think that's tempting fate."

"I see what you're saying." We reach the parking garage, and we're faced with the question of my car, hers, or separate? "How about we wait and see how the Albion pitch goes next week and think about it more from there."

She nods. "Fine. But don't expect me to change my mind. I'm willing to take *some* gambles on innovation. But I still have to keep us solvent and making smart decisions. I have to stay at least somewhat conservative."

I head for my truck, and she follows, rounding to the passenger side without a qualm. Guess we're taking my truck. She buckles in, and I will myself to not get lost in the strapboob beauty. Stay focused. This is business. And she clearly regrets—

No, no, no. Shut it down. Business.

"How about I be the innovator, the one looking into new stuff, and you be the smart and conservative one who shoots down my ideas when they go too far?"

"So…all of them?" she says with a smirk.

Is she…teasing me? I'll take it.

I pull out of the parking garage, connecting my phone to the infotainment screen. "So. Where are we going?"

She takes my phone from me, pulls up a navigation

app, and inputs a destination. "About an hour drive, one way."

Shit.

An hour alone with her in the car? I'm scared and excited at the same time. Do I dare bring up what happened? I have a thousand questions, but breaching any of them feels like grabbing the tiger by the tail.

Ten minutes of excruciatingly awkward, tense silence later gives me the distinct impression that she's wrestling with the same things I am.

I glance at her—her expression is pensive, tight. She's staring out her window, chewing on her lower lip. Hands folded in her lap, one thumbnail picking at the cuticle of the other.

I look away just in time to catch her glancing sidelong at me. Assessing me the way I was assessing her.

She doesn't know how to address this any more than I do. Kind of a relief, honestly.

Finally, tired of dancing around it in my own head, I grab the bull by the horns—and wonder what other animal-based metaphors I'm going to use in my own thoughts.

"Delia…" except I have no clue what to say.

"I don't want to talk about it, Thai."

"Yeah, see, I think that's a load of bullshit. You do, but you're scared to." I twist the steering wheel with my fist, as if I could strangle answers out of it. "How about we just…acknowledge that it happened, first."

She shakes her head. "I can't talk about this, Thai," she whispers.

"Can't, won't, or don't want to?"

"All of the above."

"Why?"

She fits her thumbnail into her mouth and nibbles on it, then yanks her hand away and shakes it, sits on the hand. "I want to pretend nothing happened. It was just a dream."

"That won't work, and you know it." I look at her. "Look at me."

She turns her head away. "No."

"Look at me, dammit. You owe me that much."

Begrudgingly, as if it's an effort of will to do so, she turns her head to meet my eyes. "There. What."

I glance at the road, then back at her. "It...*happened*. It was real. It wasn't a dream. Good, bad, or wet."

She bites her lip to hold back an unwilling smirk. "You have a high opinion of yourself, it seems."

"Is it misplaced?" I ask. "In the department we're referring to, at least."

She blushes. "I'm not talking about what happened, Thai."

I huff, roll my eyes. "Why? Are you ashamed?"

She doesn't answer. Just blushes harder.

"Delia, come on. You're not some blushing teenage virgin bride, here. You're a grown woman. You've had sex. You can't pretend nothing happened and refuse to talk about it."

"Yes I can."

"We have to work together. We have to figure this out. Because I'm not going anywhere. I'm not going to sell off and vanish, Dee. I'm in this for the long haul. I enjoy the work. I enjoy the challenge. I like being back here in River Gulch. I like being around you, even though you're prickly and uptight and still have a tendency to lash out with savage burns."

"I'm prickly and uptight?" This gets her to look at me, and not in a good way. "Are you for real?"

"Yes, I'm for real. You, Delia McKenna, are the very textbook, dictionary definition of prickly and uptight."

"Am not."

"Then quit being defensive and quit avoiding me and this whole subject, and *talk* to me."

"Why?"

"Because it's what adults do when they have sex."

"We didn't have sex."

I breathe a laugh. "I guess it would depend on your definition of sex, but sure. We didn't *fuck*. But *something* happened between us."

"You seduced me."

I laugh. "Did not. But honestly, I'll take seduced. I was worried you were going to say I, like, assaulted you or some shit."

"I wouldn't. That's a serious accusation and it's not what happened. I don't hate you *that* much."

"Thank you for that." I drive a good thirty seconds

in silence. "If I didn't seduce you, and I didn't assault you, what *did* happen between us?"

"I don't know," she whispers, refusing to even look in my direction.

"Delia, for real. What was it?" I wait, but nothing is forthcoming. "How about we take a step back. Let's just admit the facts, then. The basics of what actually occurred in your house last week."

"No."

I cackle out loud. "No? Just no?"

"Just no."

"You won't even admit to what went on?"

"I'm not talking about it."

"Why, Delia? Then answer me *why*?"

"Because I don't talk about sex!" she snaps, whirling to face me. "It's embarrassing. I'm embarrassed. Not... of you. Of me." She drops to a whisper again. "Of myself. I'm embarrassed that I let it happen at all. With you especially."

"Why? Am I such a monster, Delia?" My voice is quiet, gentle. "I used to be, and I fully admit it. I'll even apologize, and take responsibility." I pause. "Look at me for this, Dee—this is a big deal for me."

She turns her head, and her eyes are damp. "Don't."

"Too bad, I am." I meet her eyes, and then sigh. "Hold on."

I pull over, off the highway and onto the shoulder. Put it in park, turn to face her more fully. "Delia...For the first eighteen years of our lives, I was an absolute monster to you. I made your life hell. I have no excuse for how I treated you. I acknowledge that nothing I can ever say or do will make up for it, will ever mitigate the effects my treatment of you had on your life. All I can do is say I'm sorry. You didn't deserve it. I wish I could take it back. I can't. I can't make it better. All I can do going forward is try to be better. Try to do better by you."

She blinks hard, turns away, runs her fingertips underneath her eyes. Tilts her head back. "Dammit, Thai. You can't make me cry before the biggest meeting of my career. I spent an hour on my makeup this morning, and you're going to make me ruin it in less than thirty seconds." A sigh. "Do you have any Kleenex?"

I laugh. "Yeah, I keep a box of Puffs in my purse." I open the center console, pull out napkins. "I always get extra napkins when I get drive-through."

She takes them and dabs carefully at her eyes. "Thank you."

"Just napkins."

She snorts. "Not for the napkins, dumbshit. For apologizing." Her eyes flick to mine. "It really does mean a lot."

"It was years overdue, honestly."

She lets out a sigh. "Drive. We can't be late for the meeting." I pull back onto the road. After a moment, I open my mouth, but she holds up her hand. "Thai, can we just...can we table this, for now? We'll talk, I promise we will. Just...just not now. I have to be on my A-game, and I won't be if I show up flustered from this whole stupid conversation."

"It's not stupid. It's real life. It matters."

"Why is this so important to you? Maybe I'm mistaken, but I sort of had you pegged for the hump-and-dump type. You just don't strike me as someone to insist on…this type of conversation."

I growl, a wordless rumble of annoyance. "Mostly, you'd be right. But this? Somehow, this just seems different. Because it's you? Because we have history? Because you're my best friend's sister? I don't know. But it does—it matters to me."

Her eyes go wide. "You haven't told him, have you?"

I laugh. "Hell no. And I won't. It's none of his business. And it's not like he's the protective brother type anyway."

She sighs, relieved. "No, he's not. But I also know he wouldn't be happy."

"Do you care?"

"Wow, you're really poking all my tender spots, aren't you?"

"Sorry, I just—"

"Complicated, is I how I feel." She frowns, thoughtful and pensive. "He's still my brother. My *twin*."

I don't know what to say to that. "We can talk on the way back."

She shakes her head. "I need some time, Thai."

"For what?"

"To figure myself out. To figure out…" She shrugs,

throwing her hands up. "Everything. This version of you that I just can't seem to hate anymore. The problem is, I also can't just flip a switch and let go of thirty years' worth of ingrained habit. I just don't know where that leaves me."

I nod, and now when we lapse into silence, it's not as painfully tense. There's still a boiling inferno of unspoken things, still a tension.

Sexual tension? I think so.

But emotional tension, as well. By her own admission, she's still trying to hate me—but she can't. And she let me kiss her, let me go down on her. Let me make her come harder than she's ever come, unless I'm totally off base. And I don't think I am.

Point being, I can see how that would be confusing for her, at best, if not a complete mental and emotional upheaval of everything she's ever held to be true.

We're mere minutes from our destination when she speaks into the silence. It's such a quiet whisper that I almost miss it:

"You're not a monster."

What do you say to that? It's not a resounding affirmation, by any means. But coming from Delia in reference to me, considering our history? It's a definite start.

To what? No idea. But it's a start.

Chapter
FOURTEEN

Delia

THE MEETING GOES BETTER THAN I COULD HAVE anticipated. As much as I hate to admit it, Thai and I play off each other perfectly. Where I'm staid and conservative and laser-focused on the numbers and timelines and overhead and profit margins, Thai is easygoing, naturally gregarious and friendly, able to create immediate connections with everyone he talks to. He gets the lead developer, Jacob Haimovitz, to talk about baseball and they share funny stories and Jacob is put at ease and in a good mood. Then, without any kind of obvious signal, Thai turns it over to me and the conversation transitions smoothly and easily to business. With nerves smoothed and moods lifted, we're able to come to an agreement that's beneficial for everyone. Jacob finds our idea of experimenting with Tree-Free's line of products exciting and fascinating and promises to come see when we start breaking ground in a few months.

I contain my excitement until we're in Thai's truck, and then I let myself have a rare moment of girly excitement, where I screech and flap my hands. I almost never behave that way, but this deal is too big to not be excited about.

Thai just watches with amusement. "Didn't take you for the squeal and flap your hands type, to be honest."

I glare at him, but there's no real heat in it. "Hey, it's my first major deal since taking over, and it also happens to be the biggest deal McKenna has ever landed."

"The current sub development isn't bigger than this?" he asks.

I bob my head side to side. "Not really. The houses are smaller and cheaper. So even though there are more total units being built, we're actually netting less overall. Also, we developed the sub in stages. It started as twenty acres and fifteen units, and as those sold, the developer added new phases. This deal we just inked today, it's huge. We nail this development, it'll take McKenna to the next level."

"Well, you killed it," he says.

I eye him. "Hey, you killed it too."

He shakes his head, rolls his eyes. "Nah. I just played the funny man to your straight man."

I frown. "Straight man?"

"Comedy duos? Laurel and Hardy, Abbot and Costello, Martin and Lewis? It's the classic pair. One is the straight guy, not funny, not silly. Just serious, all business. That'd be Dean Martin. The other is the funny man. Goofy, wacky—that's Jerry Lewis. It only works if you have both, though."

"Jerry Lewis was funny by himself."

"Sure, and so was Costello. But when you've got the straight man to play against, it gets funnier."

"So I lack a sense of humor, is what you're saying?"

He snorts, rolls his eyes again. "Yes, Delia, that's what I'm saying. Obvious conclusion."

I hold my straight face a moment longer, and then burst into laughter. "See? Humor." I push the on button for his stereo and scroll through XM stations until I find something fun and poppy. "My point is, you loosened them up, made it feel personal and friendly. Which is something I'm not all that great at."

He smirks at me. "So what you're saying is, we make a good team?"

I look away, faking perturbation. "I suppose I can't deny that today went well, and that you did in fact contribute, in some small way, at least."

"It's okay to acknowledge my greatness," he says, sounding arch and wry.

"Yeah, okay. All hail the great and mighty Thai Bristow."

He flips his hand in front of himself and bows over it. "I humbly accept that which is my due."

I can't help but laugh. "Yes, humbly indeed."

I keep expecting him to resume our conversation

from before, but he doesn't. He demonstrates a skill I in fact lack entirely: chitchat. He can keep us talking about not much at all, and does so effortlessly. We talk about music and movies and old school friends, he tells a hysterical story about a prank his fraternity played his senior year at Yale, which involved a six-hundred-pound sow, a bucket of glitter, and Saran Wrap.

I tell him about the time a subcontractor had mistaken me for an errand girl and someone he could hit on—I'd locked him in the porta-potty, and then taken over the big excavator, suspending him fifty feet in the air. I'd refused to let him down until he begged me, in actual tears.

"He was crying?" Thai says, laughing.

"Like a baby. Apparently he was afraid of heights *and* was claustrophobic. Now, I didn't know that at the time, and I actually felt a little guilty when I found out. But when I say he hit on me, I mean he slapped my ass and told me—*told* me—to meet him at his truck after work. Like, it was an order."

"But...how could he mistake you for an errand girl?"

I shrugged. "I was dressed down. Bill, the on-site foreman back during phase one of Oak Glen, was sick, and I was filling in...so I was in jeans, a McKenna shirt, and a hardhat."

"Oh." He shakes his head. "But...even if you were *just* an errand girl—" and here Thai uses air quotes around the emphasized word, "—I don't get where he figured it was okay to slap your ass and order to you sleep with him."

"Right? I did some digging after that and found out he was notorious for it. The company he worked for was a big one, with a sizable HR department, the head of whom I happen to be personal friends with. I explained to her what I'd experienced, but she was like, I can't just take you on your word. So I set up a sting."

"Uh-oh."

"Yeah, big uh-oh. Now, this HR department was big enough that this one worker would never have met her personally. So, she did what I did—dressed down in jeans and a T-shirt and showed up acting like she was the cleanup crew or something. And sure enough, good ol' Tony the ass-slapper cornered the head of his own HR department, gave her the ass slap and the see-me-at-my-truck order."

He cackled. "I'm guessing that didn't go well for him."

I shake my head. "Last I heard, he was changing oil for eight bucks an hour in BFE, Arkansas. She fired him and had him blacklisted at every reputable and not-so-reputable contractor in three states."

"Ohhh, shit. She wasn't playing, was she?"

"Nope. Ember doesn't play around." I snicker. "I haven't even told you the best part. When he cornered her, he didn't figure in that Ember carries a taser on her person and doesn't appreciate being cornered by big smelly men."

"She tased him?"

"So hard he shit himself."

"Guess he earned it, though."

"He definitely did."

"I just can't help but wonder if that tactic ever worked for him? Like, just from a purely objective stand-point, I cannot imagine that cornering a woman at the workplace, slapping her on the ass, and ordering her to meet you at your truck would ever work. Like ever. Maybe if he was the big boss, *maybe*." He glances at me. "I'm not condoning it, just wondering if it ever worked."

I laugh. "Somehow, I doubt it. The real question is how he got away with it as long he did. There were several complaints registered against him, but he tended to move from company to company, staying just ahead of the complaints."

"Being a piece of shit human always catches up to you, one way or another."

"Well, it did for him."

We're back at the office in what feels like no time, but Thai doesn't go into the parking garage. Instead, he idles near the entrance, looking like he's thinking hard about something.

"Thai? The garage is right there." I point, in case he missed it.

He looks at me. "We just landed a huge deal. You said it yourself—biggest of your career."

"Yeah." I eye him. "What are you getting at?"

"Let's play hooky. Go do something fun."

I roll my eyes. "Thai. We're the bosses. We can't take the rest of the day off. It's barely past noon."

"If you're the boss, I'd think that would buy you at least a little leeway, right?"

"Wrong. The opposite. I have to be there before and after everyone and I have to work harder than everyone. I don't play hooky."

He frowns. "Maybe playing hooky is the wrong way to put it." He holds up a finger, dials a number on his phone. It rings, and then Cal answers. "Cal, how's it going?"

"Is that a general question, or a specific one?"

"Specific. Is there anything that needs Delia's or my personal attention today?"

"No sir, there is not. Everything is copacetic, boss."

"Thanks, Cal. I think we're both going to take the day."

"Delia McKenna is going to...*take the day*." He snorts. "Hold on, sorry, just looking outside for flying pigs."

"Um, sorry," I say, stifling a laugh. "I maybe should have mentioned that you're on speaker, with her."

He coughs. "Oh. Uh, hiya, boss."

I can't help but laugh. "What he means is, he's trying to convince me to play hooky. So far, he's not winning."

Cal laughs. "Boss, I've worked for you for ten years. In that time, you have never even been late, much less taken even half a day off. Even when—uh..." he hums as he changes tracks. "Even when you had a damn good reason to take a day off, you didn't."

He means when Dad died. I took no time off. None. Not even five minutes. Because as much as work reminded me of Dad, it was also a way to mourn him, and to get away from missing him, because I could throw myself into work. I'm still coping that way, honestly.

Thinking of Dad still takes my breath away, makes my heart squeeze painfully.

I clear my throat. "It's just not my way, Cal."

"Wasn't his, either. But I think it'd be okay if you took half a day. Not my place to tell you what to do, certainly, but…you should. Be good for you. Things are good." He pauses. "Wait, didn't you have that meeting with Haimovitz today?"

"I did—we did. And we landed the account. It's a go. Oak Glen is in the finishing stages—as soon as the last few units are dug and poured and framed, we break ground on the new project."

"Hot damn, boss, that's great news." A shout is audible on his side of the line, muffled and distant. "I gotta go, but I think you should listen to Thai. Just my two cents. Call if you need anything."

"I'll think about it. Later, Cal."

He hangs up…and immediately dials again. This time Constance answers. "Connie, how ya doing, doll?"

Doll?

She huffs, amused and annoyed in equal proportion. "Hello, Thai. What do you need?"

"Actually, I was calling to ask you that exact question."

"What do I need? A month in the Bahamas and a foot massage."

"Professionally, I mean."

"Oh, well. It's quiet around here, actually. You and Delia are out of the office, the phones are quiet, and I'm trying to make some kind of sense of Nick's godawful paperwork for the Karsten account."

"Who taught that guy to file, anyway?"

"A muppet, possibly. He could sell water to a fish but getting him to document anything is like pulling teeth."

Thai laughs. "So there's no particular reason that Delia and I would have to come back to the office today?"

"No, I'd say not."

"That's a great answer, Connie. We'll still be reachable, but we're taking the day."

"You, as in you plural?"

He chuckles. "Yeah. See, I have a pet project. I'm trying to teach our fearless leader this new concept I've been working on—it's called *fun*." He glances at me, grinning. "Before you respond, you're on speaker, and she's in the car with me."

"I *know* how to have fun, Thai," I say, deadpan.

"Oh yeah? What's the last fun thing you did?" he asks.

Constance cuts in. "Ms. McKenna, take the day off. We can call you if something comes up. We can manage half a day without you—and that's a positive commentary on your success as our CEO."

"Thanks, Constance."

"Now if you'll excuse me, I have to go back to attempting to read Nick's chicken scratch handwriting."

"Good luck with that." I laugh.

"No kidding. I'd have an easier time with hieroglyphics."

The call ended, Thai tosses the phone onto the console and eyes me, grinning. "There you have it. We are officially off work."

I frown. "So…now what?"

He laughs. "Anything we want."

I blink, and then snort. "My mind is a blank."

"Exactly." He brightens, an idea clearly hitting him. "Do you still own that little helicopter?"

I roll my eyes. "Yes, we do. I haven't used it in a while, though. I was against the purchase to begin with. I thought it was frivolous and unnecessary."

"But fun!"

"It's scary. I don't like it."

He grins, gleeful and wild. "I've been wanting a ride in that thing since Dell first told me your dad bought it."

"I'm honestly surprised you don't have one of your own."

He laughs. "I almost did buy one, a couple years ago. But then I remembered my experience with the yacht, and passed on it. My life has been too transient for it to make any sense that I maintain a crew or a pilot or anything."

"Well, you're not transient anymore," I say. "If you like it that much, you might be able to get me to sell it to you. Friends and family discount, so I'd give it to you for half of what Dad paid."

"Make the call, then," he says. "Get it ready. We're going on an adventure."

I sigh. "Fine. Just don't get me killed or arrested."

He waves a hand. "Nah. Danger and trouble aren't my jam."

I laugh as I hunt through my contacts. "No?"

"I tried skydiving, and I hated it. Bungee jumping is a hard no. The most dangerous thing I actually enjoy is driving my McClaren at the track, and that's not all that dangerous, since I've taken lessons from professionals on how to safely drive at high speeds."

"But you *are* trouble."

"Sure. With a capital T. I just don't love getting arrested—it's only fun if you don't get caught."

I snicker. "So you *have* been arrested."

"Oh, for sure. Twice. Once for public intoxication and public nudity, and the other was a nuisance complaint that, um, spiraled."

I find the number I'm looking for and make the call. "It'll be ready in twenty minutes," I tell Thai. "Now, I need the story."

"Which one?" he asks, as he heads for the airfield.

"Both?"

A sigh. "Fine. So, the first one was my sophomore year at Yale. Me and a handful of guys from my fraternity went to Daytona Beach for spring break. It was…god, wild isn't even the right word. We were out of control. Drunk from the time we woke up to when we passed out. Chasing girls, acting like privileged white douchebags. But…it was a hell of a lot of fun, and it was all mostly harmless drunk shenanigans. The story in question begins at a beachside bar."

"Where else?"

"Obviously. So, we've been wasted since, like, ten in the morning. It's been a very full day of beach volleyball, doing shots off the bellies of nubile young women, and general ill-advised carousing. It's well past midnight. We should be in the hospital for alcohol poisoning, but yet there we are, eight young men who haven't worn a shirt or been sober in over a week, and, um…someone in our group, not going to name names, decided there should be a wet T-shirt contest."

"It was you," I guess.

He snorts. "It was me." He waves a hand. "I mean, you'd have to have been there. But it was a fantastic idea. There was this whole huge group of hot girls from another college sorority, all wearing bikinis and white T-shirts. Like, literally you could not ask for a better opportunity. And, they were just drunk enough to not just agree, but to think it was a freaking amazing idea. Basically, I'm the *man*. I get the whole thing going. The band is in on it, the manager is comping shots because the whole crazy hullaballoo is bringing the crowd. Shit is wild. But then. Ohhhh, but then. My buddy Spike decides it would be even better if we took the whole party down to the beach. By this point, the whole thing is out of control. The manager is like no, no, no you can't— but who listens to managers, right? It's a stampede, like a literal riot. People are grabbing bottles from the bar, someone shows up with a freaking keg, the band cranks their amps up to fuckin' eleven, and suddenly there's this impromptu bash on the beach, with naked women and booze everywhere."

"And there's only you to blame."

"I mean, sure. You could say that, since it was my idea. But shit, that kind of thing happens all the time in spring break towns. They let it slide, for the most part, as long as it's not too rowdy. Well…this shit got rowdy." He laughs, rubs the back of his neck. "So, there I am, feeling like the king of the beach. I'm literally wearing a crown—one of my buddies gave me a crown from Burger King. There's at least half a dozen topless girls around me, like my court of debauchery. I have a bottle of Patrón in my hand, and life couldn't get any better."

"Until the cops show up?"

"On their four-wheelers and beach pickups. As the king of the beach, I obviously get arrested first, which is clearly my duty to my people." He shakes his head. "Of course, my incarceration, and the charges, are conveniently dropped when the captain gets a call from a local congressman recommending that I be let go."

"Ah, the privileges of extreme wealth."

He shrugs. "Too true."

"So, the nuisance call?"

He sighs. "That one's…kind of embarrassing."

"Do tell."

"I'd just graduated from Yale. I was bored, between girlfriends, and I'd just spent weeks cramming for my finals. So I figured a little shindig was in order. Just me and a few friends, nothing too crazy."

"Famous last words—nothing too crazy."

"It wasn't my fault. Honestly, it wasn't. I invited a handful of friends to hang out and drink scotch. I'd envisioned it as this snobby, sophisticated *soirée*. Scotch and cigars and the highbrow conversation of *Yale graduates*." He laughs, a self-deprecating sound.

"Let me guess, your friends brought friends."

"Got it in one. In fact, the troublemakers were friends of friends of friends, or something. These brainless yahoos show up, slam my fifty-year Balvenie like it's fuckin' Jack Daniels and start breaking things."

"Barbarians."

"Right? Like, have you no manners, you uncouth Philistines? Clearly not. They're out of control. I try in vain to rein them in, but once the booze has taken control, there's no reining it in."

"Never. The genie doesn't go back in the bottle."

"So a neighbor calls in a nuisance complaint. I figure, I'll talk them down, kick the offending savages out of my place, everything will be fine."

"It's not fine?"

"I open the door with my winningest smile on my face. Ready to smarm and charm the pants off those poor, unsuspecting officers."

"They won't know what hit 'em, is the idea?"

He winks at me and clicks his tongue, shoots me a finger gun. "You know me too well, my dear."

"They won't be smarmed?"

He snorts. "So, it turns out that the responding officer is a woman."

"Oh boy."

"That's not the issue. The issue is that I, um, knew her."

"Meaning, you knew her biblically."

"Correct."

"So this is where it spirals? Was she a lover spurned? Someone who didn't appreciate being humped and dumped?"

He frowns. "I made it clear from the outset that it was a temporary thing. Purely physical. She agreed that's all she was looking for, herself. We were agreed, and the activities commenced. We met a few more times after that, and I guess she started to get the wrong idea. I went about trying to set the record straight as clearly but kindly as I could. Because contrary to what you may think, I'm not the type to kick a girl out as soon as I get what I want. I'm really, really not, I promise. I just wasn't looking for anything serious, and I made that clear. But apparently, to Officer Lucas, I didn't actually mean what

I said, and clearly secretly wanted her to make me fall in love with her."

I wince. "Oh dear. That never goes well."

"No, it doesn't." He sighs. "She got upset. Her feelings were hurt, I got ticked off, and words were exchanged." A shake of his head. "Not twenty-four hours later, she gets a call during an unscheduled midnight shift to answer a nuisance complaint."

"And there you are."

"There I am. A moment of shock, and then she starts arresting me for drunk and disorderly and some other trumped-up shit. The moment the doorbell rang, the troublemakers had run off out the back door, leaving me to deal with the consequences of their behavior. And my own, I suppose. I tried to talk her out of the arrest, but...she was pissed off."

"Did it stick?"

He shakes his head. "Nah. By the time I got to fingerprinting, she'd cooled off and let me go. It was just the shock of seeing me, I guess." He eyes me. "What about you? Ever been arrested?"

I hold my nose up in the air. "I have not."

"Nothing, not ever?"

I feel my cheeks redden. "Well, I got a warning, once."

He smirks—we're pulling into the airfield where the helicopter is kept. "I sense a good one."

"Not a good one."

"Hey, I shared mine."

I sigh. "There's nothing to tell. I got caught in the back of the car with Andrew Easton, senior year, at that little spot north of here you were talking about having taken Leslie Donovan."

"You and Andy Easton?" He blinks. "Wow. Not who I would have pictured you with."

I bite my lip. "It was a short-lived attempt at rebellion I guess. Andy was the bad boy and I wanted to feel like the girl who goes for the bad boys. Not just the… the goody-goody."

He cackles. "*I* was the bad boy…he was just fuckin' trouble."

"No kidding," I say, sighing. "He's doing ten years in a penitentiary for armed robbery and attempted murder."

"Yeah, I heard that." He laughs, shakes his head. "You got caught with Andy Easton. Like, how caught?"

I blush harder than ever. Shrug uncomfortably. "I mean…"

He laughs harder. "No! The cops rolled up on *you*, naked in the back of Andrew Easton's fuckin' Monte Carlo?"

"Actually it wasn't his Monte Carlo. Apparently that was in the shop." I bite my lip. "It was his mother's minivan."

His laughter is uncontrolled now, like this is the funniest thing he's ever heard. "In the back of a minivan with Andy Easton. No fucking way." He wipes a tear away. "Did he at least cover for you?"

"Cover for me? I was buck-ass naked and on

top—and all of our clothes were in the front and we were on the back bench. *He* hid behind *me*. Let *me* talk us out of it."

"What a dick." He eyes me and then looks away, and I can't make out his expression. "Did you? Talk yourself out of it?"

"Of course I did. The cop was a client of Daddy's—we were building him a house, so I told him I'd upgrade his counters to quartz if he let me go and didn't tell Dad."

"Smooth."

I roll my eyes. "Yeah, except I couldn't ever visit the jobsite again. I mean, how do you look the man in the eyes after that?"

He laughs. "I can see how that would be awkward."

"Awkward? It was *mortifying*."

Something in the air between us has shifted, since I told him that story, and I can't place what. There's no time to figure it out, though—the helicopter is warmed up and we board, and the pilot, a good friend of Daddy's and a former military pilot, has us in the air. He asks where we're going, and Thai tells him San Francisco.

"What's in San Francisco?" I ask, through the headset.

He smirks. "You'll see."

"Oh, a surprise, is it?"

"Of course," he says. "You wouldn't agree to anything I suggest, so I'm just not going to tell you. You'll just have to trust me."

My first instinct is to make some snappy comment

about how I don't trust him as far as I can throw him. But I hold my tongue, because…is it true? Do I trust him, or don't I? I guess I do—or I'm starting to, at least. The last month he's been working for the company, he's been…consistent. Hard-working. Available. He has been…trustworthy.

Ugh. Annoying. It was so much easier to just hate him. Now I have to go around rethinking and second-guessing everything I thought I knew about him, everything I think about him. The snarky comments I instinctively make.

The flight is short, and there's not much talk—Thai is on his phone most of the ride, texting. Not sure who, and I make a point of not asking.

When we land, there's a car waiting. I glance at Thai, but he just grins at me. "What?"

It's a Rolls Royce, new and white and sleek and expensive-looking, a droptop. I roll my eyes at him. "A Rolls?"

He waves a hand. "It's not mine, just borrowing it from a friend."

"But…a *Rolls*?"

"It's fun. You ever been in one?"

I shrug. "No. But it's just a car."

"It is not just a car. It's like driving rocket-powered silk."

"I don't even know what that means."

"It means just get in and enjoy the ride." He holds open the passenger door for me, closes it once I'm in.

I shoot him a puzzled smile. "Manners, too?"

He slides in behind the wheel, presses the button, and the motor snarls to life. "Ahhh, the joys of low expectations—the simplest thing will impress! Opening a door? What a gentleman!"

"I feel like you're being sarcastic."

"Me? Sarcastic? Never!"

"Where are we going now?"

He just grins. "Surprises all the way. There's just one rule on this little adventure, Miss McKenna."

"And what's that?"

"Don't say no."

"But what if—"

His eyes are strangely serious. "You'll just have to trust that I won't ask you to do anything dangerous or flagrantly illegal."

"*Flagrantly* illegal?"

"Yeah, you know—larceny, grand theft auto, jaywalking."

I snort. "Ahh yes, jaywalking, that heinous crime." I sigh. "So you're not going to expect me to do anything too crazy?"

"No bungee jumping, no skydiving, no car racing."

I sigh. "Fine. Calgon, take me away!"

"The hell does that mean?" he asks, laughing.

"I don't even know, actually. Some old commercial, I think? For a bubble bath? I don't know. Mom used to say it when Dell and I were being crazy and Dad was working late. Which was every night."

We're back in a car together, and this time it's with the top down and the sun shining on us and the sea in the distance. Fortunately, I'd had my hair in a braid, so it's not going to get too tangled. There's surprisingly little wind noise, so we can carry on a conversation. Funny thing is, by the time we reach civilization from the airport we'd landed at, we've been talking nonstop but I couldn't tell you a single thing we talked about.

Thai is…shockingly easy to talk to.

He's funny—and laughter has been in short supply in my life, past few years. With Dad getting—not sick, just frail and tired and…old—more and more of the pressure was on me. Plus everything with Dell, and the whole company relying on me as Dad's ability to make decisions waned…

I guess I'm just now realizing how stressed I've been.

Sad.

Prickly and uptight.

Jesus, he was right.

I realize I've gone silent, and he's watching me. "Thai…" I sigh. "Am I really prickly and uptight?"

"You've had damn good reason, Delia. You've had the weight of the world on your shoulders. But I only meant it as a joke."

"I know. I guess I'm just…" I shake my head, trail off, unsure whether to say what I'm thinking.

"What?"

"I guess yet again I find myself surprised by you."

He laughs. "Like I said—it's just that you're coming

in with the lowest possible expectations. But in what sense, this time?"

"You're a lot funnier than I ever really…than I thought you'd be. I remember you never being serious and always playing pranks and acting a fool, but…I don't remember you being *funny*."

"Am I?" He makes a *huh, who knew* face. "I suppose I've always hidden my serious side beneath the whole clown persona. And when we were kids, I really was all about the jokes and pranks. And most of it wasn't actually all that funny, come to think of it. But since then, I've learned that I enjoy putting people at ease through conversation. I'm good at it. Like this morning with Haimovitz. A lot of that was calculated. When we first met with him, he was checking baseball scores on his phone—I saw. So I started talking about baseball—I can't fucking stand baseball, by the way. But we needed him loose, we needed a connection. People are more… receptive, if you create a personal connection, if you put them at ease, like, we're all just people here. Just average folks having a conversation. When you go in all tight and—" he clenches his fists and jaw and turtles his shoulders up around his ears, "—everyone around is going to mirror that. To an extent, we're all empathic."

"So…the chitchat is a calculated act?"

He snorts. "No. Not what I meant."

"Then what did you mean?"

"It's not a charade," he says. Pointing from me to himself. "This, with you? It's not an act."

"But you just said—"

"With Haimovitz, yes. You were freaking out. You were nervous. So I loosened it up with some conversation. That gave you time to realize he's just a guy, and it's just a conversation. Relax. Put your nerves back in the jar. Then you took over and went in for the kill."

"So you *were* doing it on purpose."

"Absolutely. I can't wrangle a deal like that, Delia. I don't know Haimovitz, I wasn't the one who got him on the hook, and I don't know the proposal you've been working on. What could I do? Use my conversational skills to…soften things up."

"But with me, in a personal sense…"

"I'm just…being me. Talking to you."

"Putting me at ease."

He sighs, but it's frustrated. "You're still chewing on things. I can tell. Somewhere in the back of your head, the wheels are turning. About me. About…everything." He didn't say "about what happened," for which I'm thankful. "You said you didn't want to talk about… anything heavy…so I'm just keeping it light. But it's not an act. I'm not—I'm not manipulating you."

He pulls into the drive-through lane of a Jack in the Box.

I frown at him. "Uh-uh. No way. I don't eat that kind of food." He lifts an eyebrow. "I don't! I haven't had a cheeseburger in…god, years."

He shakes his head. "So skip the bun and the soda. Just…live a little. Loosen up. Enjoy a fuckin' burger and fries, man. Once isn't going to kill you. You're not going to eat *one* burger and a handful of French fries and suddenly wake up looking like the Stay Puft Marshmallow Man. Woman. Whatever. It will be *fine*. It's the habits that get you, anyway."

We're at the order box, and he orders…I don't know. Probably a giant burger with everything on it. He looks at me, expectant.

"Fine," I huff. "Just order something for me. No onions, no tomatoes. And no bun."

He places an order for me, and we pull through, pay, and get our food. Instead of pulling into a parking space and digging in, though, he leaves the lot. I don't ask, this time. Try to just enjoy the ride, Delia, I tell myself.

We drive another ten or fifteen minutes, and then he pulls off into a little roadside park overlooking the ocean. There are picnic tables under old pine trees, a little abandoned playground with rubber-seat swings and a rusted yellow merry-go-round. He exits the car, carrying our bag of food and tray of drinks over to a picnic table.

The food, as he pulls it out of the bag, smells admittedly delicious. I honestly don't remember the last time I ate fast food.

Freshman year, maybe?

Tentatively, I nibble the end of a fry, and Thai just watches me. "Ohmygod." I eat the rest. "This is why I quit eating this shit—it's too fucking good."

"It really is. I only eat it once in a great while myself."

He rips the wrapper off a straw and shoves it into his paper cup. "This, right here, this is my Achilles."

"The soda?"

"Dr. Pepper." He takes a swig, and sighs. "So fucking good. Absolutely horrible for you—pure cancer in liquid form. But damn—so good."

He watches me eat another fry.

"These are my weakness," I say. "God, I can't believe you talked me into this. I'm going to gain literally five pounds from this."

"So what?"

"So…you don't have a clue what it takes to keep it off. No clue. None at all."

"No, I don't. I've been blessed with the metabolism of a jackrabbit and incredible genes." He takes a huge bite of a burger. "But." Another bite. "I do work hard to look the way I do. I know it's not the same. I just know, once in a while, you have to do something for you. You have to just…kick off the—I don't know—the bullshit. The rules and rigid, dogmatic formula for success. Take your hair down, take the bra off, and put your feet up."

I don't answer—I'm too busy inhaling the burger. He got me unsweetened iced tea—and it's amazing. Everything is amazing.

"Yeah, I don't do that," I say, wiping my lips with a napkin. "The hair down, bra off, feet up thing. It's not in my repertoire."

"I know," he says. "Thus…" he gestures vaguely, at himself, at me, at the food, the car. "All this."

"Thus, prickly and uptight." I eat the fries more slowly, savoring them.

"Hey, you said it, not me." He grins as he says it, though, and while the truth of it stings, I know somehow that he doesn't mean anything unkind by it.

Perhaps the opposite.

Maybe.

"I know we didn't come all the way to San Francisco for some Jack in the Box."

His grin widens. "Nope. Not even remotely."

We finish eating, and there's more of the conversation that just winds and twists and rabbit trails until I don't even remember where we started out. Back in the car, and into downtown.

To a mall.

I laugh when he parks the hideously expensive car way in the back, away from any of the other cars.

"A mall?"

He shrugs. "When was the last time you bought something for yourself, just because?" When I blink and try to remember, he laughs, and pokes the front of my shoulder. "Exactly. Now come on, we're going to go spend a colossal shitload of money."

He's so freaking good at manipulating me—we're at the mall for over two hours, and he's the one dragging me into a bazillion stores, shoving things at me to look at and try on...until I finally give in and let the feeling wash over me.

He pays for everything—a new leather coat,

Louboutin sandals, a skirt, earrings and a matching neck-
lace. Not only does he pay for it all, he refuses to let me
look at the prices, and covers my eyes when the total
comes up on the register. It becomes a game—see if I
can get a peek at how much I'm spending.

It's honestly intoxicating.

And through it all, he's funny. The mean-spiritedness
I thought was his trademark is nowhere to be found.

After the mall, we shop more near Union Square,
and he continues to coerce me into buying shit I don't
need.

At some point, I stop him. "Thai. You better not be
trying to...make up for...for anything."

He just laughs. "There's not enough money in the
world to make up for the past, Delia." He says this without a trace of irony or humor, just matter of fact. "This
is for fun. You need fun, and this is fun. Is it not?"

I can't help the smile on my face. "Yeah, it is. But
you don't need to spend all this money—"

"I thought you understood—I'm fuckin' *rolling* in
it, babe. This? It's not even pocket change. Don't give it
another thought."

"But you haven't gotten anything."

He waves a hand. "It's more fun this way. The one
time a girl dumped me, and it actually hurt? Her name
was...um. Claire? See, I've already forgotten. But anyway.
We'd been seeing each other for a while, junior year at
Yale. Couple months. It wasn't serious, but I liked her.

We had fun, we clicked. And then, apropos of nothing, she just told me she was bored of me and that was it."

"Why are you telling me this?"

"Because I caught a jet to Paris and spent a week buying everything in sight. I mean, it was legit crazy. Tens of thousands of dollars every day."

I shake my head. "Crazy."

"My point is, that shopping spree meant nothing. Not a dent. And I've got more now than I did then, because investments."

"You just...hopped a flight to Paris."

"Yup. Why not? I was pissed. Irritated, more than hurt. Like honey, don't you know I'm the one who's supposed to dump you? You can't out-asshole me, asshole."

I laugh at that. "But she did. For no reason?"

"Right. Said she was bored. I'm not boring! I know I'm not. I'm a lot of things, but boring isn't one of them."

"That's for sure."

He sees a store, and his eyes light up. "Here. Come on."

Hermès.

"No, uh-uh, no way."

He laughs, grabs me by the hand and hauls me in. "Yes, uh-huh, yes way."

I have nice things. I do treat myself once in a while, but never anything crazy. My most expensive purse is a Louis Vuitton.

A Birkin is...not even on the same planet.

Yet here they are, in all their glory.

Oh god.

He grins at me. "Pick one, or I'll pick for you and then you'll be stuck with the one I picked."

I grin. "This was your idea, and I'm not comfortable with you buying me freaking *Birkin*, so you pick. If I hate it, I'll tell you…" I look around. "But pro-tip, you can't go wrong."

He peruses. He's followed by a store clerk, and there's a flurried exchange of whispers, and then the clerk vanishes. Returns with a bag in hand. I only get a brief glimpse of it—

This is no ordinary Birkin. This one…

Oh my.

It probably costs more than a nice car.

There are waiting lists.

Celebrities can't just go get one.

This one was in the back, and is clearly…

Thai eyes me, and his smile goes megawatt. He hands the clerk a heavy-looking black card, and the clerk whisks away before I can really examine the bag any further.

"Thai, what the hell?" I whisper. "This is crazy."

"It really is," he agrees. "That was a moment of extreme serendipity. Some A-list celebrity reserved that bag—she wouldn't say who, but implied it was someone I'd definitely know—but on seeing it, decided she didn't like it all that much—and it's, like, some one-off, custom, there will never be another like it ever kind of bag. It literally just happened, minutes before we walked in, and she guaranteed me it'd be gone by end of day."

"That's not what I mean, Thai."

He waves me off. Winks. "Having fun yet?"

"Paupering you? Yeah, it's a blast."

He just laughs. "Paupering me. Good one." He wiggles his phone. "Wanna go buy a Bugatti? I know a guy."

The clerk comes back with a discreet little folder and a Mont Blanc pen, and Thai scribbles something like a signature, and then I'm holding an elaborately wrapped package which contains not just a Birkin, but a one-of-a-kind Birkin.

I'm dizzy.

Faint.

I want to rip it out of the wrapping and just hold it.

Instead, Thai leads me back to the Rolls Royce, and we're off again.

He stops by a liquor store and comes out with a single bottle of wine, two glasses, and a corkscrew. Pops them in the back seat.

Drives on.

It's evening, now, sunset.

He drives us across the bridge. It's quiet, and the sun is brilliant orange and bathes the world golden. We don't talk, this time, and I'm fine with it.

He's following directions on his phone, which is on his lap rather than plugged in—but I have no idea where we're going.

Apparently, to an exclusive gated community, where the houses are on multi-acre plots facing the ocean.

He pulls into a specific house—not one I've ever seen.

"Whose house is this?" I ask.

"My friend's, who owns this car." He gets out. "Come on."

"Where? What are we doing?"

He doesn't answer, just walks backward until I exit the car and join him, trotting to catch up.

He leads me around the side of the house, to the backyard, which backs up to the sea. It's crashing noisily, and gulls caw.

The nearest house is around a bend, out of sight.

He pauses at the water's edge, where the waves lap at the toes of his shoes. "These are vacation homes, second or third places for…well, people with more money than they know what to do with. So, no one is here. Not for a mile in either direction."

I frown at him. "Okay?"

He pops the cork out of the wine bottle, tosses the corkscrew with the cork still on it into the sand. Takes a long drink right from the bottle. Hands the bottle to me.

Grins, wild, mischievous.

I immediately know what that grin means.

"Thai, no." I take the bottle, but just hold it.

He's wearing tight gray slacks, tailored and perfect. A white button-down, also tailored. Expensive shoes. It's all bespoke, fits him like a glove.

He unbuttons his shirt. "Thai, yes." The shirt comes off, leaving him in a white ribbed tank top.

That comes off, too.

I shake my head. "You're nuts. I'm not doing this."

"It's private property. No one lives in either house—shit, I'm pretty sure all of these places are empty right now. We're the only people for miles."

"I don't have a bathing suit."

"Me either." That wild grin again.

"No."

"Yes."

"We don't' have towels. What are we going to do? Drip all over your friend's quarter-million-dollar car?"

"Over a million—it's special. There's actual diamonds ground up in the paint, or something ridiculous. And he gave me the code for the door. There's towels inside."

I watch him peel out of the tank top, and he's shirtless—that insane, magnificent torso is rippling and perfect. My mouth waters—I've never seen anyone in real life who actually looks like that—carved out of marble, magazine-worthy.

But he's not done. Shoes get kicked off, one flying one way, the other another. Socks balled up and tossed.

He pauses, hands on the fly of his pants. "Come on, Dee. Don't make me do this alone."

"You're serious?"

He grins as he undoes the button; my tongue sticks

to the roof of my mouth. "Nope. This is the opposite of serious—this is *fun*."

I roll my eyes. "Smartass. You know what I mean."

He steps out of his pants, tosses them aside.

Holy mother of damn.

His thighs are...he does *not* skip leg day, that's all I can say.

"Thai..." I whisper.

He steps close to me. "Just skinny-dipping, Dee. Doesn't have to be anything else."

I shake my head. "Can't."

"Why?"

Blushing so hard it hurts. "In public? *Outside*?"

"Not public. Just you and me and the birds."

"But outside?"

"Yeah." He grins. "You've never been naked outside?"

I bite my lip. "I don't even like being naked with the lights on."

He sighs. "Well, it's about time you get over that."

I frown. "Self-consciousness isn't something you just *get over*, Matthais."

His eyes are fiery, fierce. Heated. "I think I've already demonstrated rather clearly what I think about your body."

My eyes squeeze shut. "We're not talking about that, remember?"

I hear something, but leave my eyes shut. Gather my courage.

When I open my eyes, he's naked.

The most beautiful male I've ever laid eyes on, in real life certainly and even on any screen. Every line, every angle is perfect, sculpted.

Of course, my eyes go *there*.

And god in heaven, there's a fucking lot of *there* to look at; I've seen a few…errr, male members, obviously. But Thai's is by several orders of magnitude just the most…beautiful. He's not fully erect, yet, but getting there. Thickening and lengthening as I look at him, going from at-rest and dangling downward to pointing straight out, and then lifting upward.

He's not just big—he's *beautiful*.

He just stands, hands at his sides, seeming unselfconscious, despite being naked while I'm clothed. While I'm staring at him with unabashed amazement.

And desire.

"God…*damn*, Thai."

He shrugs. "What? What'd I do?"

I swallow hard. "You look like *that*."

He grins. "And *you* look like *that*."

"We're not on the same planet."

"Nope, I'm from Mars, you're from Venus." A cocky little grin at his dumb reference.

"You know what I mean."

"What I know is that you have an absolutely incredible body, and you'd better start taking clothes off and go skinny-dipping with me." He steps toward me. "Or I can help. But if I start helping, I can't guarantee there won't be a repeat of what happened last time, and I'm trying like hell to make sure that doesn't happen, just so you can have time to think or process or whatever, and come to the conclusion I've come to."

"Which is?"

"You and I were made for each other."

"Quit seducing me and go back to being funny," I whisper.

"Fine." He jogs backward. "Last one in is a rotten egg!"

And then he sprints full tilt for the ocean.

"Fuck it," I mutter.

Take a long slug of wine—it's damn good wine, a thick rich red. Not the chugging kind of wine, but the sipping slowly kind. I chug anyway, and feel it burn in my throat and warm me all the way down, and I immediately feel it in my head, feel it loosening me…just enough.

Setting the bottle in the sand and twisting to keep it lodged in place, I yank the zipper of my skirt down, shimmy out of it. Peel out of my shirt. Bra off, wiggle out of my underwear. Shoes off.

Naked, outside.

Naked, outside, during the day…

Naked, outside, during the day…with Thai Bristow.

Who is also naked.

Is this my life?

Before I have a chance to rethink, I jog for the water.

Thai is in the water, hair wet, up to his waist—watching me.

Hungrily watching me jog naked into the surf; as

is to be expected, there's a lot of bouncing happening as I run.

I squeal as I hit the frigid water, and then throw myself into the waves. Under the water, stroking along the seafloor toward Thai.

Surface...

An inch from him.

Stand up, water streaming off me, the water is just above my navel.

His eyes rake over my body, then finally fix on mine. "You are..." He swallows hard. "You're simply breathtaking, Delia."

My eyes sting, blur.

Thai Bristow thinks I'm...breathtaking?

My body acts of its own accord—I find myself in his arms, my hand in his wet hair and the other on his face, and I'm kissing him.

My body nestles against his as if puzzle-made to fit.

I can't breathe...

Because kissing him is the most perfect and beautiful thing I've ever felt.

And that terrifies me.

Chapter
FIFTEEN

Matthais

THIS IS DANGEROUS AS HELL. NAKED IN THE SEA WITH Delia—her body flush and soft against mine, her mouth greedy and desperate as she kisses me with furious intensity.

I want her.

I *want* her.

Need.

I'm hard as a diamond, wedged between our bodies, pressing into her belly. A dip of the knees, lift her up slightly, and I'll be buried inside her, sinking to the hilt into her soft wet slick heat. I can almost feel her wrapped and clenching around me.

My hands have a mind of their own, clutching ravenously at the glorious weighty roundness of her ass, and I focus on kissing her, keeping it a kiss, nothing but a kiss.

Because I want so much more.

Everything.

But the way I want it…is not accidental. Not just because she's overcome with lust and can't help it. I want it in such a way that she knows what she's doing. That she can talk about it.

She can do this, but she can't even talk about me going down on her?

Her hands, like mine, seem to be moving as if guided more by instinct and raw carnal desire than eyes-open intention. She buries them in my hair, clawing at my scalp to crush me closer for a deeper, harder kiss—her tongue stabs into my mouth and her lips crash against mine, slip and scour. Then, her hands are all over my arms and shoulders and back, devouring the hardness of my muscles. Her body is against mine, breasts and belly and hips. Waves crash cold against my back, swelling up between us.

She moans into my mouth.

Then, with a gasp, she wrenches her lips from mine. Foreheads touching, she pants, staring down between our bodies.

"Delia," I whisper. No clue what to say, then, what comes next.

I fill my hands with her ass, clutching and kneading and clawing—can't get enough. Want her huge incredible soft tits with those thick puffy pink nipples and wide dark areolae, but she's still pressed up against me, gasping for breath.

I bring my hands to her face, intending to pull

away so I can get my hands on her breasts, but she has other ideas.

She grips my wrists, and her eyes meet mine. Her eyes are wide and blue, fierce and electric with wild desire. She's holding my hands in place. Telling me with her grip on my wrists and with the plea in her eyes—*don't ruin this by talking; give me my way and don't ruin the spell with stupid talking.*

Deep breaths lift her chest, scraping the tips of her tits against my torso. Her hands drop from my wrists, drift to my chest. Her fingernails—I just notice for the first time that they're long and perfectly manicured and painted a pastel candy pink—trail lightly down my chest, over my pecs, over my abs. I know what she's doing, and I'm torn between desperate desire to feel her touch and a conflicted, almost self-sabotaging need to make sure she knows what she's doing, what she's getting herself into...that I'm not capable of just accepting a quick handjob and moving on, of ignoring the palpable wildfire chemistry between us.

Yet my voice is blocked. My intention to be a gentleman about this thing between us—to, for the first time maybe ever in my life, not just take what I want and move on—is utterly wrecked.

Especially as her fingernails continue their tickling, traipsing trail down my abs. My belly sucks inward, involuntarily. Teeth clench. I'm so hard it hurts. I've jerked off to thoughts of Delia McKenna's goddess body every damn day, sometimes in the shower in the morning *and* lying down on my bed with a handful of Kleenex at night. Yet, no amount of draining myself can even touch the torrential flash flood of desire for *her*.

I swallow hard, and a groan escapes my gritted teeth when her fingers wrap around my cock. The waves swell between us, covering her hand and my aching member, and then recede back down around my hipbones. It's cold—the water is icy, but our bodies are hot, radiating and pulsing with heat. Her teeth sink into her lower lip—her head is bowed, tilted down to watch herself touch me. She grips me in a light fist, and just holds me for a moment, as if wondering at the fact that her delicate, strong little hands can barely meet around me—her thumb and middle finger just barely touch. Her hand is so warm, and her touch is… crazy-making. My breath catches—I can't even groan, now.

I'm going to stand here as long as it takes, and I'm going to let her do whatever she wants. We'll just have to figure the rest out later. Because there is no fucking way on earth that I'm going to stop her from touching me.

So hard it hurts. Aching to explode. Balls are tight, swollen with seed needing release. I throb in her hands. And still, she just holds me in one hand—the other is flat against my chest, on my pec just below my shoulder. Her fist drops, sinking down around me to the root. Pauses there. Squeezes. And then her fingers slide up me, her touch light and gentle. When she reaches the apex of the stroke, her thumb rolls over my tip. This time, my groan is a coughing expulsion of ecstasy, dragged, ripped out of me. I'm still clutching her face, hands where she compelled me to leave them. Don't dare move them.

Don't dare even breathe—between groans, I'm holding my breath, involuntarily. Pleading for this dream, this fantasy, to continue. This isn't real. I'm asleep, in bed, dreaming of this. I'm going to wake up alone and try to remember this as I jerk myself off with one rough fist.

The dream, the bubble of this fantasy, doesn't pop.

She keeps touching me, slowly plunging her fingers down around me, tip to root over an eternity. Watching all the time, lip caught in her teeth. I'm taut all over, muscles straining as if I could isometrically clench myself hard enough to bring my orgasm about, as if I can will her to get me there faster.

Except...the torture is bliss.

Slower. Make it last longer. Drag it out forever.

The moment I come, she's going to wake up, remember herself. Remember that this is me, and that she's not supposed to like me. Want me. That I'm wrong. That I'm off-limits somehow. That we shouldn't do this—because of our history, because her twin brother is my best friend, because I was awful to her way back when.

So I tighten up harder, hold back. But it's impossible, holding back. Watching her small hand with the thin fingers and pastel pink nails wrapped around my thick veiny cock is too much. Her tits hang heavy against my chest, occasionally jostling slightly with her movements—those little jiggles are nearly my undoing. Her breasts are pure perfection, in shape, in size, in movement quality. Every little moment of her body sets them quivering. When a wave splashes against my back and shoves me forward against her, they wobble and shiver. When she sucks in a sharp breath, they jolt upward, and then wave side to side in tiny quakes as they come to rest.

Good god, what would I do, what would I give to have her beneath me, taking my rough hard thrusts, making those perfect teardrop globes shake and jounce?

Anything—everything.

Now, finally, she adds her other hand to the mix. Not around my cock in a two-hand stroke, but cupping me from underneath. Clutching my balls in a firm but gentle grip, which tightens, squeezes, massages, and all the while her fist is sliding torturously down my shaft, dragging back up even more slowly.

My abs brace, hard. My ass clenches and I lift up, flexing forward into her touch. Chest rises while my chin drops, and my breathing goes ragged.

Hold back.

Make it last.

If this is the only thing she ever does to me, I'd die a happy man. This memory, naked here in the wild cold Pacific, her hands all over me, touching me until I explode—this will sustain me for all time.

I'm just a greedy bastard—I want more before this is even over.

I want her mouth.

Anyone else, I'd have waded closer to shore and guided her to her knees and taken her mouth.

But Delia?

I dare not breathe, for fear she pulls away.

If I don't come, I'll die.

So I hold utterly still except for the involuntary movements I can't help, and hope she takes mercy on me, allows me to find my completion.

Who even am I, right now? I'm a take charge, take what I want and don't apologize sort of man. This simpering, pathetic, needy creature is not Thai Bristow—Delia has reduced me to this. Such is her power over me. I just hope she never figures out exactly how much power she has over me, or I'll be the kind of man I've always had nothing but contempt for—pussy whipped. Balls in her purse.

The ache in my chest, the boiling pressure in my balls increase exponentially.

Her touch does not speed up.

I lift up onto my toes, hips grinding forward. I cannot stop this motion. I need more. Need to move. Need to thrust.

I don't.

Don't dare.

Instead, I freeze, every muscle clenched as hard and tight as possible. My jaw might crack, if I grind my teeth any harder.

My breath is hoarse and ragged through my teeth.

Helplessly, I begin to push into her slowly stroking fist.

I feel the edge approaching.

It's a titanic wave of convulsive, explosive pressure.

Hold   back,   hold   back,   hold   back —*notyetnotyetnotyet...*

Chapter
SIXTEEN

Delia

GREEDY, GREEDY, GREEDY.

Lost in lust, I want nothing but him. Nothing but Thai's fat cock in my hands, his hard body tensed and shaking, his narrow hips flexing helplessly as I torture him to orgasm. His wide, tapering upper body is heaving with gasping breaths.

He's mine—under my spell. I've never felt such… power, over anyone. I love it.

I don't know who I am, right now. I don't do this; lights off, penetrate, finish, done. That's how it usually goes in my life.

Not this.

This is erotic.

Daring.

Wild.

Full daylight, the sun setting behind Thai in a blaze

of reddening orange brilliance, staining the once-silver sea salmon and crimson and a thousand hues in between.

His body is a god's.

His lats are wide and powerful, shoulders round and thick. Arms are columns of carved ivory, abs shredded down to blocks of titanium. Narrow hips, an ass like a pair of cannonballs, hard and round and taut. Thighs like tree trunks. He's got a scrim of hair on his chest and a thicker trail on his belly from navel to groin.

And god, his cock.

It's a thing of beauty, glorious and impossible. Even in the porn I watch to get myself off, I've never seen anything so perfect. Touching it, even just being allowed to *look* at it is a privilege. Golden brown flesh wrapped tight around thick veins, so thick and so wide I can barely fit my fingers around him in a circle. The head is broad and lighter shade, almost pink, fat and bulbous and weeping a clear, trickling tear at my touch. His balls are heavy and taut. He's trimmed but not shaved, a thatch of hair slightly darker than anywhere else.

I'm living in this moment—it's all there is. There will be mental and emotional hell to pay, later. But for now? Just this.

Just Thai.

Just his snarling grunts, his moans, his breathless gasps.

All I want is to touch and grip and stroke him and watch his belly tighten concave as his hips drive forward. All I want is to feel him in my hands, feel his balls tense and pulse, feel his cock throb. All I want is to make him feel good. All I want is to watch him come from my touch. To make him explode, to know I can do that to him.

All I want is this moment. Nothing more. Nothing else. No thoughts, no feelings but this wild lust for this man's body, for his pleasure.

Now, he's desperate. I feel it in him.

It's in his eyes. It's written in every line of his tense, taut body. It's in the way he holds utterly still, barely daring to even breathe.

As if he's...almost as if he's scared I'll stop. That I'll take away my touch and leave him begging.

Could I make him beg? The great Thai Bristow, begging me to let him come.

It's a tempting thought.

But for this moment, I'm too greedy to wait.

I've never in my life wanted anything so bad as to watch that fat pink tip spurt his seed all over my hands, and to hear him groan in release.

I could almost come myself, just thinking about it.

God, it'll be so beautiful.

Instead of hurrying him to it, I torture us both, slowing my touch until my hand is barely sliding down, barely grazing upward. Barely twisting around his head before slowly sliding back down. My other hand holds his balls—as weird as they are, objectively speaking, I'm so delirious with maniacal lust for all things Thai that I find his simply beautiful, and I want to pet them, caress them, hold them, cradle them with as much wonder and appreciation as I have for his cock.

He groans, a long low rumble in his chest, and his hips flex. Once, hard, his belly tucking in, hips pushing forward, cock driving up, chest lifting as his chin drops. Eyes heavy lidded, hooded. Teeth bared in an animal rictus, lip curled in a savage snarl.

God, he's beautiful. Sharp cheekbones, chiseled jaw, and fierce, expressive eyes which burn like green fire, all the gray gone now, scorched away by the ferocity of his ecstasy. His hair is wet and pasted back over his scalp, hanging around his jaw and over his ears, sticking to his skin, messy and dripping and somehow still perfect.

My gaze drops back to his cock, the real focus of my attention—his gorgeous face was just a distraction.

Now, his movements are compulsory, need driving him to thrust.

God, yes.

Yes.

Give it to me.

Am I saying this out loud? I sure as hell hope not.

How embarrassing would that be? I barely allow myself to whimper even when coming on my own, alone in my locked bedroom, in my locked house, with the lights off and the blinds drawn. During sex? I'm almost totally silent. I sure as shit *never* talk.

But Thai just does something to me. His magnetic sexual sorcery twists me in knots and erases my inhibitions and ravages my self-consciousness into nothing—makes me wild and crazed with a need I do not recognize in myself.

I want to make this last forever, but I can't delay my gratification any longer.

His breathing is sharp and short, each breath a grunt as he drives his pulsing cock into my touch.

More.

Give it to me.

Give it to me.

My mouth is open, jaw dropped and brows furrowed as I watch my hand stroke him—still slowly, so, so slowly.

I have to look at him, again. Meet his eyes.

Our gazes lock, and I'm drawn in. I'm hypnotized. Green fury, mad desire. Desperation. Disbelief. Lust. Wonder. Attraction. Need—for *me*.

"Thai…" I breathe.

I feel a moment of terror that speaking will break this spell over us, but the reverse is true. My whisper of his name only makes him wilder, makes his thrusts harder, faster.

He's trying to hold back, I can tell. Trying to restrain his thrusts. Make it last, same as me. Scared of breaking the spell, same as me.

I can no longer keep it back, no longer keep my caressing strokes of his thick beautiful cock slow.

Both hands, now.

One fist atop the other, and still I can't contain all of him. He sprouts up over my top fist, pink head straining and bursting free of my squeezing hand.

He lifts, thrusts.

I lean forward, and what comes over me, I don't know, but I press my lips to his ear, nibble his earlobe. Whisper, in a sultry, aroused, erotic voice I don't recognize as mine: "Be still." I plunge my fists down his length. "Let me. Just hold still...let me do it all."

His groan is one of equal parts disbelief and relief and crazed, mad need.

I nibble his earlobe and kiss the shell and breathe on his ear, and then I'm kissing his jawline and throat and neck and then I'm kissing his cheekbone and eyebrow and upper lip and then I'm taking his mouth with mine and kissing him with a whimpering desperation and ravenous fury.

But I can't sustain the kiss—I need to watch. I need to see the moment he explodes.

He's panting raggedly and his hips are flexing slightly, back and forth—it's as still as he's capable of holding.

Faster, then. I plunge my fists on him, down around his thick throbbing shaft faster and faster, and I know I'm ruined for all other men, all other cocks, all other bodies. He's just too perfect, and this is a wet dream come true, my wildest sexual fantasy come true—my secret fantasy, the ones which once felt so deviant and perverse and impossible, made real, with the last man on earth I'd ever have even dared imagine.

His breathing is an impossibly fast pant, as if he's sprinting the hundred-meter dash. Wild gasps. As I drive my touch faster, his hips pulse forward in time with my downstrokes. Faster and faster, until my forearm and wrist nearly ache with the speed of it.

My god, how long can he last? How long have we been here, in the ocean, like this? I don't know, but it feels like an eternity, a glorious moment stretched out into years.

Don't end, please god don't be over too soon.

My breasts ache, tight nipples like buds of diamond, begging for his mouth. My pussy is drenched, slit clenching around nothing. Arousal slams through me in waves—need, raging like a tsunami.

One single touch and I'd come with him.

My thighs tremble against each other.

My tits ache as they shake wildly, almost painfully, as my hands blur on his cock.

"Come," I whisper. It's a command.

Thai obeys.

I gasp, an aroused, breathy, whimper as I feel it begin in him. He, for his part, snarls, and then the snarl becomes a low moan, and then the low moan becomes the roar of a maddened, feral beast. He cannot withstand the need any longer, cannot hold out any longer, cannot be still another moment.

His hands, up till now fisted at his sides, reach for me as he lets go. One knots in my hair at the nape of my neck, gripping my wet tangled hair in a death grip that somehow doesn't even tug on my scalp; the other hand goes to my hip, fingers clawed into the flesh, gripping hard.

Now, god yes, now.

I slow my touch.

Reverse the grip of one hand, cradling his balls against his shaft while with my other hand I caress him slowly with one tight circle of my finger and thumb. He pulses in the ring of my fingers, sack tightening in my palm.

"Oh *fuck!*" His voice is ragged and growling.

He comes.

It's a spurting detonation of cum, and it spills over my hands, coats my fingers. Another jet leaves him, this one rocketing hard enough to splash against my stomach—and still he's not done. I stroke him, gentling my touch.

"More," I murmur.

God, who am I? Who is this wanton thing speaking with my voice, this greedy creature, this slavering, sensual siren with my body, my voice?

Slow touches, petting his tip and tracing his length with a tickling fingernail, the other clutching him at the root and squeezing and fluttering quick shallow pumps. His body is wracked with jerking shivers, he's growling wordlessly, hips heaving.

Cum drools out of his tip, over my fingers. Again, and again.

So…*much*…cum.

My fingers are wet with it, the sticky thick wet warm seed drenching my fingers in a viscous sheen. The burst that splattered on my stomach drips downward—and then a wave sloshes up suddenly, and the receding riptide of it washes my belly clean and scours my hands clean.

I want to touch him like this for always. I almost wish the waves hadn't washed his cum off me—I liked the sticky wetness on me, liked knowing I'd done that to him, drawn it out of him. I like seeing him faint and swaying, liked hearing him groan. He dips at the knees as I continue caressing him, and still more white cream seeps out of him, little dribbles which I smear with my thumb.

I'm shaking.

Trembling all over with my own need.

Will he see it?

What happens now?

His finger touches my chin, and I tilt my face up to meet his eyes, and I know this is not going to be easy to get past—this wasn't a lapse in judgment, a frantic moment of errant weakness, like in my house last week.

This is something else. Something more.

This was just the tip of the iceberg.

His eyes are still wild. Hooded with weak-kneed post-orgasmic bliss. Locked on mine and feral.

"Thai?" I whisper. It's a question which means *what now, what's next, what do I do, what are you going to do now…*

He reaches for me, and I find out.

Chapter
SEVENTEEN

Matthais

THAT WAS THE SINGLE MOST INTENSE ORGASM OF MY LIFE. For a woman who I had pegged as a dead fish lover, she was…sensual, and erotic. She knew exactly what she wanted and took it from me. No matter how good it felt for me, what she just did to me was for *her*.

She wanted that. She wanted to touch me. To feel me. To make me come. To watch me come.

And now that she's gotten that, and I'm finished, she's starting to think—starting to feel. The what-ifs and what's next are bubbling up. The realization that she's doing this with *me* is going to hit and she's going to panic.

And I need to watch her come before that happens. I *need* to feel her come on my fingers.

I grip her by the shoulders and spin her around, walk forward so her sex is clear of the waves. Yank her backward against me, my front to her back. Nestling my subsiding cock between the soft silkiness of her ass cheeks, I slink one arm around her torso and hold her against me. Clutch her breast in my hand and feel the hard pink tips of her nipple against my palm, then tweak it with a thumb as if I'm strumming a guitar string, until she whimpers. God, she's responsive. So sensitive, especially her nipples. With my other hand, I delve my touch lower and lower, scraping my flattened hand against her belly and over her pubis and the scratchy thin layer of trimmed pubic hair, black as night and tightly curled and beautiful, in a natural wedge shape pointing down to the heaven-land of her tight sex. Her lips are swollen, the nub of her clit prominent.

I kiss her ear, breathe on it. Nip her earlobe. Play with one breast, then the other, toying with and flicking her nipples until she's gasping with it, and then cupping the weight of one breast, then the other. Meanwhile, I touch a single fingertip to her clit. She whimpers at the lightest of touches.

"You're gonna come so fast, aren't you, Delia?" I murmur.

Her head nods sloppily, as if drunk. "Yeah, yeah—ohhh, ohhh god, oh god ohhhhhh god."

I want her voice. I want her words. I want her to scream. I want her to collapse against me and beg me to stop, to let her stop coming.

I slide two fingers inside her tight channel—and if I needed any further evidence that she was turned by what she'd done to me, her wetness was all the proof I would need. She's drenched. Slick and squelching as I pierce her with my fingers, delving in with my middle and index finger, curling to scrape my touch against her inside where I discovered she likes it best—high, deep inside against her inner front wall. She's already shaking, and her knees give out until she sags into my touch, held up almost entirely by my hand on her breasts and the fingers inside her. Plunge my touch hard and fast inside her, against her, rubbing my palm against her taut clit.

She whines, a high tight noise in the back of her throat, and her head hangs backward on my shoulder, and she gives in fully to letting me hold her up, spearing herself hard on my fingers. Faster, and faster, and she's screaming now, thrashing, hips wild against my hand, on my fingers.

She comes apart with a shrill, deafening scream, wordless and breathless at the end—when she runs out of breath, she sucks in another lungful of salt air and then instead of screaming again, she growls, and holy fuck is that savage growling snarl the most erotic, hottest thing I've ever heard in my entire goddamn sinful life.

I feel something spurt against my palm, and the long low growl breaks apart into a delirious gasp, a disbelieving whimper.

I don't allow her to stop.

I withdraw my fingers and smear her essence onto her clit and whirl my two sticky fingertips against her sex, faster and faster, but still a light touch.

She thought she was done.

Her second orgasm takes her by surprise, rips

through her with sudden bashing ferocity. "Ohhhhhh *fffff*-fuckfuckfuck*fuck*," she growls, "oh god ohh fuck, *Thai*—what are you *doing* to me?"

It's over as fast as it hits her, and now despite the cold water and cooling air, she's coated in a sheen of sweat, and she's gasping breathlessly and whimpering, trembling.

"Holy shit, Thai."

I keep touching, greedy for one more. Her knees give out spastically, and she grabs my hand with wild strength, gripping my wrist to stop me.

"Stop, stop, stop—no more, please, no more." She spins in my arms. Collapses against me, and I encircle her with my arms. "Any more and I'll…god, I don't know. I just can't take another one."

I smell her hair, the sea and the damp hair smell. Feel her soft pliant skin under my hands and against my skin. Her breasts are flattened against my chest. Her nose is buried in my throat.

"Thai?" Her voice is a small, quavering whisper.

"Hmm?"

"When I came, the first time…" smaller voice yet, embarrassed. "Something…um. Came…out…of me."

I grin against her hair. "Yeah, babe. You came so hard you squirted."

Nuzzles harder against me, as if to disappear against me, as if it'll nullify her embarrassment. "I thought that was a myth."

"Guess not."

Silence.

"I'm cold," she murmurs.

"Me too." I cling to her, arms tight around her, one arm barred around her shoulders, the other low on her opposite hip. "Deep breath, Dee."

"Wha—" She has no time to complete the question.

I'm already throwing us backward, and she barely manages to suck in a breath and hold it, and then we're under the surface and I kick backward, away from shore, keeping her on top, and then I plant my feet and stand up.

We're in up to my chest, now, and she's in my arms, kicking to stay afloat. Instinctively, her legs go around my waist.

God, this feels good—her, wrapped around me, wet skin clammy and soft and cold, yet somehow warm at the same time.

I walk shoreward, supporting her with my hands under her buttocks.

She wiggles when the water is lapping around my calves. "Put me down, I can walk."

I just hike her higher. "I want to carry you. I like holding you like this."

She clings to me, as if scared of dropping. "Put me *down*, I'm too heavy."

"Oh my god," I snort. "That's such horseshit."

"I am!"

I grin. "If you were too heavy, could I do this?" I squat to parallel, and then stand up. "Or this?" And then again, but this time leap upward. Not far, but I manage a jump.

She squeals. "Holy shit stop jumping!"

I laugh and walk toward my friend's house. "You are *not* too heavy."

"You can't carry me all the way there." The beach is deep, at least fifty feet from shore to the steps up to the deck.

"Can too. Watch me."

"What are you trying to prove?" she demands, even as she stops squirming and tightens the vise-grip of her thighs around my waist, and the cling of her arms around my neck and shoulders.

"What am I trying to prove?" I ask, as I reach the stairs and ascend them. "That you have a false sense of your own size."

She breathes deep against my throat. "Oh." It's quiet, barely a whisper. "You're not going to collapse, are you?"

I laugh. "No, now hold on."

There's a touchscreen keypad at the back door, so you can lock the house while you're swimming without having to bring keys or go around front to the keypad there. I input the code, hear the lock disengage, and tug the door open.

There's a full bathroom steps from the back door, for showering off the sand and salt; the house is open plan, with a kitchen, den, and dining room, all high ceilings and modern lines. It's all I really notice, though. I carry

Delia into the bathroom and set her on the counter of
the vanity. Reach over into the shower stall and twist on
the water all the way hot—the spray stutters and hits
full volume.

She's shivering.

Her thighs are a V around my hips. I can't help a
quick, appreciative glance at the pretty, delicate pink
flower of her sex, and then meet her eyes.

She's fearful, nervous, turned on, excited—too many
emotions to keep track of. God, how do women feel so
many things at once?

Yet, I'm boiling with a bunch of feelings myself.
The same mixture of worry and nerves and arousal and
excitement.

She cups her breasts in her hands, covering herself,
shoulders turtling forward. Hunching, closing off.

I grab her wrists and pull her hands away. "No way,
uh-uh. Don't you dare cover such beautiful perfection,"
I whisper. "Look at me, Delia."

Her eyes lift to mine. Wide, electric blue, flitting in
the back-and-forth search of my gaze. "I'm not perfect."

"Nobody is. But you look perfect to me."

"Not what you used to say," she murmurs.

"I used to be the world's biggest idiot *and* the world's
biggest asshole, all at once." I cup her face, and her hands
clutch my wrists; I love that gesture, her hands on my
wrists like this. "I've seen the error of my ways."

"Just like that?"

"No, not just like that. It took ten years and very winding path to come to this conclusion."

"What—" a catch in her voice, as if she's afraid of the answer. "What conclusion?"

"That I have never, ever been so attracted to, so turned on by, so…so *enthralled* by a woman. Any woman, ever. I've never wanted anyone as much as I want you."

"That's not possible."

"Why not?"

She squeezes her eyes shut. "It's just not."

Tears leak out.

"Don't overthink this, Delia. Please."

"I'm not overthinking," she whispers. "I'm…I'm over-*feeling*."

"Focus on what I'm telling you *now*." I cup her face, rub a thumb over the dampness at the corners of her eyes. "Look at me, Dee. Hear me."

Her eyes open, hesitantly, fearfully. "What?" Her voice is wet and thick with tearful, overwrought emotion.

"You're beautiful."

She shakes her head.

"You are," I insist. "Back there, in the water—didn't you feel beautiful? Didn't you feel how incredible I think you are? There's no way you could have missed it."

Steam writhes out the shower, skirls between us.

She nods, a small, shallow bob of her head. "Yeah." A pause. "But that was…during…sex. Or whatever that was."

"You think it's going to stop being true afterward?" I ask.

A miserable shrug. "I dunno."

"Tell me the truth, Dee. No matter what it is, how it sounds. Hurt me with the truth, if that's what it is."

Her eyes fix on me, and now tears stream down in rivulets. "I'm scared."

"Of what?" I know, though.

A swallow, a deep breath. Gaze drops. "I'm scared that…that once you're done with me, you're gonna go back to…to being mean." Eyes up to mine, then, giving me the full force of her tumultuous flood of emotions. "I'm scared this all a game, some…some long con you're playing. A big, cruel joke."

She shakes her head, shrugs again.

"I know you feel guilty for how you were, Thai. And I do believe you've changed—that you're genuinely working to become a better person. And that's great." She swallows hard, and she can't quite look at me, tears dripping off her chin. "But that doesn't erase how you made me feel. It doesn't change or undo the damage you did. I *want* to like you. I *want* to trust you. I *want* to let myself just be attracted to you and believe what you're saying about me."

"But?" I whisper.

"But…it's not that easy. I'm sorry, but it's just not." A shudder, as of a suppressed sob. "You nearly fucking destroyed me, Thai. You don't know. You don't *know*. It took years of therapy just to be able to look at myself in the mirror. To trust that a guy could actually *like* me. Be attracted to me. Thai…the scars you left go deep. You wounded me. Damaged me. And then you just left and forgot all about me. And then when you finally waltz back in ten fucking years later, it *seems* like you're this brand-new, changed, amazing guy. And I *want* to believe that. But to the wounds you left on me, the last ten years of time and space may as well have not happened. The fear and the hurt all come sweeping back in, fresh as the day you left for Yale."

She squeezes her eyes shut even more tightly, and tears trickle in a sudden freshet.

Then, her eyes open and meet mine.

"So, I guess…I know you're trying, Thai. I do. I see it—" She's trying like hell to keep it in, to hold it off. But she can't.

The tears and the shaking of suppressed sobs—it breaks. She breaks.

Hunches forward, shaking her head and covering her face with her hands, shoulders heaving, sobbing. Trying to talk through the sobs. "I'm trying, Thai—I—I am—but…but you just—you hurt me *so* fucking bad— for *so* fucking long."

My throat closes. I knew I was an asshole. But I think…maybe I've underestimated how badly I really did hurt her. My eyes burn. Guilt is acidic inside me.

"I'm sorry, Delia." My voice is ragged. "I'm so sorry. Please forgive me."

"I'm trying." Her shoulders rise and fall in slow,

deep, calming breaths. "I'm trying. It'll take time, but I'm trying."

"Nothing I say can fix it. I can't take away or change what I did. I know that." I trace my thumb over her lips. "Just…give me a chance, Delia. Please, *please*, give me a chance to prove that I'm not that person anymore. That I really have changed."

"No one ever changes as much as you have—as much as it *seems* like you have."

"It's been almost two months that I've been back." I pause, reach out to add some cold to the shower stream. "You're giving me *way* too much credit as an actor if you think I can keep up an act this involved."

A tear-wet laugh. "Maybe."

"Just give me a chance," I say, searching her gaze and offering her the fullness of me, in my own expression. Nothing hidden. All my cards out on the table. "Please, just…just give me a chance. That's all I'm asking."

"A chance for…what?"

I shrug. "I dunno." I swallow hard. "This?" I grip her hands in mine, squeeze. "You and me."

Her eyes search me, looking for duplicity, probably. She won't see it, because there isn't any.

Tears stand in her eyes, and her chest lifts with a deep, shaky breath. "I'm still here, aren't I?"

I smile. "Yeah, you are."

She blinks hard, clearing the tears, takes one hand back to dash her wrist against her eyes—and then re-takes my hand. "Baby steps, Thai. Take the win you've got, okay?"

I nod. "Yeah, I hear you."

"I don't know that I fully trust you, yet. But…I'll… I'll try. That's all I can give you. But you have to know, Thai—you have little margin for error. *No* margin for error. Hurt me, and I—I won't get this back."

"I know." I swallow hard. "Just remember that I'm not perfect, okay?" I squeeze her hand. "I don't want to ever hurt you, ever again. I've hurt you enough for a thousand lifetimes, and I regret it more than anything, wish I could take it back more than anything. But as much as I'm not that guy anymore, I'm still not perfect. I'm not…"

She laughs, a delicate, fragile huff. "I don't mean a misunderstanding or an honest mistake." Her eyes cut back and forth still. "You have a capacity to hurt me like no one else, Thai. That's what I mean." She lets go of my hands and wiggles forward toward the edge of the counter. "Now, let me get in that shower—I'm *freezing*."

I pick her up and pivot, setting her on her feet under the spray. She twists sideways and cuts the cold water back, intensifying the wreathing steam. I step back and reach to draw the glass door shut, but she stops the door with a hand.

Her smile is…

Complicated.

Still fraught with emotion, but striving for something brighter, higher, deeper.

"Where are you going?" she says, that smile crooked and so beautiful.

"I—"

I don't get to finish my thought—she grabs me by the hand and drags me toward her.

"Get in here," she says. "I'll wash your back, you wash mine."

The gleam in her eyes is a spark of joy, a fragment of glimmering heat. A promise of what could be...

If I'm very, very lucky, what *will* be.

Chapter
EIGHTEEN

Delia

HOURS LATER, I'M HOME. ALONE. MY LIVING ROOM IS PILED to the dang ceiling with bags and boxes. All by itself on the coffee table, however, is the shining star of the entire absurd haul: the Birkin.

Before I open it and stare at it and treasure it as my very own, I ask myself a serious question: Did I do what I did with Thai in the ocean this evening as any kind of payback or expression of gratitude for all the stuff he bought me?

I hate having to ask myself that question.

Mostly because it means, if the answer even smells like a *yes*, I have to return everything. To him, and let him deal with it, or just give it away, or something. Including the Birkin. *Especially* the Birkin.

I give it true, honest consideration. I search my heart, let my gut speak to me.

The materialistic side of me is gratified when a pretty solid *no* percolates up within me.

Not just my appreciation of expensive things, however—my pride, my dignity…my willingness to keep exploring this whatever-it-is with Thai.

If I had done anything physical with him in some slutty attempt to say, "thanks for buying me shit," I'd be hugely disappointed in myself.

I pass no judgment on anyone else, only on me. If your boyfriend or husband or girlfriend or whatever buys you something nice and you want to say thank you in a physical way, go for it. Do you. But I personally don't do that. I don't believe sex should be in any way transactional—this for that, you did this so I'm going to do that, and it especially shouldn't be I *won't* do this if you *don't* do that.

That's just me.

So, fears assuaged, I set aside the barrage of other questions batting around in my head and heart like moths trapped in a lampshade. Answer them later. Do more self-reflection later.

For now, I can enjoy all this stuff knowing it represents gifts freely given to me by Thai for reasons known only to him, and that our hanky-panky in the Pacific was enacted purely out of raw human lust.

As much as I want to, I don't rip the packaging away like a rabid animal. I unfold the tissue paper and delicately remove the purse.

White crocodile Birkin 35…and all the hardware

is encrusted with diamonds. Not little ones, either, or cheap ones, but big, real, expensive ones. The kind of diamonds that normally go on an engagement ring or wedding band.

My heart literally stops. More than a nice car? Try more than a nice *house*. Jesus.

If he dropped less than half a million on this bag, I'm a three-legged goat named Bob.

That didn't make any sense. But then, with this bag in my hands, nothing makes any sense.

My entire freaking house *and* my resto-modded vintage Bronco aren't worth as much as this freaking bag.

I can't take it.

He has to return it.

Involuntarily, my hands tighten on the rolled leather handles, as if they're saying *hell no, you're not giving this back.*

I immediately call him. It rings four times, and then he answers. "Hey. Didn't I just drop you off and you're already calling me?"

"Thai, this bag."

I hear the grin in his voice. "Let me head you off at the pass, here, darlin'. No, you can't give it back. No, you can't give it away. No, you can't put it in a safe and never wear it or use it or whatever. No, it's not my way of apologizing. I apologized in words, and I'm going to prove to you I meant it with my actions. Buying you that purse—and all the other stuff along with it? That was for *me*, Delia."

"In what upside-down universe is you buying me tens, if not hundreds of thousands of dollars' worth of stuff something you would do for *you*?" I ask.

He laughs. "I've spent my whole life being all about me. Truth is, Dee, I'm a selfish fucking prick. Always have been—no excuse, but it's how I was raised. I buy things for me. When I was hooking up, it was about me. Everything was always all about me."

"You're not making a very good case for yourself, right now, Matthais," I say with a laugh.

"Not trying to make a good case for myself," he answers, his tone matter of fact. "Just being truthful about the person I've been." He pauses. "A friend of mine—and no, it's not a euphemism for me—was an alcoholic. I watched him struggle with it. He'd be out partying with us, and listen, we were out of control, all of us. We all had problems with binge drinking. But the rest of us could sort of pull back, sometimes. Enough to get through classes. Lunch with our parents. Dates with girls. Exams, interviews. We knew we couldn't be hammered all the time. Dre? He didn't have that. He was *always* drunk. I wasn't close enough to him to ever find out what it was he was drinking to escape, but it was something deep and dark, right?" A sigh. "Okay, so the point. Eventually, he hit bottom. Made a big ruckus at a restaurant at like ten in the morning, embarrassed himself and us and it got recorded and put on social media and he was arrested…it was ugly. And for him, when he got sober enough to realize what had happened, he was like no—no more. So he went through rehab and did the AA twelve steps thing. So here's the point—he had to face the reality of his problem. He had to admit to himself that he had a problem."

I let out a long breath. "And you're saying you had to do something similar."

"Exactly. Not at all the same as what Dre went through, but it's just a loose analogy. I had to be real with myself about who I was, who I'd been."

"And when did you do this?"

He sighs. "Not sure I can pinpoint a precise moment. It's sort of been an ongoing thing. There was a day I woke up in a condo I didn't recognize, hungover as hell, a girl I didn't recognize at *all* on either side of me, bottles everywhere, and I was just like, man, what am I *doing* with my life? This is all I ever do anymore. And then later that day I called a buddy of mine, Adam Prince. Successful as hell. The first of my group of friends to cut the partying and really knuckle down and make something of himself, while I was still douching it up all over the place. So I called him, for, like, support. I'd been hoping he'd cheer me up, like *no*, Thai, you're not a useless dick."

I laugh. "Not what happened, I presume."

"Not intentionally, but no. I asked him how he was, how things were going, and he told me. He was engaged to a girl he loved. Had a good position doing a job he enjoyed. He was happy. He was contributing to society. He was…" He trails off.

"Everything you weren't," I finish for him.

"Exactly." He sighs yet again, pensive and thought-ful. "That was when I sat down and looked at my life and started trying to do things differently. Stopped partying quite as much. Stopped hooking up with, well, anything with a pulse and a pair, if I'm honest."

That puts my gut in a twist—a feeling I'm self-aware enough to recognize as the awkward, niggling discomfort which presages jealousy.

"So…" I can't help but hold the Birkin on my lap, touching the diamonds and the rolled leather handles. "Bring this whole big story back around to how you buy-ing me stuff is for you."

A laugh, a deep genuine belly laugh. "It's simple, Delia—there's even a trite, cliché phrase for it that people trot out around Christmas."

We say it in unison: "'Tis better to give than receive."

He continues. "But for the first time, I understand the truth of that statement. It really is. As much as I like going out and buying a new pair of sneakers or a nice watch or a fast car, it's way more fun to buy stuff for you. It just…*feels* better."

"Well…" I sigh, laugh. "Thank you, Thai. Doesn't seem quite enough considering how much money you spent, but…thank you."

"You're welcome." His voice is quiet.

I can sense the welter of emotions and thoughts and questions in his silence, but he voices none of it. Maybe he senses that I need time to process. To accept that there's something happening between us, and that simply because it's *him*, I just need time to work through my feelings. Which are supremely complicated.

"Okay, well…I just wanted to…." I laugh, unable to find the right words. "I don't even know. Tell you you're crazy for the purse alone, let alone everything else. And thank you."

"I…" A pause. "Today was…" Another pause; Thai is never tongue-tied, but he is now. "Thank *you* for spending today with me."

"I had a lot of fun. Which for someone as prickly and uptight as me, that's saying a lot."

He groans. "It was a joke, Dee, god."

He's calling me Dee, and I…don't hate it.

"I know." I laugh. "But also, you weren't. Because I am—was…am. I don't know. I don't really unwind and let myself have fun pretty much ever, and that's the truth, so the fact that I was able to with you says a lot." My throat is tight, and I cough, trying to clear the lump from it. "Especially since, um…" I let out a harsh breath, force myself to say it, despite the sharp lance of pain the words bring. "Especially since Daddy died, having fun has just seemed…impossible. If not wrong. Enjoying anything. Doing anything but work has been…impossible and wrong."

"I can't say I knew your dad *super* well, but I have a hard time believing he'd want you to be a workaholic monk with no life, never enjoying yourself, never doing anything for you. He loved you. He was proud of you,

I know he was. And he'd want you to…*live*. Not just…
exist. Not just wallow along and be miserable."

"Goddammit, Thai," I croak, throat tight and
clogged. "How is it you can make me cry so damn easily?"

"Delia, I…shit. I'm sorry." A swallow, audible across
the line. "I'm sorry."

"No! I…in this case it's…well, not a good cry, like
crying from happiness. But—I dunno. I guess because I
know you're right, about what Daddy would have wanted
for me. He said as much, before he passed."

I remember some of the last words he said to me:

"Have fun. You work too much…and get laid."

His voice echoes in my head, gruff, but faint. Loving.

I'm not sure anything I've done with Thai counts
as getting laid, per se, but…I think it means I'm trying.

I hear him, again—still:

"For your next trick, try being…just a girl."

"I don't know how."

"You'll meet a man who can show you. Let him."

"Okay, Daddy."

"Promise."

"I promise."

*"That's a promise you're making me on my deathbed,
Delia. You break it, I'll haunt you."*

I'm trying, Daddy. I swear, I'm trying. But it's hard—
so hard.

"Lost you, I think," he says.

"Sorry," I say, trying to sound like my voice is more
solid than it is. "I just…I was remembering some things

Daddy said to me, before he passed. Advice a lot along the same lines as you're saying he'd want for me. Don't work so much. Don't forget to have a life."

"Is that what he said? Or is that a paraphrase?"

I laugh. "It's a paraphrase." I don't believe my own ears, that I'm saying what comes out of my mouth. "What he actually said was—" I make my voice as deep and gruff as it will go, in my best impression of him, "'Have fun. You work too much. And get laid.'" I break into something that's equal parts laughter and tears.

"Your father, on his deathbed, told you to get laid?"

"Yes, he did."

"Sounds like classic Mr. McKenna. He was an irreverent old bastard." A clearing of his throat. "Coming from me, that's high praise."

"I know. And he was." I swallow hard. "The rest of what he said is...well, it's pretty private, I guess. But you aren't wrong in that he'd approve of today—of me taking the day off to have fun with you." I laugh. "He'd approve of *everything* we did, if it meant I was doing something that made me happy, that I enjoyed. He just wouldn't want to know the details."

"Did it?" he asks, his voice quiet. "Make you happy? Did you enjoy it?"

"You know I enjoyed it," I whisper, too embarrassed to speak any louder. "And...yeah, I think it did make me happy."

"Which part?"

"Both." I'm red in the face, squirming on the couch. "For different reasons."

"If you had to pick only one part do all over again, which would you choose? The first part, or the second?"

"Not a fair question," I answer.

"Maybe not. But still. Which one?"

I try to pick, but it's impossible. "I can't pick, Thai." I can barely hear my own voice. "I liked both. I…I want to do both again." I try to speak louder, more confidently. "I want to do more of both with you, Thai. A lot more."

I try to summon the uninhibited wildness I felt in the ocean, touching him and being touched by him. Heat unfurls in my belly, and my voice loosens, just a little, and I manage to bring a tiny fraction of the fire and desire I feel for him into my words.

"I want to do more than what we did today," I continue. "You make me want things, Thai. You make me… you make me want things I didn't know I could ever want, make me comfortable doing things I never imagined I'd feel comfortable doing."

"God, Delia." His voice is tight and thick, now. Heavy. "You have *no* idea what it means to hear that. I was worried you'd…I dunno. Wise up. Decide I'm no good after all. Decide it was all a mistake." A huff, a rough clearing of his throat. "I want you to feel comfortable with me. Safe. I want you…well, full stop, there. I want you. But I want you to feel safe exploring…I don't know how to say it. Yourself?" He pauses, and I wait through the silence, dearly wanting to know what else he's going to say. "You are so beautiful, Delia. And I hate that I'm responsible for making you feel shitty about yourself, in your body. In your, um…in your sexuality. I want you to be…free. Safe. Comfortable. In your body, and your sexuality." He sounds embarrassed, and I can't manage words to reassure him, because I'm too fraught and choked up to speak. "And—um. If…if I can be the one to help you explore all that, to open up and do whatever makes you happy and makes you feel good and makes you feel like… like a powerful woman in tune with yourself, then… then I think that would be the most…unexpected but incredible kind of redemption I could imagine."

"Wow," I breathe. "You really have a way with words, Thai."

"I'm not just saying that." I hear the tab of a can crack open with a hiss, and he takes an audible sip. "This is just water, by the way. I don't really drink to get drunk much anymore."

"You don't have to explain that to me, Thai."

"I guess I kind of feel like I do. I want you to…believe in me. Trust me." Another sip, and I hear a sliding door open, close. "Anyway. I wasn't just saying that to sound good. I meant every word with every fiber of my being."

"I know you did. I can tell." I laugh, but it's an awkward, weird laugh. "Here's the weird thing, that I'm kind of struggling with in all this—I have a hell of a bullshit detector. I can smell a fake a mile away. There's nothing so obvious or noxious to me as someone who isn't genuine, and a liar is the absolute worst thing you could be, to me." I speak my truth to him, because at this point, I want it all out there. "Aside from being just plain mean, that is. Mean people really suck."

"Oof," he huffs. "Bullseye."

"I don't say that to hurt you."

"Don't hold back, Delia. I'd rather know you're being honest and truthful with me."

"It's kind of where I'm at, too, honestly. I'd rather say what I really mean. So there's a clean and open slate between us." I stand up, move outside onto my front porch and sit on my rocking chair and listen to the frogs and crickets. "What I was getting at was that I can tell you're being genuine. If you were to say something just because you think it sounds good or it'll…I dunno, win me over somehow, I'd know."

There's an oddly companionable silence between us. Thai breaks it, after a moment or two. "Delia…I want you to know that you are, without a doubt, the most amazing person I know. I truly cannot think of another person who could go through what I put you through, all the mockery and pranks and cruelty and all that, and—and turn around, even a decade later, and give me the time of day. Let alone…trust me, much less…the other stuff. Trusting me with your business, your time…your body."

"It hasn't been easy," I admit.

"Tell me."

"Really? You want to hear this?"

"Absolutely." A pause. "If you can talk about it."

"No, I think I can, now." I rock in the chair a moment and think. "Work was easier, once I just accepted that I couldn't get rid of you. And then you started proving that you really were here to work, to contribute, to be a real member of a team, and that you really did have something to contribute. That was the first hurdle." He's quiet, waiting for me to continue. "Then, I had to admit—or start to admit, *try* to admit—that you really have changed, and that you really aren't such a bad guy. Hurdle two, and a much bigger hurdle. I'm mostly over that one. It's just still an odd thing mentally to accept that you, Thai Bristow, whom I've spent my whole life hating and whom I long considered to be the evilest, shittiest, douchiest human being I've ever personally known—*you*…are a decent guy."

"A decent guy." He laughs.

"I just mean—"

He cuts me off. "No, for real, coming from you, that's a lot. Two months ago, I would never have imagined you would ever call me even that, *a decent guy*."

I swallow hard. "Admitting to myself that you're *more* than just a decent guy is another hurdle, and I'm still working on that one. But honestly, you're making it easy. You really are more than just a merely decent guy, Thai. I'm…slowly, maybe—and this might be more on me than you—but I'm slowly starting to see that…that you're actually…" I almost laugh as I hear myself say it. "A good man."

He's stunned, I can tell.

More than stunned.

His voice, when he speaks, is thick. "No one…no one's ever accused me of that, before."

I laugh, to lighten it. "Well, now you stand accused of being a good man, Thai Bristow. How do you plead?"

"Trying," he whispers. "Trying like hell."

"You don't have to…make anything up to me. I hope you understand that."

"I realized that myself, actually. Although, it was more that I realized I never could. Since I can't change the past, can't take back words or actions, I also can't make up for it. I have to just stand on my feet and accept the reality that I did what I did, and how it affected you." A pause, and I hear him swallow. "I can't make up for it. I just have to…be better. Be different. Do the right thing, and be honest, and be real. Show you who I…I want to say who I am, but I think it'd be closer to the truth if I said who I'm trying to be."

"Who you are, Thai." I repeat it. "Who you *are*."

It's kind of freeing, in a weird, almost disorienting way, to not have the burden of hatred for him that I've carried for so long. And I'm realizing in this moment as I talk through all this with him, that the burden of hate was…it was fucking exhausting. It was a huge weight, an acidic lump inside me, eating at me, holding me back.

"If I could offer you a piece of advice I've learned from my own journey," I say, "it'd be that you have to not just admit your faults, but you also have to speak into yourself the solution. You have to say that you *are* who you *want* to be. For me, I had to—*still* have to—repeat to myself that I'm…healthy. Strong. That I *am* a runner. I *am* an attractive person. Worthy of accepting myself. Worthy of…being wanted. That my body is mine, and I *like* it. I have to tell myself that I *like* my hips. I *like* my butt. I like my waist. I even like the stretch marks. I *like* my thighs." I swallow, realizing I'm talking to myself, now, more than him. "I have to look at myself in the mirror—some days this is harder than others—and I have to look at the parts of me that I *don't* like that day, that I'm self-conscious about, and I have to say that I like them. That they're beautiful—that *I'm* beautiful. That I'm sexy. That I'm rockin' it in the miniskirt, with my chub-rub thighs and all. Even if it feels like a lie, I say it. Out loud. Because if I can't convince myself of it, if *I* don't believe it…who will?"

"That takes a hell of a lot of strength," he says.

"Yeah, it does." I smile, and I figure he can probably hear it. "But it's worth it."

A brief silence, which I break.

"Thai, there's one more hurdle that I'm working on."

"What's that?"

"Admitting to myself and accepting…and even maybe learning to embrace that…that I'm really, *really* attracted to you. That the things we've done aren't wrong. That I have no reason to be embarrassed by anything. That I want more with you."

"Sounds like a pretty big hurdle," he says.

"The biggest of all," I admit.

"There's no hurry, Delia. You don't have to jump over that hurdle all in one day. The horny part of me is crazy fucking impatient to get you naked again and...to do a lot of very bad things to you. But I can wait. I want it to be right. I want you to feel comfortable and ready and...yeah—I want you to be ready."

I bite my lip, closing my eyes in anticipation of mortification and embarrassment. "If I was more fully over that hurdle," I whisper, "I'd ask you what kinds of things."

His laugh is low and amused and wicked. "Strip you naked and bend you over my bed—or yours, I'm not picky—and lick you until you scream. Or...beg you to wrap those sexy, sassy, smart lips around my cock. Put you on your hands and knees and fuck you from behind, so hard your beautiful ass shakes. Maybe even spank you until that ass is nice and pink." He groans, a tortured sound. "And more than anything? You, on top. Riding me. Sinking down on me, those big lush tits swinging in my face." Another pause, a harsh sigh. "Fuck, now I'm hard as a goddamn rock."

I moan. "Holy shit, Thai," I whisper.

"Too much?"

"Hell no," is my immediate answer. "Not enough." I blow out a breath, taut with new and nascent desire. "I want that. All of that."

"I've...let's just say I've dreamed about that. A lot."

"You have?"

He groans, a gruff grunt. "Yeah, Dee, I have." A muffled sound, as of him shifting the phone to the other hand. "Want the truth?"

"Always."

"When I say I've dreamed of it, what I mean is I've fantasized about it. All of that and so much more."

"I'm your fantasy?"

"Yeah."

"I had no idea." I force out the question I'm really thinking. "What do you do…when you have these fantasies about doing that stuff to me?"

"You know damn well what I do," he growls. "I picture you, doing what you did to me today. I do that to myself, only it's not anywhere even close to as good as how it felt when it was actually you, actually your hands on me instead of my own."

"I think about you, too," I whisper, face burning but voice confident, bold. "I touch myself. I think about you, and I make myself come." A fraught silence. "And Thai?"

"Yeah, babe."

Babe? From Thai.

I don't hate it.

"The orgasms are *way* better. Even just thinking about you and touching myself, the orgasms are so much better than I ever imagined they could be." Say it, I order myself. Be bold. "And when it's really you? When *you* touch me? When it's…your mouth? Your fingers? It's like dying and going to heaven."

"Do it," he commands. "Right now."

"What?" I sound slightly frantic.

"Touch yourself."

"Thai…"

"Touch yourself. Make yourself come."

I groan. I've never done anything so daring. Never obeyed when a man gave me a command. "I'm still wearing my skirt and underwear."

"Take 'em off. Just the panties. Take 'em off, right now."

"Okay," I whisper. "Hold on."

I set the phone aside, on the table beside my rocking chair—after a moment of considering, I put it on speaker. "Can you hear me?"

"Yeah."

"I'm on my porch. Sitting on my rocking chair. It's almost totally dark, except the light from the window behind me. You're on speakerphone. Obviously, I'm alone."

"Keep talking. I love hearing your voice, Dee. Keep telling me what you're doing."

"You too," I say, sounding hesitant.

"Me too, what?"

I embolden my voice. "You do it too. Touch yourself. Right where you are."

He laughs, a low growl. "Okay. I'm putting you on speaker."

"There's no one around you?"

"Nope, not that I know of. Don't really care if there is, though. This is fucking hot."

I laugh, and swallow hard. "I'm…uh…I'm going to take off my underwear."

"I didn't actually see them, earlier. What do they look like?"

"It's, um, a thong. Yellow, and ahh, really kind of small. Barely there. My skirt is tight, so I had to wear a thong, because there's no way I was going commando under a skirt this short."

"Try it, next time. Wear it when I take you on a date, and don't wear anything under it. And don't tell me."

"Don't tell you?"

"Nope. I'll find out for myself."

I huff in arousal. Suit action to words, reaching up under my skirt and wiggling my thong off. Set it on the table near my phone. "My thong is off."

I hear rustling. "Pants are unzipped…I'm pulling them down, around my knees." An awkward laugh. "You know what? Fuck it. Just take them off." Another pause, a rustle. "Now I'm not wearing a damn thing from the waist down—just my tank top. Which is kind of stupid. So…off with that too. And now…I'm buck naked on my balcony. It faces the woods, and I'm top floor, on a corner. So, as private as it gets, in a condo building."

I lick my lips, and then let out a laughing sigh. "Fine. I'll play." I sit forward, reach behind me and unzip my skirt. Wiggle out of it. "My skirt is off." I can't believe I'm doing this—any of it. Phone sex, let alone getting naked outside on my porch.

It's freaking hot. I'm drenched, soaked with arousal.

I peel off my shirt, make short work of my bra. "I'm naked," I whisper.

"Fuck, I wish I was there to see it."

I almost invite him over, but stop short. I like *this*. It's hot, and it's daring, and it's honestly just *fun*.

Instead, I moan as I touch myself. "I'm picturing you. Your fingers instead of mine." I whimper, biting my lip. "Are you touching yourself, Thai?"

"Yeah," he growls. "Wishing my hand was yours."

"Remember earlier? How I was touching you nice and slow? Do it like that. Not rough…gentle."

He growls something like a laugh, or a grunt, or something. "You ever watch anyone jerk off?"

"No," I admit.

"We're not…gentle." A laugh. "Not how we do it."

"Oh." I bite my lip. "So…how *do* you do it?"

I hear sounds—my imagination fills in what they are. His hand sliding roughly down his cock. "Hard. Fast. Rough. I squeeze, *hard*."

"Does it…feel good?"

"Yeah, mostly. You always wish it was a woman's hand. But the goal when you're alone is to just get there as fast as possible. For me, at least. Just…get it over with. Be done." A groan. "Talking to you, remembering how I felt when it was you, earlier…imagining your incredible body…I'm going to come so hard, so fast, Dee." Another groan. "Talk to me, honey. Tell me what you're doing. Tell me how it feels."

"I'm, um…my fingers are on my…my pussy.

Sometimes I dip inside myself to…you know. Get some… some wetness. It feels good…but nowhere near as good as it felt when it was you."

"My fingers or my mouth?" he asks, his voice impatient and rough.

"Mouth." I close my eyes and remember…how he knelt down in front of me and held me up, how his tongue slid inside me and circled me, how he devoured me as if I was his last meal. "Today was incredible, but that? When you did that? Went down on me? Thai, that was the hottest orgasm of my fucking life."

He groans, a low crazed hum. "Delia…Dee. Fuck. I want you on your bed, spread out for me. I want to eat you out all fucking night. I want to give you a thousand orgasms with nothing but my tongue, all night fucking long."

"God…*please?*" I whimper. "Even just one. Once more, with your mouth. I'd die for it, right now."

He seems to know I want this, just this tonight, despite what I'm saying. He doesn't suggest anything else.

My fingers fly, and my whimpers escalate to gasping shrieks, and I can barely remember to talk through it. "Thai, ohmygod, Thai, I'm—god it feels so good. Pretending it's you, and I'm—I'm gonna…" I can't remember the words, dizzy and wild with burgeoning climax.

Masturbation has never been so incredible.

I didn't know it could be this way, I truly didn't. I was doing it wrong all this time.

Or maybe, I just didn't have Thai.

He's grunting, a low series of groans. I hear the sounds—as I'm sure he can hear the sounds of my fingers on my sex. "Dee, I'm so close. I want you to come. Right now—fuck, fuck, right now, Delia. Come for me, same time as me, fuck, right *now*."

"Oh god!" I scream. "I'm coming!"

He snarls and I come and I curl in on myself and my thighs shake and my breasts tremble and I see stars and I don't stop until I'm unable to bear my own touch anymore.

He laughs. "Well. Now I'm a mess."

"Yeah?" It's a prompt, to tell me more.

"It's all over my hand and my stomach."

"As much as earlier?"

"Nah," he says. "Only you can bring that out of me, like that."

"What...um. Maybe this is a naive question, but... what determines how much you come?"

A laugh. "Not naive. I, well...? A lot of things. But mainly, how long since I last did. I didn't this morning, so then this evening, it was a lot. But now, since I just did a few hours ago, it's not all that much."

"So...If you were to not come for a day or two?"

"My balls would ache, and if you were to make me come, it'd be a bucket. A fucking river."

I swallow hard. "Thai?"

"Yeah."

"Will you...will you do something for me?"

He doesn't quite laugh, as if he knows what I'm about to ask. "What's that, babe?"

"Don't...don't come. At all. Until the next time we...we're together." I go for broke, for as bold as can be. "Don't come until it's with me. Promise. My hands. My mouth...my pussy." I've never used that word out loud, ever.

God, I'm such a proper little princess.

But...I *like* being dirty and inappropriate.

But, *is* it dirty? Is it actually inappropriate? Doesn't really seem like it. It's just hot.

"God, you dirty girl." A deep dark laugh. "I love it."

"You promise."

"I promise." A pause. "If—"

I finish for him. "I won't either. Not until it's you."

"So then the obvious question is...when can I see you again?"

I just laugh. "True story, and a sad one: I have to go to LA for the weekend. A convention. It's going to be long and stupid and boring, but I've gone every year and I can't skip."

"*After* I promise to stay totally celibate, you tell me this?"

I laugh. "Yeah, sorry. Trapped you. But hey, I'm going to keep my promise too." I pause. "And when I get back, which'll be late Sunday night, we can...you know. See each other."

"How late?"

"Usually well past midnight."

"I have an idea."

"Okay?"

"When do you leave?"

"Early tomorrow morning."

Weird—I'm just sitting naked on my porch, jellied in a post-orgasmic haze, having a conversation with my... Thai. My Thai. Whatever this is, whatever we are. I'm not ready to label or box it yet.

"I'm going to put an envelope in your mailbox. It will have my address and a key for my condo. Before you leave, get it. And when you come home Sunday night, just let yourself in."

"A key?"

"Yeah." He pauses. "Never given anyone a key, and never had one, either. But let's not make too big a deal."

"It is, though. For me and you. And just in general. But it's big, because it's the same for me, never given anyone a key, never had one."

"I trust you." Thai laughs. "And I'm saying right now, this is your open invitation to come over whenever you want. I have nothing to hide. I'm not scared of this. Whatever it is." A pause. "And, when you come in, Sunday night. Just get in bed with me. You'll be tired, so...it doesn't have to be anything physical. That can be in the morning. We'll take the morning off, go in late. Or not at all."

"I..." I swallow hard. "I actually really like the way that sounds."

"Good, me too." He chuckles. "Now, I have semen going crusty on me, so I'm gonna go clean up."

I laugh. "Ew. Okay."

"Delia?"

"Hmmm?"

"I'm really glad you called."

"Me too," is my answer. "Me too."

"Bye," he murmurs. "Have a safe flight."

"Thanks." I pause, and I hope he hears the smile on my face; it's a big one. "See you Sunday."

"Cannot fucking wait."

This time, goodbye is followed by the call ending.

I gather my discarded clothing, toss them in the hamper.

Put on pajamas—which in this case is just a T-shirt.

And then a thought strikes me.

Before I can reconsider, I act on it.

Chapter
NINETEEN

Matthais

I RINSE OFF IN THE SHOWER, BECAUSE WHEN I TOLD DELIA I made a mess, I hadn't been kidding. Big mess.

Clean, I put on some shorts and a T-shirt, grab my spare key from the junk drawer in my kitchen, and stuff it in an envelope with a hastily scrawled note:

Delia,

I can't wait for you to crawl into my bed Sunday. Be safe. I already miss you. Yeah, I said it—I'll miss you.

See you…well, not soon enough.

—Thai.

I seal it, and write her name on the front.

A thought occurs to me, and I act on it before I have time to reconsider: I call a friend in LA who specializes in rare books. I tell him what I want, and I tell him to name his price, just get what I asked for delivered to me, here in River Gulch, by Sunday; I receive a promise that he'll come through.

Drive over to the old neighborhood, halt at the mailbox—to my surprise, there's an envelope in there already. With my name on it. Her handwriting is…magically neat.

I put my envelope for her in there, and then consider opening hers for me right now. Instead, I decide to take it home. Probably just a key, maybe a note too. But it's something.

It's late when I get home again. The envelope feels heavy, somehow. I sit on the edge of my bed staring at the envelope in my hands. It's just an envelope. Four letters in blue ink. She formed the letters of my name with fancy flourishes, curlicues and long swoops and—I'd never admit this out loud even under pain of torture—my favorite part, a little heart for the dot over the 'I.'

She'd even filled in the center of the heart with a dot of pink Sharpie.

Lame, lame, lame. I'm so lame.

Getting all sappy and giddy over a fucking heart on an envelope.

I feel an absurd compulsion to do something overly macho. Punch myself in the face. Crush a beer can on my forehead. Something idiotic like that.

Instead, I just let it wash through me, and recognize all this for what it is: I'm catching serious feelings for Delia.

The thought of not seeing her at all from now—late Thursday night on the cusp of Friday morning—all the way until Sunday? Legitimately makes my heart sink.

And I can't even escape into fantasy-land, because I promised her I wouldn't do anything until it was with her.

I'm thirty years old. I was twelve, nearing thirteen, when I started to notice girls. Noticing that I liked looking at girls swiftly transitioned into noticing particular aspects of female anatomy made me feel funny in my swimsuit area. Like any hetero teenage boy first hitting puberty, that quickly took off into figuring out how I could get a look at what a fully developed girl looked like underneath her clothes. Turned out—fortunately for me, I felt at the time—my dad had a stash of *Playboy* magazines "hidden" in a crate in the basement. Which means I've been jerking off every day of my life since I was twelve. Normal, I figure. Sometimes twice a day, maybe a little less normal, but how am I supposed to know? It's not something guys typically discuss, you know. Point being…since I discovered that looking at naked girls made my willie get big, I haven't gone a day without it. I think back…of course there have been days spent traveling, days during college when I was in classes and cramming that there just wasn't time or energy.

This is the only time in my life that I have voluntarily gone not merely a day, but several days, without doing that. Shouldn't be a big deal, but…it is.

Because I'm doing it *for* someone. She asked me, so I will.

What this indicates to me is that there isn't much I won't do, if Delia asks.

I sigh.

Just open the damn envelope. It's not a love letter, it's a freaking key.

I open it, sliding my finger under the flap. Within, a 3x5 notecard with a key taped to the blank side. On the opposite, lined side, a note.

Here, her handwriting is still magically neat and garnished with fancy flourishes, but smaller, more cramped. As if rushed. As if she was putting the words down before she thought better of what was coming out on the page.

Thai,

I honestly can't believe I'm giving you a key. I guess this means I kind of trust you, doesn't it? Should this be such a big deal? It feels like it is. I mean, it's not like we're moving in with each other or anything. Just offering each other access to our homes. The thing is, I do trust you, Thai. I'm really putting myself out here, with you. So...please, please, please don't be playing a trick on me. I couldn't handle it if this amazing new version of you isn't the real you. Because I like this Thai Bristow.

A whole lot.

See you Sunday. In bed.

—Delia

P.s.: If you were to be sleeping naked, I wouldn't be too mad. ;-)

I read the note until my eyes blur and the letters start swimming and the words stop meaning anything.

My throat is clogged, and my eyes burn. I've never really cared until now whether anyone likes me. I've always been perhaps a little *too* confident in myself, and in my place in the world. Friends have always come easily. Popularity was a cinch. Dell has been my best friend from birth, and I've never questioned that, he's just always been there, always been my dude. Girls? Pssh. I've literally arranged a hookup with a girl with nothing more than a look—I caught her eyes, smiled, darted my eyes and jerked my head at the door. She'd nodded, smiling shyly yet eagerly, and that was that.

That's the amount of effort it takes to get a girl into bed.

But being *liked*?

It's never crossed my mind.

Because I've been an arrogant prick. Just assuming people like me, assuming I'll get what I want because I always do, because I *deserve it,* simply because I'm me.

It's never been important that someone liked me.

But it's important, suddenly and shockingly, that Delia likes me.

That she approves of me. That she thinks I'm a good person. It's important—maybe more important than anything has ever been—that she wants to be around me. To be my friend. To maybe even be more.

Claire, the girl who dumped me and spurred a week-long spending spree in Paris, is the closest I've ever come to having a girlfriend, and we sure as hell never put that label on it. We just met after classes for coffee, went to my room at the frat house for sex, maybe caught a movie or a party together on the weekends. It wasn't... *important*. It didn't mean anything to me and clearly meant even less to her—my being upset had more to do with the unexpected and unfamiliar shock of being the dumpee rather than the dumper than any real emotional pain.

This whole thing with Delia is on a whole other planet. Shit, another freaking universe.

Her opinion of me counts for...god, everything.

How it happened, when it happened, I can't even pinpoint. Buying out Dell was impulsive. Maybe in the back of my subconscious it *was* another prank to play on her. Or maybe it was the opposite—maybe, in my subconscious, I'd known for years that I had to make things right with her. Maybe the guilt over my awful mistreatment of her had been niggling at me for years. Maybe buying out Dell and taking the position as co-owner of the company was my way of trying to make restitution, an in to start making things right.

It hadn't been conscious, I know that much. Things had just developed. At first, I just wanted to prove to her that I wasn't useless. Then, I wanted to change her opinion of me. Just a little. Get her from not actively hating me to where she could be in a room with me and not verbally eviscerate me.

And then, somewhere along the way, I realized I care about her, and I care deeply about her opinion of me—not only do I want her to see me as competent, not only do I want her to not hate me...

I want her to forgive me.

I want her to *care*.

The lust—our physical chemistry? It's gravy. The moment I laid eyes on her for the first time in ten years, it was obvious she'd blossomed into a truly breathtaking beauty.

I'm already sick of this phrase, but—for the first time, I care more about the personal, emotional, and psychological elements of our relationship than I do the physical. I know that stuff will happen, and from the two instances of intimacy we've shared, I also know that they will be earth-shaking and heart-stopping and be-all, end-all incredible. I'm eager and impatient and wild for her.

But…I can wait.

This note is bringing up inside me the stark, sharp reality that with Delia McKenna, I want the emotional foundation of a real relationship more—*far* more—than I want sex.

I barely recognize myself.

But, to echo what she said to me in the note—I *like* this Thai Bristow.

The arrogant, selfish prick is dead—

Long live the decent guy.

❧

It's a long, shitty, miserable weekend.

Delia is in meetings and lectures all day and having working lunches and dinners with other top executives in the construction and building industry. She texts me a handful of times, quick and clearly distracted. I don't push it, and don't worry about it.

I spend Friday at the new development site with our architects and planners and Cal, laying out how the subdivision will work best in conjunction with the landscape. Saturday I spend at the office, trying to get ahead on what I'd need to do Monday, in hopes I can convince Delia to take at least the morning off with me.

Sunday, I get a text from her while I'm out for a run—it's an image, and I didn't bring my phone on the run, just my cellular-connected watch. So the image has to wait till I get home.

When I arrive back at my condo, sweating like a pig and gasping for air, I beeline for my phone and bring up the thread with her.

It's a selfie—she's in a foyer outside a conference room, earbuds in, hair in a loose ponytail, minimal makeup; she's snapped it from high up at a downward angle, so I can see her whole outfit. Long, loose, flowy white skirt with a sapphire blue sleeveless top, in a shade that almost exactly matches her eyes. She's smiling as if at me, with affection.

That smile is for me? The squeeze on my heart is almost painful.

I take a selfie in return, me in my shorts, sweaty, earbuds still in, backward ball cap keeping my hair out of my face.

Me: *Out for a run, so I can keep up with you.*

Me: *also, you are so F ing beautiful. I can't even.*

Delia answers after half a minute: *no, YOURE beautiful.*

Delia: *Last lecture of the weekend, then a dinner party which I'd rather stab myself in the eyeballs than attend, and then I catch my flight and drive home and finally see you.*

Me: *good conference, though?*

Delia: *Meh. Never really get much out of it, but the networking is important. Some new ideas coming out, updates to code, new products. Boring as hell, and I'm one of the only women here, and the youngest person of either gender by at least twenty years. So that's fun. I've been hit on at least six times, outright propositioned twice, and I can't count the number of times and different ways I've been dismissed, ignored, or otherwise treated with suspicion, because why would a 30yr old female be at a conference for construction executives.*

Me: *I'm sorry you're experiencing that. You deserve better.*

Delia responds with an eye-roll emoji and a crying laughing one.

Delia: *Like it's new? It's what every woman experiences, in every profession, no matter her age, appearance, experience, or credentials.*

Me: *Oh. Still shitty.*

Delia: *true, it is. But I'm used to it—I just don't put up with it.*

Delia: *On to more pressing matters. Have you been a good boy, Matthais?*

Me: *I have. Been keeping busy, so I don't have time to think about you too much. Because if I think about you too much, I'll start thinking about things that'll get me in trouble.*

Delia: *So what you're saying is, keeping your promise has been HARD?*

Me: *so hard it hurts. Literally.*

Delia: *Wait, blue balls is a real thing?*

Me: *Absolutely. Well not literally. They don't turn actually blue but they do start to ache.*

Me: *full transparency here, this is my first experience w it, bc this is the longest I've ever gone. Intense dislike. 0/10 do not recommend. But...I have no doubt it'll be more than worth it.*

Delia: *wait, for real? Three days? You've never gone longer than three days without sex?*

Me: *Not without sex, without self-relief. If you know what I mean.*

Delia: *Oh. So just curious, and don't need details and you can choose not to answer. But how long is the longest you've gone without actual sex?*

Me: *Well, that depends on your definition. Without any sexual contact of any kind? Or without actual SEX sex.*

Delia: *Both, I guess. I'm just curious.*

Me: *Coming back to River Gulch is the answer to both. My last hookup, which means any contact of either definition was about two, maybe three weeks before I got the news about your dad and the company and the will. I'm not gonna call it a breakup bc it wasn't that, but I ended things with someone. And then I was just kinda busy with looking into investments and such, traveling, whatever. And TBH, the thing I ended sort of marked the end of an era, where I was hooking up just for the sake of the physical connection. I was just tired of it. Like I was tired of wasting my life, as we've previously talked about. So then I heard the news and Dell called me to meet for drinks so he could complain about unfair it all was, and he made the offer and I shocked both of us by taking it, and came back to RG. And until the thing happened with you in your house, I hadn't had anything with anyone since I ended things with Destiny. Long answer I guess but the truth.*

Me: *You?*

Delia: *haha months. Not as long as a whole year, but close. I think eight months?*

Me: *damn. And that doesn't include solo sex?*

Delia: *No, I, um, fly solo regularly, let's just say. Flown solo more than I hook up with others throughout most of my life. Basically, when I get tired of my own company and my vibrator, I go on the hunt for a date.*

Me: *Tell me if I'm prying, and I'll shut up. But follow up questions, here: are you typically a second date girl? Third? More? And when you go on the hunt for a date, what does that mean? I honestly just want to know these things about you.*

Delia: *rather personal questions, here, Mr. Bristow.* *winky face emoji* *Four dates minimum before a new guy can get to what a high schooler would call home base. If it's someone I already know and have been on dates with, it's different. Going on a hunt for someone new usually means going down to SF. I have a little network of people I wouldn't necessarily call good or close friends, but people I know and can meet for drinks. They usually have friends, cousins, brothers, or co-workers they can bring along. So then it goes: drinks with friends in SF—>new guy—>date—>hookup.*

Delia: *What about you? How do you find your hook-ups? I've always sort of pictured it as you going to a bar, choosing the best-looking girl there, and crooking your finger at her. Then bam, her panties fall off, and you're in like Flynn.*

Me: *you have a clear idea of what you think my game is like, clearly. Haha*

Delia: *Am I wrong?*

Me: *honestly, no, you're not too far off base. There's no finger crooking, and I've never actually had a girl's panties spontaneously fall off in my presence. But usually, it's along the lines of what you said. Go to a bar, find someone I'm attracted to, talk to her. And then, you know. The rest.*

Delia: *have you ever had to actually work at it? Getting a girl to like you, I mean.*

Me: *Haha I was thinking about this earlier, actually, and it's a more complicated question for me to answer than you might imagine*

Delia: *oh?*

Me: *Yeah. Basically, you're conflating two different things, in my world, or my previous world. LIKING me is not the same as willing to hook up with me. So, getting a girl to hook up with me? Honestly, no, never really had to work at it. Just being honest. But getting someone to LIKE me? That's a much different question, and has a whole other answer.*

Delia: *meaning*

Me: *meaning I've never really spent much or any time really caring whether people liked me. It just didn't matter. I had my friends and I knew they liked me, because they hung out with me and we had fun. If they had opinions of me beyond that, I never bothered to find out. As for girls? Their opinions of my character was never in play. I did have female friends in college who I didn't sleep with, and they fell into the category of friends I hung out with and I just assumed they liked me. But girls I slept with, I never asked what they thought of me, how they felt about me because feelings never entered the equation. And honestly, if I started to get a whiff of feelings from someone, I bolted.*

Delia didn't answer for a long time. Over an hour, during which time I twisted in the wind of fear and worry that I'd said too much, that I'd scared her off.

Then a text came through.

Delia: *Sorry, the presentation ended, and I had a whole social hour to suffer through. New presentation so I can talk again. Thank you for sharing that with me, Thai. That's pretty deep personal stuff.*

Me: *thought maybe it was too much personal stuff, or something.*

Delia: *No, not at all. Share things with me, Thai. Whatever it is. Because what I'm realizing is that even though we've known each other our whole lives, we don't actually KNOW each other very well.*

Me: *Damn, though, that's the truth. Weird.*

Delia: *It is weird, isn't it? How you can know someone your whole life and not actually know them on a personal level. Like what makes them tick, things like that.*

Me: *You make me tick. Like a time bomb. This has been the longest weekend of my life haha*

Delia: *same, Thai, trust me. This is no easier for me. Going without sex is not the same as going without ANYTHING, even my own fingers. Normally on these things I have my buzzy little friend to help me out.*

Me: *can't think about you doing that.*

Delia: *Sorry, not trying to tease you. Question: you said you've never been worried about whether people like you. Is that still true?*

Me: *no*

Delia: *care to elaborate?*

Me: *You. I want you to like me. I care what you think about me. Your opinion of me as a person matters to me. More than pretty much anything has ever mattered to me. Like, ever.*

Delia: *I'm developing a pretty positive opinion of you, I can tell you that much. But let's not go fishing for compliments, shall we? LOL.*

Delia: *I'm not making light of what you said. It's just still a little strange for me to realize that I also care about what you think of me. Maybe I always did, and that's why it hurt so much when you were mean to me. I don't know.*

That's something I'd have to really think about more. But I care.

Me: *I couldn't possibly have a higher opinion of you. Although, the more I get to know you, the higher my opinion of you goes. I think you're incredible. You're smart, but I already knew that. Successful, but again, a known quantity. Things I'm learning about you: you're incredibly sexy. You're strong. You're brave. You're daring. You're GOOD.*

Delia: *Wow, you do think a lot of me. Good in what sense, though?*

Me: *Good as in a moral sense. You're a truly and genuinely good person. It's a rare thing.*

Delia: *thank you. And Thai? You're a good person too. You really are. I mean that.*

Me: *Well, I'm trying at least. It's a work in progress.*

Delia: *We're all a work in progress, Thai. It's called the human condition.*

A few minutes later, another text from her came through: *Did you get my envelope?*

Me: *I did. Thank you. It means more to me than I can say.*

Delia: *the key or the note?*

Me: *Both. The key for what it represents: your trust. And the note because, well…that's what prompted the realization that I've never cared whether people like me, and that I care that you do. It was a pretty big epiphany, tbh.*

A few minutes go by, and then a text: *Thai? I miss you too. The presentation is wrapping up, so I'm gonna have to go. A couple more to sit through, then the stupid dinner, and then I'm done.*

Me: *okay. I'll let you pay attention, then.*

Delia: *I probably should, huh? I paid money to be here so I may as well TRY and get something from it, other than a sore butt from sitting on these godawful hard chairs and some cheap swag.*

Me: *I'll give you a massage when you get home.*

Delia: *a butt massage?*

Me: *Hell yeah. Your butt is one of my favorite physical attributes. Didn't you know?*

Delia: *Weird. When I say I run my ass off every morning, I'm speaking out of hope that I actually will run my ass a size or two smaller. But I'm glad you like it. I grew it myself lol* *crying laughing emoji*

Me: *When I say it's my favorite physical attribute, what I mean is first among equals. I like all of you equally. But your ass is particularly amazing. And now I'm thinking about your ass, and massaging it.*

Delia: *With your hands?* *winking emoji*

Me: *With whatever part of me you'll allow near you.*

Delia: *Allow? Try demand.*

Delia: *Okay, got to go. I'll see you in a few hours. Thanks for making my Sunday a little better. Or a lot better. Bye for now!*

She leaves me on that note? FRUSTRATION!

Demand?

She'll *demand* my body near her? Be still my beating heart.

Be still my beating *everything*.

Is this my life? *This*, with Delia McKenna? I would not have believed it, not all that long ago.

I wonder if she thinks I'm going to be actually asleep when she gets here. Like I could possibly sleep. I'm not going to push anything because after the weekend she's had I imagine she'll need to just relax and crash.

Chapter
TWENTY

Delia

G OD, I'M TIRED.
I never sleep well anywhere but my own bed, and this stupid convention starts at 8 a.m. every morning which means if I want to run and get breakfast, I have to be up at ass crack of dawn. And then the presentations go till dinner and then there's the dinner shitshow which always gets dragged out into a cocktail hour that lasts several hours, in which there's always at least one drunk guy trying to get in my pants. And all I want to do is go home.

Home, to River Gulch.

Home, to Thai.

Weird, how quickly he's infiltrated my life. How quickly I've grown used to him being around.

The flight is uneventful. I brought a book to read, but when I've read the same page a dozen times and remember nothing, I give up. My mind is not on the book, as good as it is—even those sexy Alaskan brothers can't hold my attention, right now.

My mind is on Thai.

Being away from him has only forced me to some serious and scary revelations. One, that I do indeed miss him, and a lot. Two, that it seems to be possible to develop feelings for someone without realizing it until it hits you all at once, and that this can happen in a matter of weeks. Three, that until Thai, my sex life was lame, and that I've been seriously out of touch with my own real desires and needs.

That last one is a doozy.

Don't get me wrong, I like sex. I always have, ever since I discovered masturbation as a pubescent girl, and then gave my virginity to—well, it was such a forgettable experience that I prefer to not even dwell on it. But since then, solo sex is a daily must, and while I've never wanted or had a serious boyfriend, regular partners are also a must. I'm not a one-and-done type. I've always liked to go out with a guy for a few weeks or months. I'm too busy for a boyfriend, and my focus has always been on my career, on the business. Honestly, I'm not actually all that different from Thai, in that regard. Weird.

But…I've never wanted anyone like I want him. No one makes me feel the way he makes me feel. The realization that's bowling me over? It's not all Thai. It's me. I've been sort of accepting that I like and need and want sex, but…god, how do I even put it?

I haven't examined what I really want. Deep down.

I never let myself feel how badly I want to be *wanted*.

There, that's it.

My sexual partners have been a matter of relief. Mutual release, fun, a little bit of feeling good naked.

But no one has ever made me feel truly, deeply desired.

Needed.

No one has ever put my pleasure ahead of his own.

No one has ever made me feel crazy, wild with desperation. Out of control. Willing to do kind of crazy things.

Thai does all this.

And in spades.

He sees me.

He sees what I want. Knows what I need even when I don't understand it myself. And he gives it to me.

The craziest thing is that I know all this and I haven't even actually had sex with him.

I get a little shaky at the thought of finally, actually having sex with Thai. How good will it be? If it's anything like what he can do with his hands and his mouth…I may never recover.

Heat blossoms in me, pooling low in my belly, settling in a fiery ache just above my sex. My thighs press together in a vain attempt to relieve the ache.

I should not have thought about the things Thai

did to me with his mouth—what he did to me with his hand. What I did to him with *my* hands.

How I want to do it again. With my mouth.

How I want to climb on top of him and ride him until I'm half paralyzed.

Stop, stop, stop.

I close my eyes and grit my teeth and press my thighs together and will Thai Bristow out of my mind.

I know he'll be asleep when I get back—my flight was delayed due to some mechanical issue, so I won't be walking through his door until after one in the morning.

Maybe when he feels me climb in bed, he'll wake up, and we can do things.

Is that selfish?

Being selfish isn't something I'm good at. But with Thai, I feel different. Maybe I'll feel comfortable enough waking him up and asking him to make me feel good. However he wants—his choice. I'll for sure return the favor, because I'm as manic with the need to touch him as I am with the need to be touched.

That's another part of the realization: I've never craved a man the way I crave Thai's body. Never craved his pleasure. Never found such intense sexual—and yes, emotional—joy from making *him* feel good. Watching him come apart under my hands in the ocean was one of the most erotic experiences of my life—the other is the moment he kissed me that first time, and then dropped to his knees and gave me an orgasm I have not forgotten and still wake up with wet dreams about.

"Hey, um, ma'am?" A voice to my left, male, elderly, and confused. "Would you mind letting go of my hand?"

I start, and realize I've grabbed the hand of the man next to me, in the window seat. He's about seventy-five or so and seems perplexed. We're still on our approach to land, and it's not like I'm scared of flying. But yet I was gripping his hand so hard I left white fingerprints.

"Ohmygod, I'm so sorry!" I yank my hand away and shove them between my knees. "I'm sorry."

"Not a fan of flying?" he says, sounding sympathetic.

"Actually, I'm fine with flying. It's more…" I wonder what to say to this random stranger. "I'm just eager to get home."

He smiles, kindly and understanding. "Someone waiting for you?"

I smile back. "Yeah. My…" I swallow hard when I realize the next word is the truth. "My boyfriend."

"Had to think about that one, eh?"

I laugh. "It's new, and still developing."

"And you're not sure if you want to put it in that particular box, just yet?"

I look at him in surprise, and he just laughs.

"Things were different when I was young," he says, "but when I met my wife of forty-two years, we saw each other every day and we'd take drives and do the kinds of things young kids do, you know." A knowing, naughty wink. "But when she wanted to tell people we were going steady, I balked."

"What changed your mind?"

He tapped the armrest between us. "I went on a trip. Out east, to interview for college. And when I was gone, I realized I missed her something awful. If you miss 'em, it's something worth naming."

"If you miss them," I repeat. "It's something worth naming."

"You missed him?"

"Yeah. A lot."

"Putting a label on it, putting it in a so-called 'box'—he puts air quotes around it—"doesn't really *change* anything. Just changes your perception. I think it just means you're scared of committing to it. If there's no label of relationship, of boyfriend and girlfriend or what have you, then you're not committed to it. It's less real." A shrug. "That's just you lying to yourself. You can be all the way committed to something—to some*one*—and not realize it, and not have it in a nice neatly labeled little box. It's still what it is, you just haven't named it yet." He glances at the ceiling as the pilot announces that we're making our approach for landing and to fasten seatbelts; we both put ours on, and then he continues. "Naming things gives them power. That's where the fear comes from. If you name it, it feels more real. But then, the flip side is, when you name it, you take away the unknown, to a degree. And that should, once you accept it, make you less afraid."

I nod. "That makes a lot of sense, actually."

He pats my hand. "And most of the time, there's

nothing to be afraid of anyway. If he's worth missing, then he's worth naming the relationship for."

"Thank you for the advice."

He waves a hand. "It's not really advice, it's just some things I've learned in my life."

"Well, it's appreciated, whatever you call it."

He just nods, and the conversation ends there.

But I'm left thinking, as we land and taxi to the jetway. When we disembark, I wave and smile at my seatmate, and head to collect my luggage. Back to my car.

The drive home is a little over an hour, and I spend it thinking about Thai, about what we are, what we have. What it is.

He's my boyfriend.

I feel a little giddy, at that. But it's true. And I like it.

I've never been so glad to put my car into park. I sit for a moment, and just breathe. I'm not at home—I'm at Thai's condo.

I'm going to use the key he gave me, let myself into his house—where I've never even been—and I'm going to climb into his bed with him.

I stomp my feet and shake my hands and my head and let out a little scream of…well, everythingness. Nerves, fear, excitement, eagerness. Pure, raw, somewhat unstable horniness.

I'm not tired, all of a sudden. I'm wired. I mean, yeah, behind the adrenaline of excitement is the fact of exhaustion, but…it's faint, right now.

I shut off the motor, collect my purse from the

passenger seat and then my suitcase and carry-on from the trunk. Lock my Bronco, and head for the entrance. I already have his key in my hand.

Top floor, last one on the left.

The building is newer—McKenna was in the running to build these but lost out at the last second. They're nice, though—Tyler lives in a different building of this same complex. God, I'm glad that's over, honestly. He was so *boring*.

Strangely, it's only since meeting Thai all over again that I've realized exactly how boring Tyler really is.

The elevator is thankfully quick, and I'm dragging my suitcase at a power walk toward his door. There it is. My heart thumps loudly in my chest.

My hand is shaking.

Unlock the deadbolt, then the knob, and push it open.

I'm so tired, wired, and nervous that I almost trip over it: a box on the floor in front of his door. I figure it's a delivery for him or something, so I pick it up and tuck it under my arm—or, at least, that's the intention. It's heavy, though, so I have to use both hands to carry it inside with me.

I expect it to be dark, or maybe a light in the kitchen left on for me to see by.

I let the door close behind me and absently toss the key into my purse.

There are no lights on at all, but it's not dark.

Because he's lit candles.

Dozens of them, little tea lights in a parallel line, leading across the open-plan main area to his room. My heart, already in my throat, now threatens to completely clog my airway. Leaving my bags by the door, I float, weightless, along the candle-lit path. I hear music—low, percussive jazz, a bass, a piano, a trumpet. I hear water running—and then shut off.

His room is lit with candles as well, more tea lights. This is some *Bachelor* kind of thing he's got going on, and my heart is melting even as it hammers in my throat like a tribal drum.

Wide king-size bed, neatly made, gray comforter, navy pillows. I honestly don't register the rest, other than the usual dresser, TV mounted on the wall opposite the bed. Balcony.

The path leads to the bathroom.

The door is open, more tea lights flickering.

Barely able to breathe, even less able to contain my tumultuous admixture of feelings, I hurry the last few steps into the bathroom.

He's standing in the center, wreathed in candle-lit steam. A huge claw-foot soaking tub is filled with steaming water and bubbles. Candles ring the tub, line every surface.

I told him to be sleeping naked, but he's done me one better—*way* better.

He's wrapped in a towel.

His golden hair is loose around his jawline, brushed and clean and beautiful. The towel is white, hangs to his knees. Tucked tight at the waist, low. His abs ripple, glisten in the moonlight. His body, god…this man's body is sculpted by Heaven for my viewing pleasure.

He's holding a single red rose.

And he's on the other side of a massage table.

I stop on this side of the table, blinking hard. "Thai?"

"You didn't really think I'd be asleep, did you?"

I laugh, sniffle. "A little, yeah. It's after one."

He snorts. "I'd wait up all night for you, Delia."

I glance at the table. "What's…what's this?"

"A massage table."

"You have a massage table?"

"I do now."

I lick my lips. "Um, why?"

He rounds the end of the table and wraps his hands around my waist, tugs me to him—the box is between us, awkward and poky. "It's comfy to sleep on?"

I laugh. "Smartass."

"Because I told you I'd give you a massage."

"Yeah, a butt massage."

He touches my chin with a fingertip. "I can include a butt massage."

"Thai—" I don't even know which way is up. "The candles, the bath, the massage table…" I swallow hard. "You did all this…for me?"

I'm still holding the heavy box in my hands, but I've all but forgotten about it.

He nods. "I've been keeping the water hot and the

bubbles fresh for about an hour. I'm going to rub you down, and then you're going to take a bath and relax. And then you're going to bed."

I nod. "I see, I see." I smirk. "One suggestion, however, if I may?"

He lifts an eyebrow. "What's that?"

"Bath first, and then massage?"

"I figured the bath would wash the oils off."

I shrug. "True, but three things—one, baths are not for getting clean, they're for relaxing. I mean, you can't really get clean in me-soup, you know? Two, the bath is hot and bubbly now. Third, once I'm done being bathed and massaged, I'm going to be a puddle of so much useless jelly, and it'll be easier to get me from the table to bed than from the tub to bed, all wet and soapy."

He nodded, rubbing his chin. "Points taken." He gestures at the box. "You haven't opened it, yet."

I frown. "Oh. I was so surprised by the candles and everything that I—" I cut off abruptly. "Wait? It's for me?"

He laughs. "Yeah, didn't you look at it?"

I do so: The shipping label reads *To Delia McKenna, c/o Thai Bristow*, with the address to this condo. The return address is Los Angeles, a name I don't recognize.

"What is it?" I ask.

He snorts. "Open it and find out?"

I set it down on the massage table pick at the edge of the packing tape until I can peel it off. Within, a long, crumpled wad of thick construction paper used as packing material. I pull it out—underneath, stacks of books.

Transparent archival-quality protective sleeves sheathe hardcover books. I pick up the top one: *Harry Potter and the Half-Blood Prince.* Hands shaking, I gingerly withdraw the book.

I glance up at Thai, but his face is impassive.

I open the cover, and there, on the blank page, is J.K. Rowling's signature. The copyright page indicates this is a British first edition, first printing.

"Thai…" I breathe.

"Keep going," he murmurs.

I slip the book back into the sleeve and set it aside on the table. The next book is the same. An autographed first edition, first printing copy of the next Harry Potter book. All eight. All signed. But wait, there's more— signed first edition hardcover editions of the entire Twilight series, as well.

My eyes water. "Thai, are you for real?"

He nods, shrugs. "I mean, yeah." He smiles, but it's uneven, uncertain. "In this case, I *am* trying to make up for the past. I destroyed at least one book that I remember. I saw the missing book in your house, and I just…it stung, you know? Like, you still have all your favorite books, you know? You clearly treasure them. And I know it doesn't make up for what I did then, but hopefully those will go at least a little way toward…" A shrug, as he trails off. "I don't know. Showing you I'm serious." A hard swallow. "About you. About us."

"It does," I whisper. "It goes a long way. All of this does."

He sets the rose on the table with the books; it has one of those water vial things on the cut end keeping it watered, so I don't bother with taking the time to put it in a vase. There are other more pressing concerns, at the moment.

Such as his hands trailing over the buttons of my blouse. One button, two, three buttons, four…and then the blouse is on the floor and I'm in a skirt, plain white utilitarian bra, and a pair of flats. I swallow hard, because I've been naked with him twice now, but it's still nerve-wracking at first, to let *him* see me. To let anyone see me naked, fully lit, flaws and all. And he's in no rush. Once he has the shirt off, he just runs his hands over my shoulders, down my arms. Catches my waist, holds there, hands wrapped around me just above my hips. His eyes take me in, travel slowly from eyes to throat to breast. I lick my lips and meet his gaze, letting my own hunger for him, my own appreciation for his body fuel my confidence in myself. But the thing that shifts me from self-conscious in my half-dressed state to confident? Him. His eyes, on me. His expression.

Has any man ever been able to so clearly tell me how beautiful he finds me with no more than a *look*? No more than an expression on his face? Thai hasn't said a word since peeling off my blouse, but his eyes say all that needs to be said.

He wants me naked for him, but he's dragging this

out on purpose, savoring each moment of the journey from clothed to nude.

I rest my hands on his shoulders and wait for him.

Instead of going for the bra next, his fingers travel around the waist of my skirt and seek the zipper. Find it. Slowly lower it, inch by inch, until the garment is loose, and then with a flick of his wrists, the skirt floats to pool around my feet. Kick off my shoes, toe them aside.

With each garment I lose, I feel more confident. More in need of his touch. His eyes on all of me. I want to be naked with him. I want that stupid towel off, but I make myself wait. Delay my own gratification.

He bites his lip, and I somehow know he's trying to decide what to take off me next—bra or underwear.

I guide his hands to my waist. "You handle these," I say, and then reach up behind my back. "I'll handle this."

He grins, shoving my underwear down. "I like this plan. Gets you naked faster."

"I thought you'd like that." I unhook the clasps and shrug the bra forward and off, stepping out of the underwear at the same time. "Your turn."

"I figured—okay." His protest was cut short as I yanked the towel off him.

I slide my fingernails down his abs, over his navel, to his burgeoning erection. "Hey, I missed you too, you know. You're not the only one with needs, here, buster."

He hisses as I wrap my hands around him. "But I had plans for you. You're gonna derail them, if you keep that up."

"You had plans, huh?" I feel need swelling inside me, expanding in my chest, blossoming in my belly, soaking my core. Making my hands greedy for him. "What if I had plans of my own, Thai? Did you ever think of that? Huh? What if I've spent the entire weekend dreaming about *this*?" I squeeze him, not bothering to stifle my groan of pleasure at the feel of his thick hard flesh in my fist. "What if I spent the entire flight and the whole drive here trying to decide what I wanted more…"

I ply him with both hands, now.

"Doing this…" I say, with a squeeze and a twist. "Or…*this*?"

I drop to my knees, crumpling my skirt under my knees for padding against the tile. Pull him away from his belly and kiss the tip, a brush of my lips, as if I was taking the first bite of an ice cream cone.

"Ohhh fuck, Dee." His hands bury in my hair, knotting convulsively. "Jesus, your mouth."

I stroke him, both hands, twisting. Lick the tip. "Want to know something about me, Thai?"

He hisses, then groans, and his eyes flutter into the back of his head. "Whazz'at?" God, he's gone adorably stupid.

"I don't…do this, a lot." I pause, plunge my fists down to his root, and then pull him toward my face and take a mouthful of him, bobbing down on him until I'm swallowing around him. "But not for the reasons you may think."

"What reasons…uhh…what reasons do think I would assume?"

"That I don't like doing it. That I'm too prudish for it."

He gathers my hair in his hands, two fistfuls of my black tresses, piling it on my head. His head tips back as I pull my mouth off him, lick the tip, then up the side facing me from midway to the tip, and then take a mouthful of him and bob down around him again.

"You…you wouldn't be wrong. Clearly, those assumptions are—are incorrect, however."

"Very much so."

"Enlighten me?"

I kiss the head, then suction my lips around the head and suckle while swirling my tongue against him. "It's a kind of contrariness, you might say." Another kiss, another lick. I watch his face, enjoying the expression of *his-brain-is-a-puddle-of-goo* intensifying with each movement of my mouth on him, each touch of my tongue.

I caress him with my hands while I answer him. "Most of the time, I get an impression like it's expected of me. Which is like a light switch for me—immediate turn-off. No chance."

"I don't…I don't expect anything."

I rub my thumb over the tip, my other hand slowly pumping at his base. "I know, Thai. And that's why I'm doing this. You were all set to do all this amazing stuff for me. You never even hinted at what I might want to do for you, or what you want me to do to you."

"Because I'm more concerned with what we can do together." He meets my eyes. "I'm more concerned with how I can make you feel good." He attempts to pull me to my feet. "You had a long weekend. I want to pamper you. Relax you." He swallows hard, brows furrowing when I resist his attempts to pull me away from him. "Make you feel good. Show you that I—show you how much you mean to me."

"What you've planned for me is not lost on me, Thai—trust me. And you will do everything you've got planned and more." I palm his balls with one hand and massage them gently, smirking and biting my lip around an amused huff as his eyes literally cross. "After I've gotten what *I* want. Because when I tell you that I had wet dreams and daydreams about doing this to you, all weekend long, I am in no way exaggerating."

I plunge my other hand around him, a little faster now. Smile up at him as he swallows as if doing it requires active concentration. As if he has to remind himself to breathe.

"Why?"

"Why?" I laugh. Put my lips around him and swirl my tongue against him and then plunge him to the back of my throat, as far as I feel comfortable. Swallow around him. Back away. "Same reason you're going to enjoy going down on me, once you've got me on that table. It makes me feel good. And you get off on my pleasure almost as much as you get off on your own."

"More," he whispers. "Your pleasure is more important to me than my own."

"I know," I answer, in a whisper of my own. I stroke him, one-handed, still cupping his sack with the other. "Now. Stop asking questions and let me focus on making you feel good."

He groans a ragged sigh as I continue the gentle massaging cradle of his heavy balls and begin a slow rhythm with my mouth, up and down, licking at the apex and swallow at the bottom of the movement.

Faster.

He hisses through gritted teeth. His eyes wrench open and his brow furrows, watching as his cock disappears into my mouth, my jaw stretched wide to accommodate his immensity. "Fucking hell, Dee," he growls.

I smile around him, or try to communicate a smile without being able to actually move my mouth—it's otherwise *fully* occupied.

He's tensed, now, and I know he's close. I'm learning him. He doesn't want it to end and doesn't want to forget himself and start thrusting and risk hurting me, so he freezes and goes tense all over, muscles isometrically clenched.

I want his orgasm. Now.

It's all I'm focused on. The taste of him, salt and skin and musk of pre-cum. The feel of him sliding through my lips. Against my throat. Filling my mouth until I have to swallow around him. The way he groans continuously. The way his hands snarl in my hair as if only just barely holding himself back from pulling me onto him harder, faster.

I don't know that I'd mind if he did. I want him unbridled. Fierce and unrestrained.

"Oh god, Delia. Dee, fuck, fuck, your mouth is fucking…fucking heaven." His voice is a ragged, broken thing.

I taste him nearing the edge.

His hips flex, now, helplessly.

I grasp his cock in both hands and stroke him, just beneath my lips, helping him to the end of his control, to the end of his ability to hold back.

In the split second before he comes, he does something unexpected, and in so doing, makes one of my fantasies come true: he rips himself away from me, staggering backward with a hoarse grunt of wild effort, every muscle strained and his breathing deep ragged gasps as if he just sprinted a hundred meters full out. Stomach heaving. Abs braced hard. Cock straining, standing flat upright against his belly, leaking at the tip.

His eyes are wild, almost angry with the ferocity of his need. "I *want* you, Delia." He's a raging god of sexual primacy, muscles veined and bulging, a sheen of sweat coating his body as if the sheer physical demand of pulling away and holding off his climax required a herculean effort. "*Need* you."

I stand up and prowl toward him, and when he catches back up against the massage table, I throw myself against him, bury my fingers in his hair. "Thai, you have no fucking idea how hot that was." I feel him throbbing between our bodies. I could lift up on my toes and take him into me, right now, so easily.

The temptation is intense. My whole being demands it.

NEED.

My plans, his plans, it all goes out the window. Especially when he kisses me. Surely, he must taste himself on my breath, but he kisses me so hungrily either he doesn't notice or he doesn't care. Or he likes it. I don't know. And it doesn't matter, because my breath is stolen and my very soul is taken by him, swept up in the savage need of his kiss.

God, I need him.

It would be so easy. We fit together just right. We line up as if…as if our bodies were created to fit together like two pieces of a puzzle.

I'm on birth control, and I never miss. Never.

I want him.

I need him.

I wrap my arms around his neck and just lose myself in his mouth, in breathing him and tasting him and being pressed up against the hard cliff face of his body, the springy give of his dense muscles. His hands take my body for his playground, scraping down my spine to clutch my ass with greedy strength.

I moan into his mouth. "Thai…."

He grips me, hips pressing to push against me. He

needs this, every bit as desperately as I do. "God, Delia, I want you so fucking bad, right now."

I rest my forehead against his, lean against him, crushing my breasts against his chest. One arm clings to his shoulders.

I give in.

I need him too badly.

He makes all my fantasies come true, and I need this, right now. Not in the thirty seconds it would take to get protection. I know he's clean. I know I am. All these thoughts are not just secondary, they're tertiary, distant, vague. All I know is my need for him.

I rise up on my toes, tilt my hips toward him, and feel his thickness scrape against my sex. Hold on to his neck with one arm and lean against him with all my weight. Both of his hands are clawed into my ass, and he helps me rise. Lifts me. I wedge a hand between us and guide him to me.

It happens all at once, in a single smooth slide.

The head of him drags against my slick sex, and then catches against the opening, and I grasp him, fit him to me, and I feel the moment he enters me.

I whimper as he fills me.

He matches my whimper with a rough groan of surprise. "Delia, my god...my Delia."

Sink down on him, take him fully, and I'm split apart. Destroyed by perfection, ruined by the ecstasy of our union.

No fantasy, no wet dream, no daydream could ever

have prepared me for this reality. It's too wonderful for words, too incredible to articulate. I cannot even breathe for the way he feels inside me. Full doesn't begin to describe it. I *ache* with him.

"Thai," I whisper, and sag on him, let him take my weight in his hands, on our joining, and I gasp at the deepening. "I need this. Need you. Need *more*."

He takes my lower lip in his teeth, nips hard. Then kisses my jaw, my throat, tilts my head up to kiss from the underside of my chin all the way down, and then he dips at the knees and lifts me into the air. My legs lock around his waist and I hold on. He takes two long strides across the bathroom and kicks the door closed with a loud slam. Pins me against it, hands underneath my ass holding me in place. Buried to the hilt inside me.

"I was gonna do a whole thing with rose petals and candles in the bedroom. Take my time with you, nice and slow and gentle. Romance you."

I curl my arms around his neck, one hand gripping his opposite shoulder while the other cradles his jaw, his cheek. "Hold that thought, Thai—I want that." I roll my hips. "But right now, I need *this*."

He groans, and pulls away, lowers his head to take my nipple in his mouth. Licks, kisses, suckles, releases. Repeats on the other side, and then straightens to claim my mouth again.

Drives his hips forward, surging deeper into me— even though I hadn't thought he could get any deeper.

When he does, a growl of surprised bliss is torn from my lips.

"This?" he asks, powering up into me once more. "This is what you need?"

I cling to him for balance, brace on his shoulders and use my thighs around his hips to lift up. Meet him on his upstroke by letting myself fall onto him. "Yes, god yes, Thai. That. All of that."

He's still going slow, gentle. "Fucking hell, Dee, you feel so fucking good."

"Show me how good, Thai." I roll with him, lowering myself hard onto his upstrokes, breathless with the wild delirium of him inside me. "I'm not delicate," I whisper. "I'm not fragile. I'm strong."

"I know," he murmurs, rising up against me, growling as he buries into me as deeply as our union allows. "I know you are."

"So show me." I bite his lip, sharply, and he hisses in surprise. "Show me, Thai. I can take everything you can give me. I want it all. All of you. Don't hold back. Don't you *dare* fucking hold back, Matthais Bristow."

"God, Delia. You make me so fucking crazy," he growls, surging harder into me.

I meet him thrust for thrust, taking him and rolling my hips harder to demand more. "Good. *Show* me. I want your crazy."

He snarls. Adjusts his grip on my ass, tugging me farther apart, so he can go deeper. "How can you be real?" He gasps for breath, and even that is a helpless groan of delirious desire. "How can you be mine?"

"How can *I* be *yours*?" I whisper. "I don't even know. But I am. And you are. This is real. We're real. And I want more. Fucking *more*, Thai."

With a wild, desperate sound of abandon, his mouth crashes against mine and our tongues tangle and our breath is a fusion. He hikes me higher and presses me hard against the door and now he truly lets go. His movements become desperate and crazed, his thrusts beautifully rough, almost violent. I'm shaken by his thrusts. I cry out with pleasure at each one, throwing my head back as he snarls gutturally each time he drives into me, surging home. My breasts jounce with his thrusts, bouncing upward, and his hips slap loudly against my ass. I cry with each thrust, and each cry is louder, wilder.

I can't move, now. Can't do anything but hold on and take it, cling to him and delight in each new pounding thrust.

"Thai!" I scream. "Ohmygod...*Thai*, yes, god yes!" My chants break into sobs, then, wordless and shattered as I dissolve into an orgasm that builds and builds.

It's as much emotional as it is sexual, this climax of mine.

Of *ours*.

Because he's there with me.

"With me, Thai," I beg, gasping, lips against his.

"With me. Now, now, please now, please come with me, come with me Thai, I want you to come with me."

He makes a sound I can't interpret, like a gasp or a growl, or something in between. There are no words to it, because there are no words for this.

He pushes up into me, and I roll my hips to take it, to meet it. Try to lift and sink, to make it more, to make it better, seeking deeper connection. I'm gasping, crying, and I feel tears on my cheeks, wet trails on my chin, so savaged by this endless mad climax am I—and Thai is moaning, thrusting, and his groan breaks, and I feel the emotion in him.

Touch my forehead to his and then kiss his temple. He surges, and I feel him stagger, not under my weight but the breaking of his own strength, under the ravaging intensity of his swelling climax as it builds to meet mine. I kiss his cheekbone, his jaw. I kiss his eyes, and I taste salt.

I open my eyes and pull back, meet his gaze.

He ducks his head as if to hide the evidence of his emotion, but I cup his jaw and prevent him from hiding it. I smile at him and I kiss his eyes and his cheeks.

His face crumples, and his mouth drops open, and a groan rips from his throat, and he surges up against me, sliding as deep as possible, and then I feel him explode inside me.

He shakes all over, clutching me, desperately fighting to stay upright, to hold me in place. I'm filled with him as he gasps raggedly and thrusts again, and again, each one accompanied by a snarl and a groan, and I come around him, teeth gritted as I scream with clenching, smashing explosions, racked and battered by a thousand waves of ecstasy.

Finally, he can't stand up anymore.

We sink to the ground, and I go to my back and accept his weight and somehow I never lost him—I couldn't explain how we made it from standing to missionary on the floor without losing our union, but here we are and it's not over…I'm shaking, every muscle trembling, sex spasming and rippling around him, tightening and quivering.

He's braced above me, helplessly driving into me, as if he cannot stop until he's chased every last drop of heaven out of each of us.

I wipe at his cheeks. Smile.

He shakes his head. "I'm sorry, Delia. I don't know what—"

I cradle his ass in my hands and pull him closer. "Don't apologize, Thai," I murmur, kissing his chin, and then his cheeks, still damp. "I love it."

He frowns. "I…It's…"

I touch his lips to shush him. "It's manly. It's masculine. It's powerful." I gnaw on his lower lip, smiling as I do so. "There's nothing so intimate and sexy as a man who can be vulnerable."

"It's you," he says. "You…" He laughs. "You bring out the best in me."

"Why do you laugh when you say that?" I ask.

"Because it's gotten flipped. Used to be, you brought out the worst in me."

I pet and massage the taut hardness of his ass, just enjoying that I can, how it feels. "Let's make one rule, right now, going forward."

"Okay?"

"No more talking about what used to be. Okay?" I kiss his lips, delicate and tender and slow. "It's over. It's past. I don't care about it anymore. I care about *now*. I care about *you*." I pause, hesitate, swallow hard. "Us."

He blinks hard. "Us, huh?"

I bite my lip and nod. "On the plane home, I was talking to this older guy next to me, and I referred to you as my boyfriend."

Chapter
TWENTY-ONE

Matthais

M Y HEART, ALREADY STUTTERING FROM THE INTENSITY OF what just happened, stops completely. "You… did?"

She nods, her fingernails tickling and scratching in circles on my buttocks. "I sure did. It just sort of popped out and shocked the hell out of me. And then I was just like…oh. Okay."

I lever backward and upright, scooping her up—she ends up sitting on my lap as I sit cross-legged on the cold marble. "You're my girlfriend."

She grins, nods. "Sure am." Her brow furrows in a frown even as her lips curl up in a smile; it's a confused expression. "I've dated quite a few men, but I've never self-identified as anyone's girlfriend. And I've certainly never claimed a man as my boyfriend."

"How does it feel?"

Her eyes hunt mine. A shrug, which does delightful

things to her breasts. "I like it. It's still weird, that this is happening at all, and that it's happening with you." She clasps her hands behind my neck. "But I really like it. It just feels…right."

I tuck her hair behind her ears, touch her face. The more I look at her, the more I marvel at her beauty. I hope she sees it in my expression, because I simply don't have words for it. "It doesn't feel right to me."

She frowns, confused, the beginnings of hurt creasing her face. "W—what? What do you mean?"

I smile, not quite laughing. "I mean, it feels too good to be true." I run my thumb over her lips. "I can't believe I get to be here with you. That I got to experience that with you. I keep waiting to wake up, for this all to be a dream." I swallow hard, emotion yet again welling up in me and threatening to take over, to make me a blubbering mess. I rule it, but just barely. "I don't deserve you, Delia."

"You may not think so," she says, "But I do."

Her expression so soft, so understanding, so…accepting, that it cuts into my ability to remain dry-eyed and stable. It just cuts my heart open and exposes all the soft gooey shit that I've kept bottled up my whole life. The need to be accepted. The desire to be the center of someone's affection. The desire to belong to someone.

My parents cared about me. But their way of showing that was material. Not verbal, not physical.

"Tell me what you're thinking, Thai," she whispers.

"Please. I can see you thinking, and I can tell it's deep, and I want you to share it with me."

I swallow that lump—or try to, yet again. "I…"

She touches my face. "I have a better idea? How about we talk in the tub?"

"The bath was for you."

"Overruled. The bath is for us." She smiles, caresses my hair away from my face. "You ever taken a bath?"

"Not since I was a toddler."

"So you've never taken a bath *with* someone?"

I snort. "Not hardly."

"Me either. So this will be a nice first for both of us" She kisses my chin. "Help me up so I can pee." A wince. "I'm, um, juicy."

I stand up with her, set her on her feet near the toilet, which is one of those that's in its own separate little room.

I turn away to give her privacy, but she doesn't close the door. It's oddly, endearingly intimate to hear her pee, to hear the rustle of toilet paper. I'd always thought that once you crossed that particular Rubicon, the mystery of the relationship was over.

But…

I find myself even more enamored. She's even more real, even more human. Sharing something as intimate and personal as that makes me crave her even more, to know her even more. It's a privilege, to be allowed so far into the inner workings of her life.

She emerges, washes her hands. "Was that weird?" she asks. "Should I have closed the door?"

I shake my head. "No. I was just thinking about how much of an incredible privilege it feels like, that you're letting me so close. I don't mean physically, but that way too. I just mean…sharing the intimacy of life."

She leans against me, her hands still damp from being washed, not bothering to dry them. "It almost seems like you're self-conscious, in a way, Thai." A puzzled frown, thoughtful. "That's not quite right. Not self-conscious. It's like you don't quite see your value to me."

She takes my hand, leads me to the tub. Swishes her hand in the water. Twists the hot water on, opens the drain to let water out while it refills with hot water. In a moment, she closes the drain and shuts off the water. Tests the temperature again, and then nods. Glances at me.

"After you," I say.

She climbs in, moving gingerly to avoid splashing or causing an overflow. I watch each and every movement greedily, hungry for every angle, every curve. The arch of her spine as she bends, hands on the sides of the tub. The bend of her thigh as it swells to become her buttocks. The delicate fold of her belly, the taut muscles visible— she's *powerful*, strong, vibrant. She lowers herself into the water, steam wreathing around her face.

A sigh escapes her. "Get in," she murmurs, her eyes on me. "It's hot."

I put my feet in, sitting on the edge. She opens the drain again, and more water gurgles out, and when I brace my hands on the sides and lower myself in, the overflow drain sucks noisily. She closes the drain once I'm settled, and the water hovers right at the point of sloshing over, the overflow drain working overtime.

I have my knees drawn up, and Delia smirks, reaching forward to pull my legs to either side of her, extending her legs over mine, feet against the crease of my hips.

Her hands rest on my knees, mine on her thighs. This position isn't sexual, but it is the most intimate I've ever been with anyone, in a way.

A moment of silence.

"Thai, I just want you to know…" Her cheeks are tinged pink. "That wasn't planned. But I don't regret it."

I don't know what to say. Guilt and worry have been percolating. "Delia, I…I shouldn't have—" I shake my head. "Number one, I'm clean. I've never… I've never been like that with anyone. Unprotected, I mean."

"Thai…" She grabs my hand, and water sloshes over the side. "It was *my* idea. I wanted it."

"I just…I should have asked if you were sure. If…I assumed you're on birth control, but I just feel irresponsible for not making sure."

She huffs, an actual laugh. "Thai, you're not responsible for my choices—I am. I knew exactly what I was doing." Her toes tickle my ribs. Flick against my member, threatening to start me up again. "I *am* protected, just so you know. But it wasn't a moment of weakness, or a lapse in judgment. It was a conscious choice. I *wanted* you." She holds my eyes. "Hear me, Thai. I needed you inside me, and I took what I wanted. And I don't regret it. I...I fucking *loved* it. More than anything, literally ever. I'm still shaky."

"I just...I wanted our first time to be...romantic. I had this whole thing planned, you know? I'd give you a massage and you'd take a bath and I'd make you come a few times, and then in the morning we'd have slow sleepy romantic sex."

She grins, bubbles around her chin, rosebud tips of her breasts poking up out of the water, a thin scrim of bubbles sliding down the slopes. "I still want that, so you'd better deliver now that you've promised me that." She keeps rubbing me with her toes, wherever her feet reach. "But. You need to understand something."

"What's that?"

"That I'm just as needy and horny as you are. That I want you every bit as much as you want me. That I'm not just...*allowing* you to do things to me. Or *giving* you little moments, little pieces. It's not an exchange, or a transaction. Like, you gave me an orgasm so I *suppose* I'll let you have one, too. Or, you went down on me so I *guess* I'll let you have sex with me." She smirks, sniffs a laugh. "I want you. I want things with you. Since things started with you, I've had fantasies of you. I've struggled with that, too. That it's you. That I shouldn't want you. That I shouldn't be attracted to you. But I am, Thai. I do.

I can't get enough. I really can't. I'm still all quivery from the last orgasm, but I already want another."

I grin. "I can oblige."

"I know you can. And believe me, I invite you to take every available opportunity to make me come. Give me as many orgasms as is humanly possible, *please*. I want them, all of them. Wake me up with them, tease me, surprise me, challenge me, dare me. I want it all—you make me want things I didn't know were possible. You make me feel…crazy, daring, wild. Thai, you bring out the best in me, too. More than you can know." She shakes her head, emotion swirling in her eyes, in her expression. "I was…I think I was only half living until you came along."

I can reach her sex, so I trail my fingers along her seam. Tease her, touch her. "It doesn't seem possible, but I'll take it. I'll earn the trust and faith you're showing me."

She sits up, more water splashing over the sides. Takes my hands and grips hard. "Thai, no. Listen, okay, listen. Like I said earlier, the past is past."

"I know, but—"

She shakes her head. "*No*, Thai. There's no earning." Her expression is fraught, wild blue depths blazing with meaning and intensity and purpose. "Maybe you need to hear the words—and maybe I need to say them: I *forgive* you, Matthais."

I'm choked, eyes burning. Duck my head, instinctively. "Thank you, Delia. I…"

She forces my head up. "No hiding."

I blink. But I can't hide it. And she doesn't flinch away from my emotions. If anything, it draws her closer. Opens her up yet more. I shake my head. "I don't know what to say," I whisper, eventually.

"How about you tell me what you were thinking about earlier."

I duck my head and laugh, then meet her eyes again. "I'll try." I go back to what I was thinking about—acceptance and affection and all that. "So, warning…it's pretty deep. Maybe even heavy. Definitely personal and…I don't know. It's a lot."

"I can handle it, whatever it is."

"I know you can. It's just stuff I've never really thought about too much, and certainly never shared."

"But you're gonna share it with me?"

I nod. "I am."

She settles backward again, water up to her chin. "I'm listening."

"So, my parents." I sigh and keep going. Once the words start, it gets easier. "They care about me. I grew up with a sort of understanding that Mom and Dad care about me. Right? Like, they're my parents, of course they care about me. But…they're not…emotive people."

She laughs. "No kidding. I have noticed this." She tilts her head to one side. "Funny thing is, in some way, I probably know them better than you do. Your parents, I mean. You left for college and you rarely came back. Whereas I've lived next door to them my whole life, and I see them pretty frequently, when they're in town. They come over for drinks and we play pinochle." Her face falls. "Or, we did, before Dad passed. Hard to play five-hand pinochle with only four people. And it wouldn't be the same."

She brightens, shakes her head to banish the sad reverie. "Anyway. Sorry, I hijacked the moment. You were saying?"

I smile at her. "So anyway...they never said that they cared. Or rarely. Certainly not Dad." I shrug. "They showed me in other ways. Bought me literally anything and everything. Took me on vacations. Put me in karate and fencing lessons and riding lessons and all that shit, whatever it was I expressed interest in. But I never had to stick with anything. If I wanted to quit because I was bored, I quit." I laugh, wave a hand. "Point is, that's how they showed me affection. Buying me stuff, giving me what I wanted, when I wanted it. They...physical affection wasn't something they did either. Once I was too big to be carried, and too old to need hugs and kisses when I hurt myself, that kind of stuff stopped."

"That's...actually really sad, Thai. Everyone needs hugs and kisses."

I nod. "I'm not excusing, or even explaining, except maybe to myself. Maybe that's why I turned to hooking up the way I did. Why I've never had a real relationship. Showing emotions, talking about emotions—it's hard for me. Accepting it is even harder."

"So, when I touch you, like nonsexual affection..."

I shrug, uncomfortable and hot under my skin and working hard to keep the honesty going, to give her the real me when so much of me wants to shut down, to distract, to avoid. "It's...I don't know what to do with it, Dee. It makes me feel like I'm..." I shake my head, searching for the right expression. "It makes my heart feel like it's breaking open. But...because it's so full. It's kind of scary but..."

She smiles, beautiful, tender—that daring, emotional smile which makes me feel like my whole soul is going to overflow, burst out of my skin. Because it's so lush and so lovely and real and beautiful and delicate and soft and it's meant for *me*, and I want to hide from it as much as I want to hoard it and inscribe it on my mind and my heart so I never forget that *she* can smile at *me* this way.

"Thai, I'm noticing something, here."

"Okay?"

"You used the word 'care.'" An arch of her eyebrow. "Your parents care for you. Showed you they care."

I'm not following. Or...that's what I'm trying to convince myself of, at least. "Okay, and?"

"And, you're stopping short."

I swallow hard. "Of what?"

"The correct word." She rubs her forehead, and leaves bubbles trailing down her face; I brush them away, only to make it worse, and we both laugh. "I know my parents *love* me, Thai...my dad *loved* me. He showed me he loved me, told me he loved me."

My skin feels too tight for my face. My heart is hammering so hard it hurts. Under the water, my hands shake. "Dee…"

She sits upright, scuttles closer to me, hooks her legs around my waist and hers around mine. Clings to me, our soapy bodies slippery and warm against each other. "So when I do and say things that show you I…*care*…" She runs her hand over my hair. Soap trickles down my neck. Her breath is light and warm on my nose. Her breasts are soft against my chest. Her thighs squeeze my waist, like a hug. "That makes you uncomfortable?"

"Not uncomfortable, I just…it's unfamiliar." Truth requires bravery. "I crave it, Delia—but it's scary."

"That's okay," she says. "I'm not asking anything of you—and listen, it's new and different and scary for me, too. We can take this slow."

"That's what's scary, though, Delia—it's not going slow. For me, in here." I tap my chest.

She cups the back of my neck. "I know. Me too."

"I know what it's developing into, and I just…I can only do my best to be man enough to show you how I feel. To maybe even…say it." I laugh, a sharp huff. "God, why is that so hard?"

"Because it's unfamiliar and it's vulnerable. It means I could reject you, or somehow otherwise hurt you. I could change my mind. I could meet someone better." When my face shows my obvious turmoil at this, she just smiles and clings tighter, with arms and legs. "But I won't."

"No?"

She shakes her head. "Nope. I won't change my mind about you. I won't reject you or hurt you—at least not on purpose, but I'm no more perfect than you are, and at some point I'm going to do or say something that's gonna hurt you. But it won't be on purpose." She bites my chin, then kisses my lips. But before I can kiss her back, she keeps talking. "And I sure as hell won't ever meet anyone better."

That blows my mind. "You're crazy."

She nods. "Yeah." A nuzzle of her nose against mine; this is the stuff that makes me feel like my heart could explode. "About you. You're amazing, Thai."

I shake my head, but it's in amazement, not denial; I don't even know how we suddenly got here, to this place of tenderness and open affection, but I like it. A fucking lot.

"It feels amazing to hear you say that," I say.

"I mean it."

I rest my forehead on hers. "I care about you, Delia. A whole hell of a lot."

"I know." A smirk, a laugh. "I care a whole hell of a lot about you too, Thai." The smirk turns into a grin. "I think I'm ready for that massage, now."

I stand, step out of the tub, bubbles and water streaming off me—and the look on her face as she watches me tells me her words about wanting me were not idle, or empty. The appreciation and desire on her face is undeniable.

I towel off quickly, then wrap the towel around my waist, but Delia has other ideas.

"Leave it off," she says, taking it and tossing it aside. "What's the point in a sexy massage if I don't get to look at you naked."

"As you wish," I say, and then take a fresh towel.

She stands up and I lift her from the tub and take my time drying her, paying perhaps inordinate amounts of attention to drying her breasts and buttocks.

Eventually, she laughs. "I think I'm dry, now, Thai."

I give her left breast one last scrub. "There. Now you're dry."

Setting her rose on the sink, I replace the books into the box and put it on the floor of the bedroom just outside the door, and then I drape another clean, dry towel over the massage table. I guide her to it, lay her down on her stomach, arms at her sides.

For the next forty minutes, I use everything I know about massages, which, admittedly, isn't much, but I do my best, beginning at her scalp and ending at her toes, front and back. Slowly, her body loosens and relaxes, and she goes heavy, limp. When I've massaged all her muscle groups, she's on her back, breathing slowly, eyes closed. Not asleep, I don't think, but close.

Her eyes flicker. A tiny, faint smile curves her lips. "Do you do happy endings?"

"You're my happy ending," I say.

"Tease."

I bend over her, standing at the side of the table,

and touch my lips to her. "What kind of a massage did you think this was?"

She hums, a relaxed version of a laugh. "You *did* mention the possibility of an orgasm as part of this romantic massage experience."

"I think I remember saying something along those lines."

She grins, licks her lips. "I'm not too proud to beg, Thai."

I touch my lips to hers again. "You *never* have to beg, Delia. I'm the one who should beg you for the privilege of being allowed to touch you."

She grins, following me with her eyes as I round to the end of the table, running my hands up her shins, to her thighs. "Go on."

I lean over her, kiss her knees, her quads. "Delia, I beg you, please, let me make you come."

She parts her legs, draws her feet up to her butt. "I'll allow it. But on one condition."

"What's that?" I ask, playing along.

"You may only use your mouth."

"Challenge accepted." I haul her to the very end of the table, fold a towel under my knees.

Grab her ankles and drape her legs over my shoulders, and then cup her ass, lift her. She shivers, watching, eager, anticipating. Biting her lip, hips tilting up. Flexing up toward my mouth as I bring my lips to her inner thighs, teasing nibbles and licks and kisses upward toward her center.

"Please, Thai—please. I want it so bad. Give me that mouth, Thai—you make me so crazy."

I moan at her words. "You know what makes me crazy? You, talking dirty. That makes me go nuts."

Her teeth clamp on her lower lip as I abandon the pretense of teasing her. "You like it when I talk dirty?" She gasps when I flick my tongue against her. "When I tell you how much I love the things you do with your mouth?"

"Drives me crazy." I lock my lips over her clit, flick my tongue against her, and she moans.

"Ohhh god, Thai. Your mouth—your tongue. Fuck, oh god, don't stop."

"I won't stop till you beg me to stop."

She knots her fingers in my hair, and her hips flex. Tilt, grind. Her moans are loud and wild and abandoned, wanton and free. "Thai, yes, god…don't stop. Oh fuck, that feels so good."

"What feels good? Tell me. Say it."

"Your mouth on me."

"Where? On you where?" I tease, now, light flicks, slow circles.

"On my pussy."

I growl, and give her what she wants, my tongue, fast and stabbing and licking until her hips are gyrating.

"Thai, oh *god*…ohgodohgod—" Her eyes wrench open. Meet mine. "Fingers. Need—your fingers. Inside me. Do—do the thing with your fingers while you lick my pussy."

"You said only my mouth." I smirk.

"I was an idiot," she says. "It sounded hotter than it is. The thing with your fingers…I fucking need it. It makes me come *so* hard."

I slide a finger inside her and curl, massage where she likes it best.

"More," she demands. "More fingers."

I laugh and oblige. Two middle fingers, deep inside her, curling and plunging, and now she's moaning nonstop, and her hips are rolling to drive her sex against my mouth. Her legs lock around my neck, toes hooked around her heels, and I lift her, help her move, bring her closer. She's frantic, soon, chasing the edge, and I push her over with everything I've got.

When she starts screaming, I moan. Her hips flex madly, grinding against me as I pursue her farthest extremes of ecstasy, making her screams break into moans, and then breaking her moans down into gasps, and still she comes, hips bridged upward, whole body quivering and tensed. Her gasps have dissolved into a breathless silent scream, chin trembling, tears pooling her tight-squeezed eyes.

And then she gasps for breath, finally, sucking in a ragged lungful of oxygen. "Oh my *fuck*, Thai. I'm dead." She goes limp, boneless.

"Oh my fuck," I echo, laughing, sinking back to sit on my heels. "That's a new one."

"*That* was a hell of an orgasm," she says, then cranes

her head up just enough to meet my eye. "Come up here."

I stand up. Round the side of the table, plant my hands on either side of her face. "Hi."

She scratches my jaw. "Thank you."

I frown and laugh. "Why are you thanking me?"

"For all of this. For the candles, the rose. The books. The absolutely *incredible* sex. The bath. The massage. The orgasm." A happy sigh. "That was a really, *really* good orgasm."

She pulls my face down and kisses me. "Mmm. You taste like me. Not sure how I feel about that." Another kiss. "Kinda tangy."

I laugh. "I love the way you taste. Honestly, I do. You're sweet as sugar."

She hums the chords of a recent popular song involving a certain melon and sugar, and I laugh. She reaches her arms up around me and clings to my neck. "Take me to bed and hold me."

I lift her in my arms, and her nose nuzzles against my neck—she inhales, and sighs, as if the scent of me is reassuring, comforting. Holds tight. When I set her on the bed and pull back the covers, she just watches me, and waits as I go around blowing out all the candles—and let me say, it takes almost as long to blow them all out as it did to light them. Eventually, all the tea lights are out, and I climb into bed next to Delia. She rolls toward me, reaching for me; her head goes onto my chest, her thigh over mine. Hand on my belly. Breathing soft, slow.

"Be here when I wake up, 'kay?" Her voice is already muzzy and faint.

"I will be. I promise."

I have an arm around her, underneath her, cupping her hip. Somehow, my other hand finds hers, and I cradle her hand inside me, as if sheltering it, protecting it.

She's soft as silk, warm as a summer wind. Flesh and curves against me. I'm hypersensitive to every point of contact between our bodies.

I assume she's asleep based on her breathing, so I'm surprised when she speaks.

"Thai?"

"Hmm?" My own voice is drowsy; the comfort of her in my arms is like intoxication, but infinitely better.

"Don't be scared."

"Huh?"

A pause. The words sound like they're bubbling up from the depths of her, unfiltered as she tumbles into sleep. "Don't be scared, Thai…"

"Of what, honey? What would I be scared of?"

She nestles closer. Nothing has ever been more right than this, her and me. "I think I love you."

Everything inside me contracts, clenches. I know I go tense.

"Don't say anything." This is a faint whisper. More asleep than awake.

"Delia…"

Her hand leaves the shelter of my hand, drifts up.

Finds my face, my jaw, pats me. Scratches. Rests there. "I know. We have forever. It's okay."

I'm spinning.

Don't be scared…I think I love you.

I *am* scared.

But more than I'm scared, I crave her.

I…

I crave her affection. I crave her touch. Her kisses. Her body.

I crave her love.

To be loved—to be told that I am loved, to be shown, physically, to have it demonstrated the way she so bravely does…it fills the hole in me that I hadn't even realized was there.

Quietly, holding her asleep in my arms, I let myself cry with that realization.

I'm not embarrassed. It's not emasculating. It's real. It's human.

She loves me.

She's not demanding anything from me.

I fall asleep, eventually, still wondering at the marvel that is the woman in my arms.

Chapter
TWENTY-TWO

Delia

I WAKE SLOWLY, BUT MY SENSES TELL ME I'M NOT IN MY HOME. I'm somewhere unfamiliar. It's the scent in the air, the...*feeling*.

But then I wake more fully, and memories flood me. Even before I open my eyes, I'm smiling. Because as awareness of my surroundings picks up, I feel him.

Which means all those memories were not dreams. I didn't dream any of it.

I let my eyes remain closed and let the smile hover on my lips and I revisit last night.

Coming home, exhausted but excited to be going home to Thai. The candles. The rose. A whole box of signed copies of my favorite childhood books. The best sex of my entire life, bar none, by several orders of magnitude.

All the sex I ever had before him was, cumulatively, a small firecracker going off. Not even an M80, just one of those cheap crappy ones you get from a roadside stand. Last night, bare, with Thai? That was a nuclear detonation.

I sigh, remembering.

And *I* initiated it. I feel proud of that. I wanted him, and I took what I wanted. I didn't wait for him, I didn't hold back, I didn't shy away from myself, from my own needs. I didn't hide.

I've always pushed what I want and need behind the veil of what I *have* to do—work. That always came first. The company. Dad. Taking over, all of it. Thai blew into my life and knocked all the pieces of my life askew and awry, but it helped me reprioritize.

I matter. What I want matters. What I need matters.

Thai has helped me see that. Showed me that.

The bath, and the things he told me about himself.

The massage.

God, the massage.

The orgasm at the end was…beyond words.

He's behind me, arm flung low over my hip.

As I consider turning toward him, he twists to face away—and I realize I have a certain need which cannot be ignored any longer. A quick trip to the bathroom— including a rinse of my mouth with mouthwash—and I'm back in bed, bladder relieved and hands washed. This time I snuggle up behind him. Press up behind his big hard body, curl against him. Wrap a hand around his waist.

I don't quite doze, just rest like that, not quite sleepy but perfectly content to lay holding him.

After a time I couldn't put a number to, he stirs. I feel him waking. His hand covers mine.

He rolls to his back, and his eyes fix on me. "Hi."

I smile. "Hi there, beautiful."

"Isn't that my line?"

I shake my head against the pillow. "Nah. You're beautiful to me, so that makes it my line."

His hand covers my face. "Waking up with you is…"

"Pretty much the best thing ever?" I suggest. "Yeah."

"Yeah."

A frustrated expression crosses his face. "I don't wanna move."

I huff a laugh. "But you have to pee."

"So bad."

I push at his shoulder—it's like shoving a brick wall. "Go. I'm not going anywhere, promise."

He hesitates. "You better still be here naked in my bed when I get back."

I pinch his chin between finger and thumb. "Naked in your bed and thinking dirty thoughts about you."

That gets him out of bed in a hurry, which leaves me laughing. I only laugh harder when I hear him pee—I have never in my life heard a urination of that length or force. I hear him rinse his mouth too, and then he's swaggering back to me. And I watch every move he makes on the way, hungrily.

"You're looking at me like I'm something to eat," he says, lifting the covers and diving in.

"That's because you are." I reach for him, catch his hip, pull him closer.

He slides up against me, and we're on our sides, facing each other. I throw my leg over his hip, slide my hand under his neck and play with the hair at his nape. My other hand drifts between us and finds him already growing for me. His eyes search me, and the way he looks at me…it's like he's seeing the sunrise for the first time. Like he's been blind and given sight.

His palm runs from my underarm to my hip, and then he fondles my breast. My breath catches at his touch, because he doesn't just *grope*…every touch is a caress. Worship.

"Delia," he murmurs. "I can't even deal with how sexy you are."

I laugh, shaking my head. "Feel free to tell me that all the time, Thai." The laugh fades, and I give some vulnerable truth. "I'm not gonna lie: it feels *really* good, hearing that from you."

He pushes me to my back and leans over me. His mouth dips kisses to my flesh, shoulder and throat and breastbone, the valley between my breasts. I cradle his head and treasure the warm wet touch of his mouth, his worship of my body.

But his worship doesn't end with his kisses.

"Sexy isn't even close to the right word." Another kiss, to the outside of my left breast.

"Lovely." His tongue slides over my nipple.

"Divine." He nuzzles the underside.

"Heaven itself made flesh." His breath huffs hot on my belly.

"Perfection." My ribs, now, under my right breast.

"An angel." Another kiss.

"Your skin is starlight. Your eyes shine with the light of the moon." My right breast, now.

I hold his head, playing with his hair. Listen to his words, his descriptions of me, and I hear the truth in them, and my heart swells, fills every particle of me.

He's not done.

"Every breath I take is for you," he says. "What wouldn't I do for you? Walk a thousand miles? Cross an ocean? Pluck a star from the sky for you?"

"Thai…" I whisper.

"I'll go anywhere for you, Delia. Do anything for you."

"Thai." I palm his cheek. "Just be you. Just be mine."

He finds my mouth, then, and claims it. His tongue slashes into my mouth and his lips are strong and firm on mine. His hands clasp in my own, fingers twining, pressing my hands to the pillow above my head and he's above me, knees between my thighs. I hook my thighs around his hips and cling to him, lift up to meet him.

It's a kiss without end, breathing for each other— breathing each other. Tasting, delving, subsumed.

For a long moment, there's nothing but the kiss. Hands joined, lips locked, tasting each other.

But I need more, and I need him and I know how I want it.

I roll into him, leverage him to his back. Our hands still joined, I slide astride him, and now I'm sitting on him, his hands pressed to the pillow. I slide against him, stroking his hard erection between the lips of my sex. His moan is raw. I tease him with this, slowly rubbing myself on him, almost taking him inside me but never quite doing so—rubbing the head of him against my clit until I'm gasping and biting my lip and grinning with glee and wild delight, and still I tease him. He just crushes my hands with his powerful grip and holds still for it. Grunting, moaning. Grind his thickness between my nether lips, back and forth, my wetness coating him, making the slide slick and smooth.

"Delia, god, my god Delia—what are you doing to me?"

I press my weight onto our hands, leaning forward. Brush the tips of my breasts against his face, tease them against his lips, over his eyelids. Torture him with them, until he growls and nips at me, suckles my nipple into his mouth, but I laugh and pull away from his hunting, questing mouth, and go back to brushing them against his mouth, his lips, his cheeks. Then, finally, I let him have them, lowering myself so he can glut himself on me.

He's throbbing against me. I've teased him—and myself—long enough.

I grasp him and guide him to me. One hand braced on my chest, I lift up and nestle the broad round head of him to my seam. Tease him up and down the slit, until he's nuzzling in between the lips, and I sink a little closer to him. Take a tiny bit of him. Teasing us both. He's not breathing, jaw gritted, brow furrowed, chest lifted, hips flexed upward, abs taut. I brush him up and down, slowly bringing him into me, slowly letting myself drift lower—millimeter...by millimeter...by millimeter.

"Ohmygod, Delia," he breathes. "What are you doing to me?"

I don't answer. I have about half of his length inside me, and I want all of it. But instead, I flick my hips backward, so he nearly falls out of me. My hands are both braced on his chest, now. I use only the roll of my hips to tease him, to torture us. Flit up, away, and slowly, slowly lower myself around him, gradually take him again, inch by inch.

His hands roam up my thighs to my hips, cling there, and the fierce grip of his fingers in the flesh of my ass tells me how badly he wants to haul me down hard, to drive deep.

But he doesn't.

He barely moves, waiting for me.

He loves this torture as much as I do—and our eyes lock, as I pause. Just the plump tip of him splitting me open, just inside me.

I flutter there, light quick rolls of my hips.

He moans.

I do this until he's gasping and his groans are maddened and rough.

And then I clash my mouth over his and slam down onto him all at once, and we both groan into the kiss.

Away, then. Into the wild rhythm of hearts lost together, of love being made with crazed abandon.

He drives up into me and his hands grip the bell of my hips and helps me crash down onto him, and then he's holding me apart so he can slide deeper and I'm leaning forward cradled in his arms and he's using his hips and thighs to drive into me and I'm whimpering every time he enters me, deeper and deeper. Cry with the beauty of us. At the perfection of all that we are, together.

"Thai!" I cry out.

"Delia," he responds, in a rough snarl.

I lose track of everything but him slamming inside me with beautiful perfect strength, filling me until I ache with the nascent explosion, until I blossom with the sunfire heat of climax. There's nothing but us. But our union, our bodies so made for each other crashing together.

I topple over the edge and falling screaming into climax, crying his name and dripping tears onto his golden flesh and still we move together, and I'm quaking with orgasm still when he finally lets go.

There's no screaming in this—there's only my voice lost in breathless awe, only him too shattered to even whisper my name. He bursts into me and I'm filled with the hot flood, and I ride him for more, and now it's my movements that are desperate and wild, driving more and more out of him, until he's trembling and gasping and slips out of me, spent.

Finished, panting, sweating, I collapse onto him, and his hands explore my body, scratching gentle patterns from shoulders to buttocks.

I'm breathing against the side of his throat; I feel his pulse hammering crazily against my nose. "I remember what I said last night," I whisper. "And I meant it."

He palms my cheek, brings my face up so our eyes meet. "I am totally, absolutely, one hundred percent, head over heels in love with you, Delia McKenna. It scares the absolute hell out of me, and I'm okay with that."

I smile, my lips curving against his cheek. "Matthais Bristow loves me."

"Yes," he murmurs. "I sure as hell do."

There's nothing else to say, so we just hold each other.

Breathe together.

Bask in the afterglow, and glory in the lush atmosphere of possibility—the potential of what our lives together can be, will be.

Beautiful, I know that.

Filled with a *lot* of incredible sex, I know that too.

And most of all, filled with love.

THE END

Epilogue

Dell

FUCK EVERYTHING.
Seriously.

I walked away from River Gulch with nothing but the clothes on my back.

Okay, well…that may not be *exactly* true. But it feels like it.

I have no real home—the thing with the model fell apart pretty quickly and I've been bouncing around pretty aimlessly ever since.

I rented a condo in San Francisco for a while.

Got bored.

Went down to LA, rented an apartment down there.

Got bored.

Then everything with Dad happened, and…my life, such as it was, fell apart.

Listen, okay? It's not like I was sitting around

waiting for dear old Pa to croak so I could get my grubby little mitts on his pile of cash. He was my dad. I loved him. I may have had a fucked-up way of showing it, but I did—*do*—love my father.

I regret—and will regret to my dying day—that I wasn't there when he passed.

I wake up in a cold sweat, every single night, a monstrous weight of unspent grief lodged behind my eyes. I see him, in that moment when I'd known I was too late.

I listen to his voicemail every fucking day.

The money doesn't mean shit.

I've got my trust and that's plenty. Especially when I didn't do shit to earn anything I have.

It's the way he tried to trap me that bothers the hell out of me. He tried to manipulate me. Like, didn't he realize I never wanted that life? I don't know what else I could have done to make it clear that I wasn't interested in that fucking company.

I'm *angry*.

All the grief I don't know how to cope with, how to expel…it sits inside my chest like a demon, acid dripping from its fangs and claws. Poisoning me.

The poison of grief transmutes into anger.

I have my Louis Vuitton overnight bag with some clothes, and that's it. I have more shit in a storage locker in River Gulch, but none of that means anything without somewhere to *have* it.

And I'm fucking lost.

Right now, literally.

I sold my fancy half-million-dollar sports car. I sold all my watches except the Phillipe Patek Dad bought me for my twenty-fifth birthday, which I wear all the time, now. I sold nearly all the shit I spent my life up until now accumulating.

The clothes in my bag are from a department store at a nowhere mall, off the rack. Cheap.

My sunglasses are from a kiosk at that mall.

I'm driving a 1993 Range Rover with over a hundred thousand miles on the odometer.

I'm somewhere in…I don't fucking know. There are cows and horses and silos and wheat or grain or corn or some shit. I don't fucking know. I just know I'm super, super lost. Been driving for hours, took a wrong left turn at Albuquerque—yeah, yeah, I know that's in Nevada, and I'm in Illinois or somewhere. Wait—New Mexico. And maybe I'm in Missouri. Don't know, don't care.

I stopped caring, stopped keeping track of miles, and I never had a destination. Most nights, I sleep on the back bench of my Range Rover in the back of a Walmart parking lot or somewhere like that.

I'm just driving. Going nowhere, trying to run away from myself. I know it won't work. But if I stop running, I'll start drinking, so running is better.

I've already pickled my liver pretty damn well by this point, and if I go and grief-drink now, I'll never stop.

And I…want a *life*.

I just don't know what it looks like. Where it is. What to do. How to find it.

My engine sputters and dies, and I pull the big beast over to the side of the highway. It rolls to a stop, and just like that, I'm stranded.

Did I sell my phone, too? Yes I did.

No way to call anyone—not that there's anyone to call. I wouldn't call Delia for help, mainly because I think she'd rather watch me suffer than actually help me. I know that's neither fair nor true, but I already said I'm angry, okay? Nor would I call Mom, because she's essentially gone too, pining after Dad.

Thai?

He stayed in touch after Dad's funeral. Called once a week, we exchanged texts. Thai was all buddy-buddy. But god, I'm fucked up. He knows it. And he knows he can't help me fix it. We've been best friends our entire fucking lives; when I'm ready to come back, he'll welcome me with open arms. I know that, and in some ways, that anchor, the reassurance that at least I'll always have Thai to rely on…it's what keeps me going, way out here. He fixed himself. He figured his life out. And if *he* can do that? If Matthais Bristow, playboy, fuckboy, itinerant douchebag, can settle down and be a career man in our hometown with my sister? Then surely I can fix the mess that is Cordell McKenna.

And yes, I know they're together. I smelled that

drama coming a mile away, him and Delia. I suspect they're happy little homemakers by now, and I don't wanna be around to see that shit.

Gross.

My best friend and my twin sister?

Shudder.

But also…it's sweet, and redemptive, and all that gross, sappy, gooey shit that I'm too bitter and angry and sad to be around.

So, here I am. Middle of absolutely nowhere. No gas. Miles from anything. No gas can. No phone.

It starts to get hot in a hurry, so I get out of the SUV and lean against the hood—there's a little bit of a breeze, at least, so that helps.

A semi passes with a tornado of wind, honking its loud-ass air horn. Another, after a few minutes. Neither so much as slows.

A Porsche 911 whips past, way too fast.

An old guy on a tractor—and that tractor takes a full twenty minutes to from one end of the horizon to the other. He just tips his dirty John Deere hat in something like an apology and keeps going.

When someone does stop, it's a pickup older than me.

It's being driven unironically—not because old trucks are cool, but because it's all the person has.

It's red, but how much is paint and how much is rust, I don't know. There are bales of hay piled high over the cab, pressing the back end down over the wheels.

Windows are open. Country music—old, twangy, honky-tonk music—floats out of the cab.

The woman driving is wearing a white tank top, a pink camo ball cap, and black sunglasses. She stops and waits for me to approach. She's young, about my age. I can't see much else of her, but...

You ever look at someone who you can't see too much of, but you just know they're incredible-looking? I get that impression with this girl.

"Hey." Her voice is light. Her smile is bright and contagious. "Ya'll need help?"

"Yeah."

She glances at my Range Rover. "What's up with it?"

"Ran out of gas."

"Well, there ain't a gas station this side of Carthage." She smiles, and the sun seems to shine a little brighter, and I swear a bird flits by, singing a happy little song.

"Yeah. I should have stopped at the last town, but I didn't."

"Rookie mistake, 'round these parts."

I laugh. "No kidding."

She leans over and shoves open the passenger door. "Well, Rookie, hop in."

I lean into my Rover, grab my bag and keys, lock it, and head for her truck. Toss the bag on the seat between us, and slide in. It smells like old cigarettes, hay, and girl.

Meaning perfume, hair stuff, lotion—and the, mysterious, indefinable, intoxicating scent of a woman.

She eyes me. "Got a name? Or should I just call you Rookie?"

I laugh again—I haven't laughed in what feels like years. "Dell. My name's Dell McKenna."

She extends her right hand, and when I clasp my hand around hers, I get a jolt:

Don't let her get away from you, Dell. She's the one.

I hear it in my skull like an audible fucking voice.

I yank my hand away, too fast, like I was burned. She smirks, lopsided. "I know, I know, I gotta put lotion on. Tossing hay bales is hell on the hands."

I shake my head. "No! Sorry—no. It wasn't that. It's not that. I just…" I flap my hand helplessly. "There was a bug."

She snorts. "Okay…if you say so." Clearly, she doesn't believe me.

Understandable.

I look at her. Her hair is up under the hat, but it looks dark. Brunette, maybe. Can't see her eye color. Don't dare get caught copping a glance at her body.

None of it matters. She's beautiful. Her voice is beautiful. Her very presence, the sense of her in this space, near me—it's beautiful. Calming.

I'm shook.

"Gonna ask me my name?" That grin, lopsided, teasing, brighter than the sun. "Or are you just gonna stare at me?"

I swallow. "What's…your name?"

She smiles, and I think I hear an angel singing somewhere.

"Kyra," she says—*KYE-ruh*. "Kyra Connelly."

I hear that voice in my head again—it's the voice of my soul, yelling at me:

She's the one. Don't let her get away.

WANT MORE OF DELL'S STORY?
SPRUNG
Coming in 2022

Also by
JASINDA WILDER

Visit me at my website: **www.jasindawilder.com**
Email me: **jasindawilder@gmail.com**

If you enjoyed this book, you can help others enjoy it as well by recommending it to friends and family, or by mentioning it in reading and discussion groups and online forums. You can also review it on the site from which you purchased it. But, whether you recommend it to anyone else or not, thank you *so much* for taking the time to read my book! Your support means the world to me!

My other titles:

Preacher's Son:
Unbound
Unleashed
Unbroken

Delilah's Diary:
A Sexy Journey
La Vita Sexy
A Sexy Surrender

Big Girls Do It:
Boxed Set
Married
On Christmas
Pregnant

Rock Stars Do It:
Harder
Dirty
Forever

From the world of *Big Girls* and *Rock Stars*:
Big Love Abroad

Biker Billionaire:
Wild Ride

The Falling Series:
Falling Into You
Falling Into Us
Falling Under
Falling Away
Falling For Colton

The Ever Trilogy:
Forever & Always
After Forever
Saving Forever

The world of *Wounded:*
Wounded
Captured

The world of *Stripped:*
Stripped
Trashed

The world of *Alpha:*
Alpha
Beta
Omega
Harris: Alpha One Security Book 1
Thresh: Alpha One Security Book 2
Duke Alpha One Security Book 3
Puck: Alpha One Security Book 4
Lear: Alpha One Security Book 5
Anselm: Alpha One Security Book 6

The Houri Legends:
Jack and Djinn
Djinn and Tonic

The Madame X Series:
Madame X
Exposed
Exiled

Dad Bod Contracting:
Hammered
Drilled
Nailed
Screwed

Fifty States of Love:
Pregnant in Pennsylvania
Cowboy in Colorado
Married in Michigan

Goode Girls
For a Goode Time Call…
Not So Goode
Goode to Be Bad
A Real Good Time
Goode Vibrations

Billionaire Baby Club
Lizzie Goes Brains Over Braun
Autumn Rolls a Seven
Laurel's Bright Idea

Standalone titles:
Yours
The Cabin

Non-Fiction titles:
You Can Do It
You Can Do It: Strength
You Can Do It: Fasting

Jack Wilder Titles:
The Missionary

JJ Wilder Titles:
Ark

To be informed of new releases, special offers, and other Jasinda news, sign up for Jasinda's email newsletter.